Dear Romance Reader,

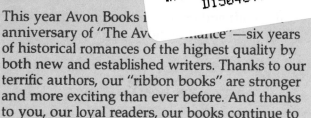

This year Avon Books is [celebrating the] anniversary of "The Avon Romance"—six years of historical romances of the highest quality by both new and established writers. Thanks to our terrific authors, our "ribbon books" are stronger and more exciting than ever before. And thanks to you, our loyal readers, our books continue to be a spectacular success!

"The Avon Romances" are just some of the fabulous novels in Avon Books' dazzling *Year of Romance*, bringing you month after month of top-notch romantic entertainment. How wonderful it is to escape for a few hours with romances by your favorite "leading ladies"—Shirlee Busbee, Karen Robards, and Johanna Lindsey. And how satisfying it is to discover in a new writer the talent that will make her a rising star.

Every month in 1988, Avon Books' *Year of Romance*, will be special because Avon Books believes that romance—the readers, the writers, and the books—deserves it!

Sweet Reading,

Susanne Jaffe

Ellen Edwards

Susanne Jaffe
Editor-in-Chief

Ellen Edwards
Senior Editor

DREAMSONG

LINDA LADD

AVON BOOKS ◆ NEW YORK

AVON BOOKS
A division of
The Hearst Corporation
105 Madison Avenue
New York, New York 10016

Copyright © 1988 by Linda Ladd
Published by arrangement with the author
Library of Congress Catalog Card Number: 87-91836
ISBN: 0-380-75205-0

First Avon Books Printing: July 1988

AVON TRADEMARK REG. U.S. PAT. OFF. AND IN OTHER COUNTRIES, MARCA
REGISTRADA, HECHO EN U.S.A.

Printed in the U.S.A.

K-R 10 9 8 7 6 5 4 3 2 1

FOR
Tim and Kathy King
and Timmy and Matt

Prologue

St. Louis
September 10, 1810

"You let her take my son?"

The voice was low and deadly, coated with enough ice to send a chill up Hugh Younger's spine. He shifted in his leather desk chair, reluctant to look at Luke Randall's angry face. He had been more than a little afraid of his wife's older brother, anyway, ever since Luke had come back to St. Louis. Anne had always defended her brother, but despite what she said, Luke had never been like other white men. He was as savage as the Sioux who had raised him.

Hugh finally forced himself to lift his bloodshot brown eyes to his big brother-in-law. Even now, Luke wore the garb of the red devils, his six-foot-five-inch frame looking enormous in the tan buckskins decorated with long, beaded fringe. Luke's terrible, unreadable green eyes settled on Hugh, disconcerting him even more. He needed a drink, he thought, reaching with palsied hands for the cut-glass decanter on the desk beside him. He poured a good-sized shot of whiskey into his glass and tossed it down with one quick motion.

1

"I want answers, Hugh, and I want them now," Luke demanded, leaning forward to brace both palms flat on the desktop. "Pete's my son, damn you!"

"It wasn't my fault," Hugh stuttered quickly, remembering well from his childhood the force of Luke's volatile temper. He nearly shook with nerves. "I told you I was drinking that night, Luke! I can't remember every detail, for God's sake! What the hell does it matter anyway? The little bitch stole him away in the dead of night! I must have tried to stop her, since she clubbed me with the poker! My head still aches from it, and it's been two weeks!"

He tipped the decanter to his glass again, drinking hastily, then closed his eyes as the whiskey burned like fire in his gullet. He looked up as Luke turned and took several impatient steps away from the desk before he stopped, running his fingers worriedly through his thick, curly black hair.

"Have the authorities picked up her trail yet?" he demanded, turning back.

Hugh's eyes shifted guiltily. "I haven't notified—"

Luke's handsome face darkened with fury. "Why the hell not?"

"Because I wanted to keep the whole thing quiet. I've got a man on it," he added quickly, "and he said Bethany Cole had some friends down on the riverfront. He thinks she might have taken the boy downstream on one of their keelboats."

"Is that her name, Bethany Cole?"

"Yeah."

"And she was Pete's nursemaid?"

"Yeah, and Anne trusted her. I trusted her, too, I guess. She seemed good enough with the boy."

The mere mention of Anne sent a pang through

Hugh's heart. His beloved wife had been dead from fever for six months now, six long, lonely, godawful months.

"I want a warrant put out on her," Luke Randall was saying in clipped, angry syllables. "With her name and age and description. And I want you to notify Andrew down in New Orleans. Do you understand me, Hugh? You let some half-grown girl from God knows where steal my son, and by God, you better hope I can find them before anything happens to him!"

The whiskey burning in Hugh's stomach gave him more courage than he normally would display. "What the devil do you care, anyway, Luke?" he muttered as he refilled his tumbler. "You haven't even seen the little half-breed in three years—"

Huge, sun-browned hands caught the front of Hugh's rumpled linen shirt before he could finish, hauling him bodily out of his seat.

"You're nothing but a weak, drunken fool, Hugh. Why my sister ever married you is beyond me, but I'll tell you this—you better pray to God that I find Pete, and find him well, or I'll be back to take it out of your worthless hide!"

Luke thrust his brother-in-law away in contempt, and Hugh dropped limply back, making the hinges on the tufted leather swivel chair squeal in protest. Luke turned, his knee-high moccasins making no sound as he crossed the expensive blue-and-crimson Chinese carpet. The door clicked behind him, and Hugh Younger slumped deeper into the cushions, cradling his whiskey bottle with one arm.

How could his gentle, lovely Anne have ever been blood kin to that savage monster? he thought. Fresh tears began to form in his eyes. Luke should have stayed with the savages, along with his little half-breed son. He dropped his head to his folded arms, leaning against the desk to sob for his wife with the bitter, heart-wrenching grief that never, ever left him.

Chapter 1

Natchez
September 24, 1810

"Beth? Does it hurt the worm when you stick in the hook?"

Bethany Cole looked down at the long purple-black worm wiggling between her thumb and forefinger, somewhat disconcerted by the six-year-old boy's question.

"Well, Petie, I hope not," she replied, her smooth brow knitting in a frown as she tossed his line back into the water.

Peeto immediately focused his intent green gaze on the tan cork bobbing erratically in the currents along the bank of the muddy Mississippi River. Bethany baited her own hook, wiping her hands on the old pair of brown linsey-woolsey breeches she wore before she swung her cane pole out over the water. She held the pole in the crook of her elbow long enough to push escaped ringlets of her long blond hair beneath her wide-brimmed straw hat. She looked around, contentment filling her as she sat on the low riverbank and enjoyed the warm sunshine of early autumn.

5

Downriver from their spot, infamous Natchez-Under-the-Hill bustled with all its notorious activities, despite the afternoon hour. But Valerie Goodrich's stables and boat landing, where Bethany and Peeto had taken refuge after their flight from St. Louis, were just far enough away that almost no one came around. Only occasionally did a keelboat or flatboat stop there to unload its cargo, usually when the river was high. Mrs. Goodrich was known around Natchez primarily for the excellent horseflesh she raised in her spotless stables.

Bethany glanced back toward the barns and riding rings where Peeto had watched her work with the horses all morning. Val was not immediately in sight, and it took a moment before Bethany saw her busily dipping a spade in the petunia bed in her front yard. Val was a small, stocky woman of sixty-five, with graying auburn hair and kind, dark eyes that missed nothing. Bethany had become very fond of her in the six weeks they had lived in their cozy little room over the stables. But, most of all, Bethany had enjoyed working with the horses. She had a real gift with them, with all animals. Val had noticed it right off. Even Bethany's father had admired her talent for handling animals, and he had liked very little else about her.

Bethany sighed. Her father had drowned when she was almost twelve, nearly six years ago, and now those early years growing up with him along the Ohio River seemed a misty eternity ago. The time since then in St. Louis seemed much more real, although she didn't like to think about the first three unhappy years, which had been spent in the orphanage. The last three years, in the Younger house, had been better, at least until the night they had been forced to flee.

Gooseflesh rose on her arms at the thought of Hugh Younger, and she glanced at Peeto, hoping he could someday forget what had happened that night. It had all been so unexpected and terrifying. Although Hugh was often drunk, stumbling around the house and yelling at them, he had never before come into Peeto's bedchamber. And never had he tried to hurt them or touch her the way he had then. Cold, clammy terror welled inside her as vivid pictures formed in her mind, images of Hugh's angry, contorted face as his fingers bit into her arms and tore at her clothes, and then the terrible, dull thud of the poker against his skull. Oh, Lord, what if he was dead now? What if they had killed him?

Please, please don't let him be dead, she thought desperately, but she remembered the blood on his head and how very still he had been when they had gathered their belongings and fled the house. She took a deep breath, telling herself for the thousandth time that they were safe with Val.

Even if Hugh had died, no one knew where they were, and if Hugh had survived, he wouldn't care enough about Peeto to come after them. He never had. It was his wife, Mistress Anne, who had been so kind and understanding when the little half-Indian boy had arrived at her big house on Olive Street. Peeto was the reason Bethany had been hired out of the orphanage, and that in itself was enough to make her grateful to the child. Peeto had been so little then, only three years old. She would never forget how lonely and frightened he had been those first months in St. Louis, hiding under his bed, afraid to come out. He hadn't even understood English then, only speaking the gutteral language of his Sioux mother.

Anger rose fiercely in great swells as Bethany thought of Peeto's father. She certainly didn't have to worry about Luke Randall coming after them. He had dumped Peeto off like an unwanted puppy, then returned to the faraway western mountains called the Rockies to trap furs. Peeto wouldn't ever talk about him, and sometimes Bethany wondered if the little boy even remembered him. Bethany had never seen him herself, since Anne hired her after Luke Randall had left, but she knew he was a fur trapper with clear jade-green eyes, just like Peeto's.

Peeto was better off with her and Val than with his father or his uncle. He had seen enough of Hugh's drunken, destructive rages. Thank goodness she had been able to persuade Captain Hosie to bring them to Natchez on the *Mariette*. Val was an old friend of Hosie Richmond, who had asked her if Bethany and Peeto could stay with her.

Bethany had been afraid to travel all the way to New Orleans on the *Mariette* because Peeto's other uncle lived there. His name was Andrew, and he was a lawyer, but that was all she knew about him. He might be as mean and abusive as his brother-in-law, Hugh. Peeto was much better off with her. She loved him more than any of his family ever could. She put her arm around the child, hugging his thin shoulders, then pressed a kiss on his soft cheek. He turned big, serious eyes to her.

"We don't never have to go back, do we, Beth? Not never?"

How many times would she have to reassure him?

Bethany wondered. Her heart twisted, but she smiled, pushing unruly black curls off his forehead.

"I'll never let them take you back there, I promise," she answered, and her reassuring words eased the anxious lines around the child's eyes. His relief soon disintegrated as he discovered that his floating cork had disappeared beneath the surface.

"Uh oh, uh oh!" Peeto cried with such a curious mixture of glee and panic that Bethany laughed.

"Now, don't let go," she warned when the cane pole dipped dangerously close to the water as the fish decided to put up a fight. "Pull him in, quick, like I showed you!"

Bethany was pleased to see that Peeto remembered everything she had taught him so diligently in their daily fishing excursions, and moments later he pulled his fish out of the water, the fat catfish flip-flopping frantically on the bank. "He's even bigger than mine, Petie!" she cried. "Val won't believe you brought him in by yourself!"

Peeto's grin was so utterly smug that Bethany had to hide her amusement, but it was good to see him happy again.

"Don't you want to show Val?" she suggested as she worked to get the heavy fish off the hook.

Peeto immediately yelled across the yard to Val, and Bethany glanced over her shoulder as she pushed the big mudcat down on the stringer stick that held the rest of the day's catch. She was surprised to see two men standing with Val at the front gate. Shielding her eyes with one hand, Bethany watched them for a moment, wondering if they were the men Val had been expecting, who were to choose from her breeding stock. When they started along the dirt path toward her and Peeto, Bethany at first thought the bigger man was one of the Choctaw Indians Val sometimes hired to help around the place, because of the fringed garments he wore. As they came closer, however, she saw that he was a white man with a short black beard, his skin deeply bronzed by the sun. The other man was much smaller, with thin gray hair.

"Look, Val, Petie caught a dandy!" Bethany called out, holding up the heavy stringer with some difficulty.

Her smile faltered at first sight of the strange expression on Val's brown, weathered face. Suddenly wary, she looked immediately at the strangers. The tall one was staring intently down at Peeto, and as the boy pressed closer to Bethany's legs, the big man raised clear green eyes to her face. She froze as if turned to stone, her heart plunging to her toes.

"Run, Petie!" she yelled, swinging the heavy stringer with all the strength she possessed.

Her unexpected action caught Luke Randall by surprise, and before he could duck, it hit the side of his head with a loud slap. Bethany and Peeto didn't wait; they sprinted down the hard-packed dirt path toward the barn as fast as their bare feet could carry them.

Terrified, Bethany dared a quick glance over her shoulder just before she slammed shut the barn door. "Hurry, Petie! He's right behind us! Hide in the loft, and I'll try to stop him!"

Peeto scampered with boyish agility up the ladder, and Bethany wasted no time scrambling to the top of the bales of hay stacked beside the door. When Luke swung the door open seconds later, Bethany shoved one of the heavy bales off the stack and onto his head. She released another one behind it as he grunted in pain and muttered an oath, then she headed for the ladder. Halfway up, a strong arm closed around her slender waist, hauling her down as if she weighed nothing.

Bethany fought as hard as she could against his immense strength, kicking and jabbing with her fists the way Captain Hosie had taught her. One such attempt finally connected with his nose, drawing blood, before she was jerked around and given a hard shake that sent her hat flying onto the straw-littered floor.

She hung limply for a moment, her head whirling like a river eddy, and Luke shook her again for good measure. Before she could gather her wits and renew her fight, Peeto came hurtling through the air from the loft, his shrill Sioux yell shattering the air. He hit Luke's back like a load of stones, and as Luke went to his knees, Bethany rolled free and grabbed the pitchfork leaning against the stall. Peeto ran behind her, and she jabbed the pitchfork in a threatening manner toward Luke as he rose slowly to his feet.

"Don't come no closer," Bethany warned breathlessly, but she had only enough time to gasp as he reached out with a quickness that stunned her, jerking the pitchfork from her grasp.

"Dammit, enough!" he shouted, flinging the pitchfork away. But apparently it wasn't enough for Bethany and Peeto, who darted in different directions. Bethany grabbed a loose board from the woodpile in the corner and swung it at him as hard as she could. Luke dodged it adroitly, then deflected her second swing with his forearm. Furious now, he dove at her, amazed to realize that he was in a life-and-death battle with a mere slip of a girl not half his size. He tackled Bethany around the waist, and they tumbled together into the nearest pile of straw. Peeto pounced on Luke's back as they landed, both small fists pummeling the top of his father's head.

Luke had had enough. He roared with rage, twisting to peel the attacking boy off his back, then held him under one arm while he pinned the girl with his leg. They both began to shriek at the top of their lungs, but even their fierce struggles were no match for Luke's strength.

"Now, hold still," he ordered from between set teeth as Val Goodrich and the small, gray-haired man finally showed up at the open barn door.

"Need any help, Randall?"

Luke gave Constable Hedger a sour look. "Yeah, you can put this little hellcat of a kidnapper in jail where she belongs."

Luke got to his feet, prudently keeping secure holds on both Bethany and Peeto. He frowned as the constable looked distinctly sorrowful.

"Sorry, Val," Constable Hedger said, scratching his gray-whiskered chin, "but the man here's got a warrant on the girl, all legal and sworn out upriver at St. Louis. Says she abducted the kid there. I ain't got no choice but to take her in. Come on, gal."

But when he took hold of Bethany's arm, Peeto went crazy, screaming for her and fighting against Luke's hold until Luke was forced to let him go. Peeto ran sobbing into Bethany's arms, and she held him close. Luke stared at his son for a moment before he gestured the constable to one side.

Bethany watched the two men with wary eyes as they talked quietly together. Fighting her tears as Val patted her back, she briefly considered making a run for the river. But she knew they couldn't make it.

Luke Randall was watching them with hawklike eyes even while he talked to the constable. There was no way she could escape him!

"It's all right, Petie, don't cry," she murmured, but her own voice sounded choked, because she knew it wasn't going to be all right. She was going to jail, and Peeto would be sent back to St. Louis, where she had promised him she wouldn't ever let anyone take him.

"Come on over here, little gal," Constable Hedger said, motioning to Bethany. "Mr. Randall, here, has somethin' to say."

Peeto clutched her tighter, and Bethany knelt to cup his face between her palms. "It's all right, Petie. Stand here by Val a minute."

Peeto glared at the big man who was trying to take her away from him. "You better not hurt Beth," he threatened with low, lethal venom before he was enfolded in Val's stout arms.

Luke drew Bethany aside with a less-than-gentle grip on her arm. She was glad to see blood trickling from his nose and a small cut on his temple. He deserved it!

"As far as I'm concerned," Luke said in a low, hard voice, "you deserve to rot in jail right here in Natchez for trying to kill Hugh—"

"He's not dead?" Bethany interrupted, weak with relief.

"No, sorry to disappoint you, but he survived, and now, since you've made sure my son is dependent on you, I guess I'll have to take you along with us. Because if I don't, he'll hate my guts as long as he lives."

Bethany gave him a contemptuous look. "Why

should you care about that? You haven't come back since he was three years old. Why did you come back at all?''

Something moved in the clear green depths of Luke Randall's eyes, something that almost frightened Bethany. ''I don't give a damn what you think of me, but for the boy's sake, I'm going to take you down-river with us. Then I'm going to feel great pleasure in turning you over to the law, and I hope they throw away the key.''

''Really? You're bringing me with you?'' Bethany asked, overjoyed to be going with Peeto, even if a jail cell awaited her in New Orleans.

Luke looked down into Bethany Cole's big silver-gray eyes, so wide and innocent and appealing, and realized for the first time that she was very, very young. And pretty enough in a tomboyish sort of way, he thought, as his eyes moved over her tanned face with the few freckles on her nose. But he wasn't fool-ish enough to trust that innocent look, not for a min-ute. The young girl standing in front of him had nearly killed Hugh with a poker before she abducted Peeto, and he would see her in prison for it just as soon as he could manage it.

Chapter 2

Luke only gave them time to collect their belongings, and he was careful to keep a tight hold on Bethany Cole's arm as they left Valerie Goodrich's stables and walked down Silver Street, the muddy, unpaved main thoroughfare of Natchez-Under-the-Hill. He rested his other hand on one of the two flintlock pistols he always kept in his belt, as they passed the saloons and brothels lining the street all the way to the main river landings. The small strip under the Natchez bluffs was not a place to let down your guard. Among the thieves, gamblers, whores, and cutthroats, murder was committed as regularly as dawn lit the morning sky. It was nowhere for Bethany Cole to have brought his son.

Luke glanced down at the top of the girl's pale blond head. She barely reached his shoulder, and she had one arm close around Pete, as if to protect him. Luke's eyes moved to the boy. He had grown so much taller and stronger since the last time that his father had seen him, and he was brave. Pete had not hesitated to take on his father in order to help the girl.

"We're going in that?" Bethany asked in surprise, as they stopped on a planked dock alongside a heavily laden birchbark canoe.

15

"That's right," Luke answered. "Don't worry, it's safe enough."

Bethany had seen enough canoes during her youth on the Ohio River to know that much, but with a giant of a man like Luke Randall aboard, she wasn't sure the fragile craft could stay afloat, much less bear the three of them all the way to New Orleans. She started to say as much, then decided against it as Luke swung Peeto into the canoe, helping him get settled on a thick, furry buffalo hide spread out near the bow.

Bethany didn't wait for Luke to assist her; she threw in her cloth valise and Peeto's small suede satchel before she stepped in to sit as close as possible to Peeto. She watched closely as Luke walked around the canoe, checking the supplies and gunpowder pouches packed in its midsection. Despite his height and powerful build, he moved with smooth masculine grace, as if he planned each footfall in advance. In that way, he reminded her of an immense, dangerous jungle cat—a black panther, perhaps, with his shaggy black hair and watchful jade eyes. She shivered. Many men would fear him, she had no doubt of that.

When Luke was satisfied that everything was in order for their journey, he lowered himself into the stern and pushed away from the dock with the end of his paddle. The canoe glided out into the swift river currents, and to his surprise, Bethany Cole picked up the other paddle, dipping an expert stroke into the water.

Luke ruddered their course, and with Bethany's steady paddling, they soon floated past the last gray shanty of Natchez-Under-the-Hill and entered the long stretch of the river that wound in a serpentine course to the Gulf of Mexico. A long-legged blue heron took startled flight from a downed log near them, and Luke watched it skim low over the surface of the water, wings outstretched in a six-foot span, before it banked upward to disappear over the forest lining the opposite shore.

Peeto had watched the bird's graceful flight as well, and Luke's eyes rested on the boy's fine profile. It was hard to believe that this child was his son. A boy he hardly knew; a boy who regarded him with hatred from eyes identical to Luke's own. But his face was very like Snow Blossom's.

Luke wondered if Peeto could remember anything about his mother. A clear vision of her rose in Luke's mind, a day long ago when they were still children, when she was six and he was twelve. She had shot his bow, then laughed when her arrow hit the center of the target. Another, less happy memory swiftly followed the first, the day Snow Blossom died. Luke heard her scream again, heard Peeto's cries as she fell. Determined not to relive that day, he thrust his paddle into the swirling eddies, hoping the boy had forgotten. Peeto had been only three, hardly more than a baby. Perhaps he was not haunted by the memory as Luke was.

"Watch the planter yonder," Bethany Cole suddenly called out from the bow. "You best rudder us clear."

Luke knew that a planter was an uprooted tree that the current had pushed along until its trunk became braced on the bottom, causing its upper branches to lie treacherously hidden just below the surface to wreck unskilled boatmen. But as he picked out the planter's telltale ripples on the surface, Luke wondered how Bethany Cole knew about them. He ruddered a wide path around it, and regarded the girl with new interest. For the first time, he wondered about her background. Hugh had told him little other than that she was one of the servants Anne had hired out of a charity orphanage.

In the fortnight he had been searching for her on the river, Luke had never once envisioned her as being so young. Her innocent appearance didn't fit at all with his image of the conniving abductress who had taken his son. Most likely, though, her youthful look had worked to dupe Anne and Hugh into trusting her. Still, she hadn't been clever enough to elude his pursuit, and that made him wonder . . .

Half a dozen boatmen along Laclede's Landing in St. Louis had remembered her. Several had even recalled her boarding the *Mariette* with Peeto. Then in New Madrid, a town on the Mississippi seventy miles below the junction of the Ohio River, he easily learned that she had brazenly entered the major trading post to buy peppermint candies for Peeto.

In Natchez, it had taken Luke a little longer to pick up her trail since the Goodrich stables were off the beaten path. Luckily, the constable had recognized her description from Luke's warrant. It seemed strange to Luke that she would abduct the boy, then make no attempt to hide her tracks.

Nevertheless, she had made sure Peeto was devoted to her. A massive frown drew Luke's straight black brows together. It would be hard to separate them, but he would have to find a way. He would see her in jail, just as he had told her.

The September afternoon was beautiful, with a clear blue sky stretching out in a dome above the river, while sunshine dappled the trees overhanging the banks. After several hours of paddling, Luke began to look for a place to stop and stretch their legs. When he saw a sunny sandbar a short distance downriver, he ruddered the canoe in that direction.

"We'll stop there on the sandbar for a while," he called out to the girl, and she angled her paddle toward the narrow beach without comment. The canoe had barely scraped the bottom when she was out with one agile leap, pulling the craft farther up onto the sand. While she lifted Peeto out, Luke picked up his long-barreled rifle and the sack of food that Val Goodrich, during her tearful farewell, had insisted they take.

Bethany and Peeto stood close together, watching Luke with distrustful eyes while he walked a short distance up from the water to have a look around. Thick forest hugged both sides of the Mississippi River all the way to New Orleans, and the woods were inhabited mostly by Indians, mainly Choctaw and Cherokee. Luke knew full well that their favorite prey were the keelboats and flatboats that tied up for the night all up and down the river. This place, however, looked safe enough with its rocky bluff just behind the strip of beach. The trees were sparce enough for him to spot even the stealthiest of the red warriors.

"Go on, sit down," he told them, annoyed by the frightened, accusing expressions on their faces. They were acting as if *he* were the criminal instead of Bethany Cole, and it irked him.

They obeyed at once, sitting together on a driftwood stump, and he dropped the sack of fried chicken and buttermilk biscuits in front of them, taking his own portion a few steps away. He leaned back against a weeping willow tree, from which he could keep an eye on them.

The wind from the river sent the drooping fronds waving to and fro, creating patterns of sunlight over the girl's hair, and Luke watched the pale blond curls glint like gold. She didn't wear her hair as long as most women did, but it swept her shoulders, thick and silky, with soft, wispy ringlets.

All of a sudden, her hair reminded him of his mother. He could vividly remember a time when she sat very close to him, her arm around his shoulders, just as Bethany was doing with Peeto. That was before Panther Dog had murdered her. Cold, loathing hatred that had possessed him since childhood roared up from the depths of his mind, but he pushed all emotion back with the mental strength he had found within himself even at Peeto's age.

Bethany looked up as Luke Randall suddenly moved away from the tree trunk and paced down to the edge of the water. What was he thinking as he bent and filled a metal cup with water, then stared out over the wide, turbulent river? His face remained inscrutable, and he looked very much like a fur trapper as he stood there, with his short black beard and fringed buckskins, so big and strong and silent.

She glanced around the clearing again, searching for a way to escape, but even if they could run away, the forests were wild and tangled with undergrowth, and there might be Indians hiding there with their scalping hatchets. She shivered, her arm tightening around Peeto.

"I'm thirsty," he whispered.

"Go down and dip some water from the river," Bethany told him. "Here's a cup."

Peeto didn't move, looking fearfully at his father's tall, intimidating form.

"He won't hurt you, Petie," Bethany said. "He is your father, you know."

Peeto's sunburned face grew harder. "Yes, he will. I hate him," he muttered, but he took the cup and moved down to the water, carefully skirting Luke's position on the bank.

To Bethany's dismay, Luke strode back toward her. He stood and looked silently down at her, his eyes bright green against his bronzed skin, until she grew uncomfortable. A little afraid of him, she turned her gaze to Peeto.

"Why did you take Pete?"

His question came suddenly, and Bethany looked up, not sure how much he knew.

"Didn't Hugh Younger tell you?" she asked hesitantly.

"He said you abducted Peeto for ransom, then nearly clubbed him to death when he tried to stop you."

Bethany could not help her gasp of outrage. "He's lying!" she cried furiously. "I didn't abduct Petie! Not for ransom or anything else!"

Luke Randall lifted one dark brow in obvious disbelief. "No? Then tell me what you call it."

Bethany's initial anger subsided, and she looked at the sun sparkling off the river. "Why should I? You won't believe me over him."

Luke's eyes didn't waver. "Are you saying you didn't take Pete? And you didn't hit Hugh with the poker?"

Luke watched her expression close up as if a shade

had been drawn down. She suddenly looked distinctly guilty.

"Maybe I had a good reason," she said a moment later. "One I'm sure Hugh forgot to mention."

"Go ahead, mention it."

Bethany watched Peeto collect mussel shells along the littered sand. She didn't know if she should tell Luke Randall the truth about that night. She didn't know if he could be trusted, or if he was as bad as Hugh. She only knew she had to protect Peeto as long as she could.

"He was drinking," she said finally. "He was so drunk that he came into the nursery and tried to hurt Petie. So I hit him, and I knew if Hugh died, they'd hang me or put me in prison, and Petie would be all alone. Petie was scared and wanted to come with me, so I took him and left."

Luke lifted the cup he held, taking a drink of the water it held before he emptied the rest on the ground. "You're right, I don't believe you," he agreed. "Come on, we've been here long enough."

For the rest of the afternoon no conversation passed between them, and Bethany was glad when Peeto fell asleep on the soft buffalo robe. He was so little, and he had been through so much in his short life. For a while, she had thought they could be happy together with Val in Natchez. Then Luke Randall had shown up out of nowhere.

Bitterness washed over her. Luke Randall would only abandon Peeto again. He was a cold, hard man, or he could never have left his own child for three long years. She had to find a way to escape before Luke took Peeto back to Hugh Younger. And this time she would be more careful. This time she would change her name, and Peeto's, too! This time Luke would never be able to find them!

When the sun sank low, painting deep, cool shadows along the shoreline, Luke discovered just the place to camp for the night. A freshwater creek fed into the river next to a sandy, well-protected clearing, and he shifted his position in order to head the canoe in that direction. The river surface at the mouth of the creek was perfectly smooth, and he was caught totally unprepared when the canoe rammed to a full, lurching stop.

Bethany barely managed to grab the side in time to keep from being thrown into the water, but Peeto was not so lucky. Bethany screamed as the child was flung headlong into the swift, cold current. Panic overwhelmed her as Peeto disappeared under the surface, and she stood up, oblivious to Luke's attempts to stabilize the rocking canoe. Seconds later, when Peeto's head appeared again and his fearful cries for help came to her, Bethany jumped awkwardly into the water, frantic to get him before he was pulled under again.

The river felt like ice, shocking her whole system to a near standstill until she tried frantically to fight her way back to the surface. She gasped for air, relieved to find that her feet barely touched the bottom. This gave her the stability to reach over to where Peeto was floundering and fighting against the current a few feet away and grab his shirt.

Struggling with all her strength, she managed to stand against the push of the water long enough to thrust him back into Luke's reach. He swung the boy into the canoe, then jumped out to tow the boat over the submerged sandbar, leaving Bethany to follow.

She didn't have Luke's strength, however, and she could not last long in the rushing current. She panicked as her feet were swept out from under her. She swallowed water, terror welling up in her as she was sucked beneath the surface.

Luke shoved the canoe, Peeto inside, a good distance up onto the sand. When Peeto began to call for the girl and tried to climb out, Luke turned, fully expecting Bethany to be right behind him. He gasped when he saw her several yards away, struggling in panic against the current. He ran into the river, then dove, a few hard strokes enabling him to catch her. He turned her bodily, getting his arm around her chest in a secure hold before he towed her to shore.

"Why the hell did you jump in if you can't swim?" he yelled furiously as his feet touched bottom. "I would have gotten him!"

"I didn't know that! I didn't know if you even cared if he drowned!" Bethany screamed back as he dragged her onto the bank. She jerked away and ran up the beach to Peeto.

Luke muttered an oath when she dropped to her knees and gathered the little boy into her arms. He whirled around as a yell drifted out across the river. He saw a flatboat at midstream, the heavy, lumbersome craft riding low in the water from the weight of hundreds of kegs and crates lashed together on its deck.

"We be stoppin' downriver a spell. You be welcome to tie up wid us," came the distant shout of a burly-looking man holding the rudder stick.

Luke lifted his arm in acknowledgment, but he didn't intend to take them up on their offer. He preferred to be on his own. He knew how to take care of himself, and he didn't trust strangers.

He walked back toward Bethany and Peeto, well aware that dark would settle quickly once the sun went down. He gathered enough driftwood to start a fire, and Bethany and Peeto moved toward it, drenched and shivering.

"You better get those wet clothes off him. Yours, too," Luke told Bethany, and she immediately started to undress Peeto, wrapping him in a warm, dry blanket. But she was not about to disrobe herself, not in Luke Randall's presence, and she stiffened, distinctly embarrassed, as he showed not a trace of modesty, stripping off his buckskin tunic in one swift motion. Her eyes fastened for an instant on his naked chest with its matting of dark hair, broad and brown and ridged with muscles, but it was the masses of oblong scar tissue above his breastbone that riveted her gaze.

She swallowed hard, wondering what horrible wound could have created such a cruel-looking mark, but even that thought fled as Luke stepped immodestly out of his buckskin breeches. Her eyes darted from the sight of his tall, steel-muscled body clothed in only a brief, Indian-style loincloth as Luke lay his damp buckskins near the flames. Peeto yawned beside her, and glad for something else to do, Bethany made him a bed of buffalo skins and lay down close beside him.

Peeto slept at once, exhausted from the emotional trauma of the day, but Bethany found it impossible to close her eyes. While Luke sat on the other side of the fire, his rifle across his lap, she lay awake in her damp shirt and breeches, staring downriver at a small flickering in the darkness. It was the flatboat people who had asked Luke to join them. If only she could get Peeto away from Luke, she could go to them. She had seen women and children on board. She knew they would help her.

A twig snapped in the darkness outside the fire, and she lurched upright. Luke was already in a crouch, his rifle ready. The firelight flickered over his nearly naked body, painting golden shadows across his furred chest and bulging, muscular arms as he scanned the shadowy trees. The sight of him sent a strange sensation racing over her flesh—fleeting but powerful, and impossible to identify.

"Did you see anything?"

His whisper was barely audible, and Bethany shook her head, suddenly terrified of whatever was lurking in the darkness.

"It's probably some animal drawn to the fire," Luke murmured for Bethany's benefit. But he had been trained much too well by the Sioux not to make sure. "Get Pete in the canoe," he told her softly, then crept out of the fireglow and disappeared into the night.

As soon as he was gone, Bethany felt alone and scared. She hurriedly gathered up the drying clothes, then lifted Peeto in her arms.

"Don't be afraid," she whispered, as the little boy roused enough to whimper. "It's all right, sweetie. We're going to sleep in the canoe, that's all."

He slept again as soon as she settled him in the canoe, and she sat in tense dread, peering around the clearing for Luke. Terrible thoughts swirled in her head as the minutes ticked past. What if they were surrounded by savages or the bloodthirsty pirates that plagued the river? What if whoever was out there had already killed Luke in some silent fashion and was on the way to get her and Peeto? She stifled a scream with her fist as a frightening shape loomed suddenly on the far side of the fire. Luke stood there, tall and silent and half naked, as primeval as the ancient forest around him. She shivered again.

"It was a deer," he called out to her. "You can come back now."

Bethany went limp with relief, then moved to obey him. She started to reach for Peeto, but drew up as a sudden thought spun into existence. She glanced downriver at the flatboat party, then at Luke, where he was busy piling more wood on the fire. This was it. This was her chance, probably the only one she would have.

After that, she didn't hesitate for a moment, but pushed the canoe out into the river. Her heart hammered with fear as she leaped into the stern, thrusting her paddle into the water. Without Luke's weight, the canoe cleared the sandbar without trouble. Then she paddled frantically as Luke's enraged bellow echoed out over the river behind her. Bethany looked back fearfully, but she had made it! She was too far out for him to stop her! And there was no way he could follow, not at night without a boat!

"Beth! Beth!" Peeto cried, sitting up in terror, and Bethany quickly took his outstretched hand.

"We have to get away, Petie! This is our only chance!"

Peeto had no complaint about leaving Luke's company, and he sat quietly as Bethany paddled steadily, using the fires downstream as a beacon. If she stayed in the calmer waters next to shore, there was little danger of capsizing or being swept away, as there was in the swifter currents at midstream.

Within the hour, she and Peeto were close enough to see figures moving around the big bonfire on the shore, and she quickly brought the canoe up behind the moored flatboat. Several men ran toward her, aiming their guns at her, while others in the party followed with torches.

"Please!" she cried. "Please, help us!"

"Who ye be?" came a suspicious masculine voice, obviously fearful of the often-played trick of the river pirates. More than one riverboat party had met its doom while rescuing an innocent-looking victim, only to be overwhelmed by murderous thieves waiting at the wayside. Bethany was quick to reassure them.

"I'm all alone with my little boy! You saw us earlier with a man. He's took off without us, and we're all alone!"

"Be comin' in then, lass," the man called, and Bethany gratefully put her hand in a strong one that helped her to shore. A different man leaned down to lift Peeto out of the canoe, but Bethany quickly took him again.

"It's over now, Petie," she whispered, and the tired child looped his arms around her neck, wearily laying his head on her shoulder.

"Oh, you poor little lassie," crooned a heavyset woman who had pushed her way through the crowd of men. "All alone on the river with a wee little one. Poor tired little angel." She patted Peeto's back. "He can sleep on deck where the other children are sleepin'. It's safe there."

Bethany was more than willing to let herself be taken under the wing of the older woman, who iden-

tified herself as Mrs. McFern, the captain's wife.
Bethany was ushered up the wide gangplank to the
deck of the long flatboat. She was tired, too, so weary
she could barely stand up. A canvas lean-to had been
erected as a makeshift tent, and she settled Peeto
alongside several other small children, then knelt beside him, rubbing his back the way he liked until he
fell asleep again.

Afterward, she stood and looked upriver, toward
where she could now see Luke's fire, at least five
miles away. He didn't have a boat, and he couldn't
cut through the undergrowth along the shore, at least
not before dawn, when the flatboat would set sail. She
walked down the gangplank toward the roaring blaze
on the bank, where the adults were congregated.

"Poor, unfortunate lamb, so young to be alone with
the little bairn. Tsk, tsk," Mrs. McFern said sooth-
ingly, putting a comforting arm around Bethany.

Bethany said little, but her thoughts were on the
morrow, when they would embark downriver again
where Luke would never, ever find them. She was
safe. Peeto was safe. And that's all that mattered.

In her safe haven, wrapped in Mrs. McFern's
motherly concern, the likes of which she had not experienced since her own mother had died, when she
was four, she sleepily began to feel almost magnan-
imous toward Luke Randall. Perhaps she would leave
his clothes and canoe behind on the bank where he
could find them when he eventually made his way
downriver. Yes, that's what she would do. He probably thought her a thief, but she wasn't one. She had
never stolen one thing in her whole life. She would
prove it, too, by not taking anything of his when they

left on the flatboat. If Captain Hosie was still in New Orleans, he would help them again.

Those were her last thoughts as her weary mind and body gave way to exhaustion. She closed her eyes, slowly dozing off, as the men and women of the flatboat chatted around her.

A long time later, just as the darkness over the river was beginning to gray into daylight, something awoke her. She sat up as Mrs. McFern gave a short scream. Bethany looked around, her bleary eyes focusing on the object of Mrs. McFern's fright. To her cold, stark horror, she saw Luke Randall striding directly toward her like some ancient, wrathful god, his brown, nearly naked body still glistening with water.

"Ooooh!" cried a young woman on the other side of Bethany, succumbing to a shocked swoon, but Bethany wasted no time on fainting spells, not after seeing the lethal look on Luke Randall's face. She scrambled for dear life, her only thought to get to Peeto. But she wasn't quick enough; Luke's hands closed around her arms. Bethany's knees turned to jelly as he held her in an iron grip, his wet, powerful body nearly touching her heaving breasts as he jerked her off the ground, shaking her like a rag doll. Just as quickly as Luke had arrived, several men closed in on him, their guns aimed at the intruder's bare chest.

"Who the devil are you, walking in here half naked amongst our womenfolk?" Captain McFern demanded furiously. "We could have shot you, thinkin' you was an Injun, dressed like that! Where in tarnation ye come from, man?"

"I floated down on a couple of logs I lashed together after this bloody little thief stole my canoe and everything else I had," Luke said, grinding out the words savagely.

"What?" McFern sputtered. "That poor little lass come to us with her son—"

"He's *my* son, dammit! She abducted him from St. Louis, and I can prove it. There's a warrant for her arrest in my buckskins in the canoe."

Bethany felt dozens of eyes swing to her in condemnation as Captain McFern sent a man to the canoe to verify Luke's story. Moments later, the man returned with the warrant in hand, and Bethany's would-be protectors backed away, leaving her to Luke's righteous fury.

Fear held her in an icy grip as he nearly dragged her after him to the canoe.

"Sit," he ordered, and she sank down obediently while he quickly donned his buckskins. His breathing was hard and rapid, and she could almost feel the waves of cold rage emanating from him.

"Get your clothes off."

"What?" Bethany gasped, looking around as if to run, but long brown fingers shot out to capture her slim wrist.

"I said to take off your clothes. Now, or I'll do it for you."

Frightened, Bethany did as he ordered, quickly slipping out of her shirt. She covered her breasts with her crossed arms, shivering in the predawn chill.

"The rest of it, too," he intoned harshly.

Bethany obeyed, cringing in humiliation, but Luke hardly looked at her as he threw a blanket at her. Bethany pulled it gratefully around her shoulders.

"You left me without clothes," he said coldly. "Let's see how you like it."

Bethany huddled in the bottom of the canoe while he strode off to get Peeto. She was embarrassed and cold, but glad the people of the flatboat party were too busy with their preparations for disembarkation to witness her humiliation. She was so furious with Luke Randall she could kill him! She never thought he could find a way downstream! On a makeshift raft? It was impossible!

She tensed all over as he approached again, carrying a fussing Peeto, but the boy quieted as soon as Luke handed him to Bethany.

"Don't ever try anything like that again, girl, do you understand me? Never."

Something in his voice terrified Bethany, and she shivered under her blanket as he pushed the canoe into the river and began to paddle.

Chapter 3

Around noon, Luke relented about Bethany's clothes. They were nearing a small river settlement where an old friend of Luke operated a trading post. They would stop there to eat and stretch their legs. Anger still churned in his gut over Bethany Cole's foolhardy stunt, even more so at himself for allowing it to happen. He had been stupid and careless, but who would have thought a young girl like her would take off on the river at night the way she had? He wouldn't ever turn his back on her again, that was for damn sure.

She was in the bow, wrapped toe to chin in the blanket. Her gaze promptly slid guiltily away and her small jaw angled upward at a stubborn slant that belied her subdued mien. He knew she would try again if given half a chance, but she wasn't going to get one.

As they neared the small, cleared bluff where Old John had his place, Luke gazed up at the scattering of roughhewn log cabins above the river. A blacksmith's shop and a small inn were set back from the trading post and livery stable. A plume of smoke rose from the fieldstone chimney hugging one end of the store, and a gaunt-ribbed cow grazed near the front porch.

Luke beached the canoe on the narrow strip of sand, then swung into the knee-deep water. He picked up his rifle and tossed Bethany her shirt and pants.

"Put them on. You're staying here with the canoe, but Pete's coming with me."

Bethany put on her clothes eagerly as Luke lifted a subdued Peeto onto his hip. She watched silently as they trudged up the hill. She wouldn't go anywhere without Peeto, and Luke Randall knew it.

As Luke reached the small, leaning porch, he heard several voices from inside the combination saloon and mercantile, and he looked around. There hadn't been another boat on the beach, so the other travelers must be riders from nearby Natchez Trace. As he climbed the rickety steps, still carrying Peeto on one hip, he saw three horses tied to a hitching rail by Old John's livery stable.

Inside, a dozen men lounged around the planked bar and scuffed-topped wooden tables, most of whom Luke recognized to be longtime inhabitants of the tiny settlement. Old John stood near the bar, but when the old man saw Luke, he came forward at once, his grizzled face splitting into a welcoming grin.

"Well, if it ain't Luke Randall hissef! Whar the hell ye been, man?"

"West," Luke answered laconically, and the old man's rheumy eyes went to the boy in Luke's arms.

"What manner of varmit you got thar?"

"This is my boy. We're going down to New Orleans."

"I'll be damned for cursin'. I ain't never knowed

you had no boy! Come over har and have a drink wid me. You still trappin'?''

''Yeah,'' Luke answered, his eyes roving the room. Two men sitting at a nearby table attracted his attention. They both returned his gaze with narrowed, speculative eyes until his unwavering green stare caused them to look away. They were trouble, bad trouble; he knew that with the sixth sense he had developed in the mountains, where a man couldn't survive without it.

''Who are they?'' Luke asked Old John, and the man lowered his voice.

''They be the Hackett brothers, and thar's not one decent bone in the three of 'em together.''

''Three?''

''One's outside somewhar or druthers. That be Smilin' Jack in the black shirt. He's the one wid the big teeth, and that one wid the red hair and skinny mustache be Bucko. The other one goes by Braid, 'cause he's got long hair all braided up with bear fat. They rode in this mornin', and I ain't turned my back on 'em since.''

''I wouldn't, if I were you.''

''Heard tell they murdered a family on the Trace awhiles back, woman and children, too, but nobody can prove it.''

Luke's hand moved to Peeto's shoulder, where the boy stood quietly beside him. He could believe the Hacketts were capable of murder just by looking at them. He ordered his supplies, suddenly anxious to get Peeto away from the hard men drinking whiskey at the table, and very glad he had not brought Bethany Cole inside with him. He had no doubt they would consider a young girl like her fair game.

* * *

On the riverbank, Bethany paced back and forth
beside the canoe, glad for the opportunity to exercise
her cramped legs. Her stomach rumbled, and she felt
as if she was coming down with a chill from sleeping
in her wet clothes. At least she had them on, she
thought. She looked up at the buildings above her,
wishing Luke and Peeto would come back with some
food. She could smell the mouthwatering aroma of
roast venison, and if this trading post was like her
father's place, there would be plenty of vegetable stew
as well. And fresh bread and ale. She stopped, staring
up at the cabin. What was taking them so long?

She frowned, walking a short distance up the hill
to see if they were coming. They were still inside,
and she turned back toward the canoe, less than willing to make Luke Randall angry again. She intended
to keep her clothes on.

Halfway down the dirt path along the side of the
bluff, a sound brought her to an abrupt standstill.
Weeping. Soft, heartbroken weeping. Her first thought
was that it was Peeto, hurt or frightened. Alarmed,
she ran back up the hill. She was very near the livery
stable, but as she stopped there to listen, she realized
it was not a child she heard.

It was a woman, she decided, and never had Bethany heard such awful, hopeless sounds of misery, not
even in the orphanage, where muffled whimpers came
in the dark of night after a new child arrived, all alone
and afraid. Even then, Bethany had always gotten up
to lend comfort, because she knew how the children
felt. She had cried herself to sleep many times, her
face hidden in her pillow so the dormitory matron
wouldn't hear and punish her, and her heart twisted

in compassion now for whoever was suffering in the stable.

She looked around warily, moving past the horses at the hitching rail to peer inside the open doors. The dim stalls were quiet and deserted, but when the crying began again, Bethany followed the sounds to the last stall. A small figure sat huddled in the corner, her face in her hands. Bethany knelt, reaching out to touch the girl's tangled brown hair.

The girl flinched, flailing weakly at Bethany with both hands.

Bethany gasped, horrified by the ugly bruises covering the girl's face. Angry welts and older, yellowing bruises covered her arms and one shoulder revealed by her torn dress, and her eyes were so swollen that it was impossible to discern what she had looked like before the terrible beating.

"Who did this to you?" Bethany whispered, catching the girl's hands, but the poor thing shrank away, as if expecting more blows.

"Please, let me help you," Bethany said urgently, afraid that whoever had abused the girl would come back.

The beaten girl suddenly grabbed Bethany's arm, and muttered hoarsely in a language she did not understand. *"Aide-moi, Jacques, mon beau Jacques. Il veut me tuer—"*

"Come on, try to stand up. I'll help you," Bethany said, draping the girl's arm around her shoulder. She had to get her out of there, Bethany thought wildly, but the girl was too weak to stand and spoke pleadingly in her own language. Desperate, Bethany half dragged the girl toward the door.

"Whar'd you come from, gal?"

The crude voice sent Bethany's blood running cold, and she whirled around to stare in horror at the tall, skinny man slouched in the doorway. He wore a filthy blue shirt and black breeches with some kind of animal skin vest, and his hair was black and oily, braided in a queue that hung to his waist. He smelled awful, of some terrible odor that Bethany didn't recognize, and when he smiled, she saw dirty, broken teeth, except for one gold tooth in front that hung down like the fang of a wolf. Her eyes dropped to the slim leather whip he carried in one hand.

"You weren't thinkin' to steal me wench thar, was ya now?" he asked, raising the whip to scratch at his braid.

Bethany sprinted straight for him, so quick that he had no time to react when her doubled fist hit him square in the nose. His head jerked back and blood spurted. Cursing in rage, he caught her by the hair as she tried to dart past him.

"Now whatcha gonna do, bitch?" he growled, and Bethany grunted in pain as she was flung to the ground near the other girl. She screamed as the whip whistled down and white-hot agony erupted in her cheek.

Luke stopped near the top of the path, as Bethany's cries echoed from somewhere to his left. He turned toward the stables, then cursed as Peeto lit off in that direction before Luke could stop him. He dropped his sack of food, following the boy at a run, and seconds later burst through the stable door just as Peeto threw himself on the man who was bending over Bethany.

Luke frowned, hauling Bethany's assailant up by his vest with one hand and sending a steel-knuckled fist into his face. Braid Hackett went over backward and lay unmoving in the straw as Peeto scrambled into Bethany's arms.

"Did he hurt you?" Luke asked Bethany, his eyes on the swollen weal across her cheek.

She shook her head. "No, but there's a girl over there that he hurt real bad."

For the first time, Luke saw the girl cowering against the stall. He went down on one knee beside her, wincing at the sight of her battered face.

"We can't leave her here," Bethany was saying. "He'll kill her if we do. Please, please don't leave her here."

"We're not leaving anybody," Luke said, handing Bethany his rifle as he carefully lifted the frail girl in his arms. He headed toward the door, but as he stepped outside, Smiling Jack and Bucko blocked his path.

"Whar the bloody hell you be goin' wid our woman?" Jack Hackett demanded.

"We're taking her out of here, so get out of our way," came Bethany's voice from behind Luke before he could reply. Luke cursed under his breath as both Hacketts turned their attention to the diminutive girl carrying a rifle every bit as tall as she was.

Expecting trouble now, Luke lowered the beaten girl to the ground. As Smiling Jack went for the flint-lock pistol in his belt, Luke lunged at him, tackling him around the waist. Bucko drew his knife to stab Luke, and Bethany pointed the rifle at him, closed her eyes, and squeezed the trigger.

The bullet struck him square in the chest, knocking him off his feet, and he was dead before he hit the ground.

When he saw the blood on his brother's chest,

Smiling Jack roared in rage. Luke rolled to one side, trying to get to the pistol in his belt, but before he could pull it out, Hackett had Peeto by the throat and was aiming his gun at the boy's temple.

"I'll kill the kid if you move, you bastard," Hackett cried, his eyes darting to the group of shouting men who'd been drawn from the saloon by the sound of gunfire.

As the men ran toward them, Smiling Jack backed away to the horses, holding Peeto tightly around the neck as he mounted. Luke made his move before Hackett could kick the horse into a gallop. He dove for the reins, and the horse reared in fright, its hooves flailing the air as Luke tried to pull Hackett out of the saddle.

Bethany screamed as Peeto fell. She tried desperately to get him out of the way of the prancing horse, but one of the sharp hooves struck the child's head before she could drag him out of the way.

Jack Hackett hung on, managing to spur the horse enough to loosen Luke's grip on his arm, then thundered away down the road into the woods, leaving his brothers behind, one dead, one unconscious.

"Petie, Petie," Bethany cried, cradling the boy in her arms as Luke fell to his knees beside her.

"Come on, let's get him inside," Luke said as he examined the bloody cut at the back of Peeto's head. "Old John will bring the girl."

An hour later, Bethany sat upstairs at the tiny inn, holding Peeto's hand as Old John wrapped a linen bandage around the boy's forehead.

"He'll be all right, missy. It ain't half as bad as it

looks. He just be needin' to be restful fer a spell, and he'll mend right up as good as new.''

Bethany gave him a grateful smile, then glanced at the girl on the other bed. ''What about her? Will she be all right, too?''

Old John shook his head. ''They like to beat her plumb to death, and we's right here close and dint even know it. Those there Hacketts are pure poison, all three of them, murderin' and thievin' and butcherin' anybody who looks at 'em wrong.''

''There's only two of them now,'' came Luke's voice from the door. ''Bucko's dead, but the one we left in the barn is nowhere to be found. How's Pete?''

''He be makin' it fine, I reckon. You best stay the night and let him have a spot of rest.''

''We'll leave in the morning then,'' Luke said, propping his rifle by the door. ''But I intend to get Hackett for what he did to Pete.''

Luke's voice sounded like chiseled granite. Bethany watched him bid good night to the stooped old man, but she swung around as the girl behind her rose into a sitting position. As the girl began to scream, Bethany went to her, and to her surprise, Luke sat down on the edge of the girl's bed, taking the frightened girl by the shoulders. He spoke to her in her own tongue, calmly, firmly, and after a moment, she suddenly went limp in his arms. Luke pulled her against his shoulder, murmuring soothing words while she wept.

Bethany stared at him, astonished to see the big, mean fur trapper display such tenderness. The girl cried and cried, all the while speaking rapidly against his leather tunic.

"What kind of talk is that?" Bethany asked after a time.

"It's Creole French. That's what they speak in New Orleans."

"What's she saying?"

"She says her name is Michelle and that she ran away with a white man. The Hacketts attacked them on the Trace."

"What do you mean about a white man?"

"She's an octoroon," Luke told her as he lowered the quieted girl to the bed. Bethany covered her with the blanket, but she still didn't understand.

"Octoroon? What does that mean?"

"It means she's one-eighth Negro, probably from a quadroon grandmother. It's one of the upper color castes in New Orleans; at least it was when I was there."

"You've been there?" Bethany asked, for some reason surprised by that.

Their eyes met. "Yeah, I've been there."

Bethany was more than curious as to when and where, and why he was acting so strange about it, but he gave her no chance to question him. He rose again and sat down at a small table by the window, laying out his brace of pistols in front of him. Bethany tucked the covers around Peeto as Luke began to clean and reload his guns. She sat beside Peeto, realizing how totally exhausted she was.

Her eyes closed wearily, and eventually her head fell back against the wall. Sometime later, when something lightly touched her cheek, she jerked back to awareness. Luke Randall was standing close above her.

"Is it very painful? Your cheek?" he asked, studying the darkened bruise on the side of her face.

Bethany shook her head, surprised he had even noticed it.

"Better get some sleep," he told her. "We're leaving at dawn."

"Are you going to let Michelle come with us?" Bethany asked.

"Yeah. John said the Hacketts will be back for her if we leave her here."

Bethany lay down close to Peeto, cold chills rising on the back of her neck as she remembered Braid Hackett, with his whip and awful-smelling hair, and Jack Hackett's cold, cruel smile. Suddenly, she was very glad to be with Luke Randall. He was so big and strong, yet he had been gentle, too, with both Peeto and the girl named Michelle. He wouldn't let the Hacketts hurt them.

Chapter 4

As they floated past the riverfront of New Orleans on the wide bend of the Mississippi River, Bethany was amazed to see the high river levees the inhabitants of the city had erected to protect their low-lying homes from the annual flood waters. The earth embankments were at least thirty feet high, and she found it incredible that their canoe rode high enough in the water to look out over the rooftops of the city.

Behind her in the stern, Luke paddled steadily, as he had since early that morning when they had left Old John's trading post. They had traveled hard all day in order to reach New Orleans before nightfall, and she had nervously watched the shoreline for the Hacketts in case the terrible brothers found a way to follow. She looked back to where Michelle lay wrapped in a blanket next to Peeto and shuddered to think of what the poor octoroon girl must have suffered at the hands of three such brutal men. Michelle was still very weak, slipping in and out of consciousness throughout the day. At the moment, Peeto slept as well, but he was much better, thank goodness. Bethany was proud of the way the boy had helped soothe Michelle when she awoke in terror.

44

Glancing back at Luke, she wondered why he hadn't taken the canoe alongside one of the landing wharves. They had passed many wharves where long rows of flatboats and keelboats were docked along the earthen levee like great stepping-stones. At midstream, a forest of masts indicated a vast number of ocean sailing ships visiting the city from places far and wide.

Bethany searched in vain for a glimpse of the *Mariette*, because it was very likely Captain Hosie was still in the city, selling his cargo before he labored to propell his boat back up the mighty river. She wasn't sure what Luke meant to do with her, because he seemed a little softer toward her now, even though he had said next to nothing the whole day. Perhaps he wouldn't put her in jail, after all. Perhaps he would let her stay with Peeto. But if Luke did decide to jail her, she would escape and find Captain Hosie. He would help her.

Bethany lay her paddle across the bow in front of her as they floated past a great open area near the river, which Bethany assumed was some kind of military parade ground. Both the Spanish and French seemed inclined to include such a place in their settlements along the Mississippi, but behind the grassy field stood a large, triple-spired church and several other massive stone buildings of Spanish design. Scores of pedestrians moved about the square, despite the encroaching dusk, but Luke still made no attempt to land along the high levee.

A short time later, they left the town behind, and the landscape began to take on an almost funereal look from the huge, thick-branched live oak trees draped with long gray moss that resembled tattered shrouds. Not long after, as the shadows of night deepened over the river, Bethany saw with relief that Luke was finally ruddering the canoe toward a wide wooden loading platform that extended for perhaps thirty yards along the river levee.

Bethany remained in the bow as Luke climbed out and gave a couple of sharp jerks to the black iron bell affixed to a weathered piling on the dock. Three loud clangs echoed in the twilight quiet, and Peeto sat up, rubbing his eyes with his fists. Michelle didn't move.

"Where are we?" Bethany asked tentatively.

"Cantigny Plantation. You help Pete, and I'll get the girl."

He easily lifted the thin girl out of the canoe, waiting with her in his arms while Bethany and Peeto stepped out; then they followed him across the dock. Narrow wooden steps led to the top of the levee, where a dirt road stretched out upriver. Not far in the distance, Bethany could see the lights of New Orleans. Cantigny Plantation was situated surprisingly close to the city.

At the sound of shouts, she looked down the other side of the embankment and saw the glow of torches coming toward them through the darkness. She stopped, holding Peeto close, as a group of people came into sight. The handsome man in the lead was tall with broad shoulders, dark curly hair, and a thick mustache. His face creased with pleasure as he greeted Luke.

"Luke! Good God, where'd you come from?" he cried, then, upon sight of the limp girl in his brother's arms, he drew up in surprise. "Who's that?"

"She's hurt pretty bad. We found her upriver at Old John's."

"Here, Micah can take her to the house," the man said, gesturing at a big black man standing just behind him. The Negro servant immediately took the girl from Luke, and his master added, "Take her to Tante Chloe, then run for the doctor."

"Tell him to bring the sheriff as well," Luke said, and Bethany's body went rigid. He *was* going to throw her into prison! She held back slightly as Luke turned, drawing both her and Peeto into the torchlight.

"This is Pete, Andy. Pete, this is your Uncle Andrew."

"You found him then! That's wonderful!" Andrew Randall exclaimed, his gaze moving to Bethany. "Is she the one who took him?"

"She's the one," Luke answered mildly, "but right now we're all tired and hungry. Let's get up to the house."

"Of course. I'm sorry," Andrew said quickly. "I've been anxious to show you around Cantigny." He turned to the handful of Negro servants still waiting behind him. "Jess, run up to the house and have Elise ready the guest rooms, and have the cook prepare food for everyone."

Luke picked up Peeto in his arms, and Bethany followed them up a graveled road between twin rows of massive oaks with the curious moss. Awed, she stared at the plantation house at the end of the avenue, its windows ablaze with light. It was as big as the mansions she had seen atop the bluffs in Natchez, where all the wealthy aristocrats lived. Six stately columns graced the semicircular portico that faced the river, and symmetrical wings stretched out on either side. Both the first and second floors had wide stone

galleries supported by long rows of columns. As
Bethany followed the men up wide brick steps set
with urns, then across the porch to a set of tall carved
doors with a gigantic fanlight, she wondered if Cantigny belonged to Luke's brother.

Inside, the first thing she noticed was the clean
smell of beeswax and lemon oil such as Mistress Anne
had used on her cherrywood tables in her sitting
rooms. Then her gaze swept across the black-and-
white-tiled foyer to where a beautiful staircase as-
cended in a graceful curve to a wide mezzanine. A
huge chandelier was suspended on long velvet ropes
from the high plastered ceiling, its crystal teardrop
prisms tinkling musically as cooling river breezes
wafted through the front door.

When Luke set Peeto down, the little boy immediately ran to Bethany, who picked him up, glad to
have his small warmth in her arms again. Her gaze
drifted again to the elegant stairway and glittering gold
mirrors. Two handsome Negro maids wearing black
silk dresses and white ruffled aprons stood waiting at
the bottom of the steps, and Bethany suddenly felt
ugly in her dirty shirt and torn breeches. This house
was much grander than Hugh Younger's estate on Olive Street, and Bethany had thought *that* was a palace
beyond compare.

"The maids there will take you upstairs, so you
can put Pete to bed," Luke told Bethany. Without
waiting for her answer, he turned to accompany his
brother across the glossy foyer to a door at the rear
of the house.

"She seems a harmless little thing," Andrew said
as he crossed the library to his desk and lifted the lid
of a silver cigar box.

Luke gave him a sour look as he chose one of the narrow Cuban cheroots his brother offered him. "Bethany Cole's a whole lot of things, believe me, but she's not harmless," he said, puffing the cigar to flame as Andrew held a taper for him. "I learned that the hard way."

"She gave you some trouble?" Andrew asked, obviously surprised.

Luke sat down in a leather armchair, his smile grim. "Well, I'll tell you this much. When I ran across her a couple of days ago, she slapped the side of my head with a string of fish and tried to kill me with a pitchfork. Then she stole everything I had, including my clothes, and took off with Pete in my canoe. Last but not least, she nearly got us all killed when she tried to rescue that poor battered octoroon you saw a moment ago."

"Is that all?" Andrew asked with a straight face, his dark blue eyes twinkling with amusement.

"So far," Luke replied, "but tomorrow's another day."

Andrew laughed. "She hardly looked big enough to cause you that much grief."

"That's right. She's not much more than a kid herself."

Andrew's expression sobered. "Not according to the letters I've received from Hugh. He's accusing her of everything in the book. He insists she's a criminal of the worst sort."

"And she says Hugh abused Pete. That's why she took him."

"You don't believe that, do you?"

Luke studied the glowing tip of his cigar, taking a moment to consider. "I didn't at first, but I'm begin-

ning to have doubts about Hugh's story. You should
see her with Pete. She loves him, there's no doubt
about that. And he loves her.''

''He's a handsome boy.''

''Yes, he is.''

Andrew grinned. ''I'm glad you found him. I've
been worried. But what are you going to do about
Hugh's warrant? The sheriff will be here soon.''

''I don't want him for her. I'm not putting her in
prison. If it hadn't been for her, I'd be dead right
now.''

''Dead! What the hell happened on this trip?''

''She shot a man at Old John's before he could help
his brother finish me off. That's where we picked up
Michelle, from three bastards named Hackett.''

Andrew's eyes darted to Luke's face. ''Hackett?
Not Jack Hackett?''

Luke turned to him. ''He's the worst one. The one
named Bucko is dead now, and the one with the braid
got away. Do you know them?''

''I know of them. Jack Hackett and his brothers
are the scourge of the Trace, Luke, and have been for
years now. It's bandied around that they killed their
own mother when they were just boys. There are other
stories, as well—so grisly I didn't want to believe they
were true.''

''Believe them. The men I tangled with are capable
of anything. They nearly beat that poor little octoroon
to death, and I want them. Jack Hackett held a gun
to my son's head and nearly trampled him with his
horse. I want him hung for his crimes. As soon as
the sheriff gets here, I mean to put a price on his
head, one so big that his own brother will turn him
in.''

* * *

After Luke and Andrew had disappeared into the library, Bethany carried Peeto up the beautiful stairs set with gleaming banisters and covered by a thick crimson carpet that silenced their footsteps. The maid led them down a wide corridor on the second floor lined with fine settees and chairs of gold-and-white striped satin.

"I bez Elise, mamzelle," the maid said in heavily accented patois, as she opened the door of a bedchamber. "Zour bath bez in de alcove le toilette, and zour supper bez by de fire, iv you pliz."

Bethany waited for the polite chambermaid to depart before she examined the spacious bedchamber. It was furnished in the height of luxury, the drapes made with some kind of rich fabric of a lovely rose color trimmed in ivory lace, but she hardly even looked at the immense white four-poster bed hung with a billowing white netting caught up at the corners with gold ribbons. A set of elegant French doors opened onto the upstairs gallery, and Bethany stepped outside, still carrying Peeto in her arms. She stood very still in the darkness, afraid to believe Luke had not thought to post a guard at her door.

The night was quiet except for the sound of the rushing river, and there was no one in sight. She could walk right out with Peeto, and if she didn't Luke would put her in jail just as soon as the sheriff arrived at Cantigny. She had to try to make it back to New Orleans. She had no choice.

Peeto lay his head on her shoulder, and Bethany patted his back. He was so tired, and his head probably still ached. How could she expect him to walk all the way back to town? It wasn't far, but he was so little. She knelt down, cupping his cheek in one palm.

"Luke's going to put me in jail if I stay here, Petie. He's already sent for the sheriff. I have to try to find Captain Hosie. I know you're tired—"

"Don't leave me here with him. Don't leave me!" Peeto clutched her neck in a stranglehold, and Bethany squeezed him tight.

"I won't, I promise, but we have to hurry before Luke finds out. Do you want me to carry you?"

Peeto shook his head, and she hugged him again before taking his hand and tiptoeing down the gallery. Behind the next set of French doors was the room to which they had taken Michelle. Bethany could see several servants hovering around the girl's bed, and she was relieved to see that Michelle was being cared for.

They slipped past silently, then hurried down the stone steps she found at the rear of the mansion. She and Peeto immediately ran out among the dark, eerie trees. When they reached the levee, there was enough moonlight to give them a shadowy path to follow.

Bethany hurried along, her heart beating with the dreadful fear that Luke would discover them gone and ring the alarm bell. After ten minutes of swift walking, Peeto began to lag, and Bethany picked him up.

"Just a little farther, sweetie. I know you're tired. Lay your head on my shoulder and rest."

Bethany trudged on, her arms aching from Peeto's weight, and she sighed in relief when she saw the first house on the outskirts of town. She set Peeto down at the first streetlamp, looking back down the river the way they had come. The imagined vision of the look on Luke's face when he found out she had taken his son again struck terror into her heart. She hurried along the wooden sidewalk beneath the levee, her goal the crowded wharves and the *Mariette*.

Tall lamps of lacy hand-wrought iron cast circles of yellow light that chased away the dark along their path. A knot of young men stood laughing and drinking ale from tankards in front of the open entrance to one brightly lit waterfront dive. They were boatmen, Bethany could tell by their grimy leather pants and red flannel shirts. Captain Hosie was well known and well liked among the rivermen who plied the mighty Mississippi, and it was likely that one of these men drinking toasts to the river might know where she could find him.

"Your pardon, sir," she said loudly, stepping into the light to address the young man nearest her, "but I'm looking for a friend, a Captain Hosea Richmond of the *Mariette*. Do you know where I might find him?"

The man she had spoken to was barely older than Bethany herself, and more than a little intoxicated, but he endeavored to answer her query in a gentlemanly fashion, and the others in his boisterous group interrupted their conversation to stare at her and Peeto.

"I don't rightly recollect knowin' the bloke, missy, but—" The tipsy fellow scowled and muttered an oath as one of his companions jostled him aside.

Bethany gasped as the newcomer grabbed her by the arm, his other hand clamping under her chin and forcing her face toward the wall lamp.

"By God, boys, it be her! Lookee here, just lookee at her face!"

Bethany struggled to free herself as another man held a piece of parchment up alongside her face.

"See thar, it be her all right. And lookee thar, lookee, thar's the kid!"

The speaker grabbed Peeto by the waist, and although the boy put up a fight, screaming Bethany's name at the top of his lungs, he could not break free. Bethany increased her own struggles and managed to strike the toe of her boot against the shin of the man holding her. It connected with a crack, eliciting a shriek of pain, but before she could land another blow, her feet were held tight, and she found herself being carried down the street amid the laughing, shouting men, while several others dragged Peeto along after them.

An hour after Luke's arrival at his Louisiana plantation, he still sat in the book-lined library, finishing his supper and going over with Andrew the accounts of the last year's sugarcane crop. Both he and Andrew looked up when there was a tap on the door, followed by the waddling entrance of Tante Chloe, the huge Negress in charge of the household staff.

"Excusez-moi, messieurs, bud men bez here. 'Bout de reward."

"Show them in," Andrew told her, then turned to Luke in explanation. "Hugh sent me a pencil etching of the girl, and I had it posted all over the city. I've already had a half a dozen false leads like this one. Now that you've found her, I'll have the posters taken down."

Luke nodded absently, glancing down at the figures

on the paper in front of him as three men were ushered into the library.

"They took Beth! They took her!" Peeto screamed at first sight of Luke. Luke's head jerked up, then he shot to his feet at the sight of the three strangers restraining his son.

"What the devil's going on here?" he demanded sharply. "Let him go."

Peeto ran to Luke when they released him, and Luke picked him up, realizing as the boy wrapped both arms around his neck that it was the first time his son had come willingly to him.

"It's all right, Pete. What happened? Where's Beth?"

"They took her away, they took her away," Peeto repeated over and over, until Luke raised chilling green eyes to the men in front of him.

"Who are you? What are you doing here?"

"They got her locked up down at the calaboose," said one of the men, "but we's the ones who saw her first so we gets the reward money. We ain't leavin' here until we gets it," he added with a wary look at the big, black-bearded man.

"That's impossible. Beth's upstairs."

"No, she ain't. We found her down on the wharf with the boy there."

"Is that true, Pete?" Luke asked, holding the boy out so he could look at him. Peeto nodded, tears running down his face, and Luke knew immediately what had happened.

"Pay them, Andy," he said, setting Peeto down on the edge of the desk, then squatting in front of him. "Beth took you into town tonight, didn't she, Pete?"

Fat tears filled Peeto's big eyes, and Luke pulled his son close.

"Don't worry about Beth anymore. I'm going to get her right now and bring her back here. You go with Tante Chloe. She'll put you to bed, and when you wake up, Beth will be here."

Peeto hesitated.

"I promise," Luke added, and Peeto reluctantly let the big Negress lead him out of the library, just as Andrew reappeared from an adjoining room.

"I paid them, but you'd better hurry. They said the girl put up one hell of a fight when they took Pete away from her. And, believe me, the calaboose is no place for a young girl like her."

Luke shook his head angrily. "That little fool! If it wasn't for Pete, I'd let her spend the night in jail, just to teach her a lesson."

Andrew heard the anger in Luke's voice and shook his head as Luke left to order the carriage. If being thrown in the calaboose wasn't enough, the poor girl was also going to have to face a good-sized dose of his older brother's formidable wrath.

At half past midnight, Luke was pacing the cold stone floor in the granite auspices of the Cabildo. He had been ushered into the small, ground-floor office almost three hours before, and if the damned police commissionaire didn't show up soon, he was furious enough to take the keys from the ignorant jailers outside and find Bethany's cell himself.

A black frown rode his brow as he prowled back and forth, a muscle twitching in his cheek at the thought of what she had done. Damn the girl! Didn't she have any sense at all? Getting herself thrown in prison! Not to mention endangering Peeto the way she had! By God, he'd damn well better lock her up in a barred room at Cantigny to keep her out of trouble!

"Ah, *le sauvage*, it's been a long time, eh?"

Luke stiffened at the derogatory name and spun around to find Monsieur Maurice Rachene behind him. He hadn't seen the rotund police commissionaire in ten years, but he looked the same, with his balding head and gray-streaked goatee. They had not liked each other then, and Luke didn't like the man now.

"That's right, Rachene," Luke answered showing no sign of that dislike.

"And already trouble has begun," Rachene stated as he carefully folded his black velvet cloak, and hung it on a brass coat tree. He studied Luke as he tugged off his spotless white gloves and placed them on the desktop. "I assure you, my wife, Adelaine, was sorely vexed when I was summoned from the opera and could not escort her home."

Luke had almost forgotten how pompous and self-important Rachene could be, but he swallowed his ire, remembering from his past dealings with the man that he would have to use diplomacy to free Bethany.

"I apologize for the inconvenience," Luke said, "but it is of the utmost importance that one of your prisoners be released. She is hardly more than a child, and her arrest was a misunderstanding."

"Indeed? Perhaps you should let me be the judge of that," the policeman said, lifting the back of his formal evening jacket before he sat down behind his desk. "Would you join me in a glass of wine?"

Luke gritted his teeth to hide his growing impatience, but he said nothing as the Creole took a great deal of time pouring two tumblers of brandy. Luke accepted the glass offered to him, and—to his further annoyance—it took twenty minutes more to convince the stupid fool that Bethany should be released into his custody. Even then, Monsieur Rachene was not particularly cooperative.

"I find this strange, I must say, monsieur," Rachene said, "but perhaps if you could assume the costs of her incarceration, we might be able to arrange something."

So bribery was still alive and well in the Vieux Carré, Luke thought in cold contempt.

"How much, Rachene?"

"Five hundred francs, perhaps, but Monsieur Younger must personally drop the charges against her. Will he be willing to make the journey downriver to do that?"

"Of course. Andrew will arrange everything. He will issue you a bank draft from the Banque de la Louisiane in the morning."

Monsieur Rachene still took his time. "I must have your signature on the custody agreement. We do want to ensure the legality of this transaction, do we not?"

Luke nodded, trying not to show how close he was to losing his temper as the Creole penned the agreement in a slow, careful hand. When Rachene had put the last flourishing touches upon it, Luke skimmed it quickly, then signed, eager to be done with the business.

"The jailers tell me the girl was distraught when

they brought her here. They were forced to restrain her, you understand.''

Luke wasn't surprised that Bethany had resisted her capture, especially with Peeto's safety in question. He remembered clearly the fight she had put up on the day they met. He was glad when Rachene finally led him from the office, then up a narrow staircase at the back of the building. After climbing more stone steps and traipsing down several long, dark corridors lined with prison doors, Luke lost patience.

''Where the devil is she?'' he demanded acidly.

''Not far,'' Rachene told him calmly, and a moment later, the jailer on duty in front of a heavy wooden door with a barred grate at eye level inserted a metal key in the black iron lock. Luke felt a wave of satisfaction when he saw the dried blood caked around the guard's hawkish nose. Bethany Cole had a hell of a right hook. The door swung inward with a scrape, and the guard bent forward to send the light of his lantern into the dark cell.

Bethany was in one corner, on her knees on the cold, dank floor. Her arms were stretched up over her head, her wrists manacled to an iron ring fastened to the wall. She looked small and helpless, and as Luke went to her, fury such as he had rarely experienced shot through him.

Bethany turned to look at him, fighting her tears. ''I guess you had to come and see me in chains for yourself,'' she said hoarsely. ''I guess it makes you feel real good.''

Luke ignored her words, turning glittering eyes on the jailer. ''Damn you, get those irons off her.''

The guard hurriedly unlocked the heavy bands on her wrists, and the chain clattered to the stones.

"Come on, Beth, I'm taking you home," Luke muttered. But as soon as Bethany's hands were free, her fingers caught at the fringe of his tunic.

"They took Petie, Luke! No one would tell me where he is!"

"He's safe with Andy at Cantigny. Now come on, let's get out of here."

Bethany let him help her up, but her legs were too numb to hold her weight. When they crumbled beneath her, Luke put an arm under her and swept her up in his arms, carrying her out without another word to Rachene or his guards. She felt like a forlorn child in his arms, he thought, tired and weak and defenseless. He was glad when he was able to step out into the cool night air. Once in the dark confines of the carriage, Bethany huddled in the corner farthest from him. Luke stared at her, realizing that for all the courage and bravado she had displayed since they had met, she was scarcely more than a small, frightened girl.

"It's all over now," he murmured. "Just try to forget it."

"I'll never forget it," she answered in a low voice as she laid her cheek against the cushioned seat, fighting her exhaustion and emotions that were tattered after spending long hours in the cold, dark cell.

As the coach rocked along the road to Cantigny, she fell into a weary sleep. A short time later, when the coach drew up beneath the river portico, Luke took her in his arms. She didn't awaken as he carried her across the gallery to where Tante Chloe waited with a candle, then into the hall where a single candelabra burned on the newel post at the bottom of the grand staircase. He was halfway up the stairs before he saw Peeto, dressed in a small white night-dress and standing on the top step, his eyes huge with fear.

"Did they kill her?" he asked with horror, his bottom lip trembling.

"No, son, she's just asleep," Luke answered softly. "She's very tired. Run and pull down the covers on her bed."

Peeto hurried away, and Luke followed, gently lowering Bethany to the sheet as Peeto climbed onto the blue-and-gold embroidered bedstool. Luke watched from the foot of the four-poster as Peeto carefully tucked the soft pink comforter around Bethany's shoulders, then lay down as close as he could get to her. Two pair of identical jade green eyes met for a long moment.

"Do you remember me at all, Pete?"

Peeto closed his eyes without answering, settling his dark curls close to Bethany's blond ones.

Long after the boy slept, Luke stood leaning against the bedpost, watching them. They were such children, both of them. It was frightening to consider all they had gone through in order to remain together. Bethany Cole treated Peeto like a son of her own womb. She could never have had any ill motives toward him, no matter what Hugh had said.

Luke sighed with a great weariness of his own, then sank down in a velvet wing chair beside the bed. As he watched the two figures sleeping so peacefully in the bed, a thought came unbidden to his mind. He promptly pushed the idea aside considering it absurd, but it returned with unequalled persistence, again and again, until he was forced to give it closer scrutiny.

At dawn, when the faraway bell clanged in the slave's quarters, summoning the field-workers to breakfast, he was still sitting there, turning the thought over and over in his mind.

Chapter 5

Bethany's eyes fluttered open the moment Elise tugged the curtains back, flooding the large bedchamber with bright sunlight. She peered groggily at her surroundings before she realized that Peeto was sitting close beside her. As she struggled to sit up, he wrapped his arms around her neck.

"I was scared you wouldn't ever wake up," he whispered.

All the terror of the night before, when she had cowered alone in the horrible prison cell, came hurtling back, making her shudder. She fought the memories, patting Peeto's back.

"I'm all right now. Luke got me out."

It occurred to her then how little she could remember about the ride home, other than that Luke had been very kind. The whole series of events was like a strange, hazy memory, and the tender understanding he had shown her was such as she would never have thought possible from a man as hard as Luke Randall.

"Marster say dad zou be wantin' a bath, mamzelle," said Elise from the foot of the bed. "Jemsy, he brode it up for zou, and he make one for lil' boy. Marster say dad you no wantin' doze clothes zou wear. He say to burn them.''

Bethany looked down at the filthy shirt in which she had slept. ''Yes, please, burn them,'' she agreed with a shiver.

''Tante Chloe done cleaned zou udder things. They be hangin' in the chiffonier dere, if zou pliz. I take de lil' Marster for his toilette?''

Bethany stared at the maid, wondering at the respectful title she had given Peeto. She hugged the boy's shoulders. ''It's all right, Petie. Go have your bath. It'll make you feel better. Then we'll see about Michelle. Have you seen her this morning, Elise?''

''Le docteur say she bez dreadful sick and dad we muss teg kyah of her.''

As Peeto followed Elise out onto the gallery, Bethany stepped down from the bed, examining her bruised wrists. There were dark blue marks on her arms and legs, too, where the men had gripped her hard. She swallowed, remembering again the terror of those long hours she'd spent in the dark. She never, never wanted to be alone in the dark like that, not ever again.

Suddenly anxious to wash away all remnants of the prison from her body, she entered the bathing alcove, slipping out of her soiled shift and breeches and stepping into the hip bath. The warm, scented water felt like a silky caress against her skin as she eased down until submerged to her neck. She had not often experienced the luxury of a long, relaxing bath, and never in a porcelain hip bath like the one in which she now sat. A wooden washtub in front of the kitchen fire was more like what she was used to, without the lovely scent of roses rising from the warm mist.

Memories of the calaboose came back, and she felt slightly ill as she remembered the way the guard had jerked her around, laughing as he chained her to the wall. She took the small bar of soap shaped like a little rosebud and lathered it up to scrub every inch of her skin and hair.

She lay back then, wishing she could soak all the haunting memories from her mind as easily as she was soaking the dirt from her body. After a time, when the water began to cool, she got out and dried herself on the thick, soft towels. As she donned her clean breeches and shirt, her foremost thought was what Luke had in store for her now. He could have left her to rot in prison. Why hadn't he? He had threatened her earlier with that fate more than once.

A tap on the outside door preceded Elise's entrance. "Mamzelle? Marster wand you," she said with a bobbing curtsy. "In de library, if zou pliz."

"Who? Luke?"

"Oui, mamzelle."

Suddenly reluctant to find out what he planned for her, Bethany clasped her hands nervously together as Elise gathered up her discarded clothes.

"Elise?"

"Oui, mamzelle?"

"Did he—the marster, I mean—seem very angry when you saw him?"

Bethany saw a flare of fear in the chambermaid's chocolate brown eyes. "Non, mamzelle. He only said dad he wand to see zou."

"Have you known him long, Elise?" Bethany asked, remembering that Luke had been to New Orleans in the past.

"Oh, non," the maid answered quickly, then busied herself with the bed linens, as if reluctant to discuss the matter further.

Bethany stood in indecision, not looking forward to going downstairs. She moved to a polished cherrywood table and bent to look at herself in the small oval mirror. She stared at the ugly, perpendicular bruise across one cheek and several other red scratches on her neck, not at all pleased with her appearance. Her hair was still wet and tangled, and she picked up a heavy ivory-and-silver brush, taking a moment to examine the exquisite flower design on the silver handle. She'd never seen anything so beautiful. She sighed, drawing the bristles through her hair. She had better not make Luke wait or he might be even more angry with her.

"Tante Chloe says lil' marster be needin' hiz breakfast," Elise said as she smoothed the creases from the fresh sheets she had put on the bed.

"Who is Tante Chloe?"

"She be de one in charge of all de house peop', mamzelle."

"All right, but tell Petie I'll find him as soon as I can, would you?"

"Oui, mamzelle."

Bethany hesitated a few more moments after the maid left the room. Then, angry at herself for her own cowardice, she walked resolutely out the door. Nevertheless, once beyond the sanctuary of her room, she decided she should peek in on Michelle before she faced Luke in the library.

The octoroon's bedchamber was very dim, the heavy draperies drawn over the balcony door. Bethany tiptoed across to where Michelle lay asleep on the bed. Her face was still too swollen and discolored for Bethany to make out much of her features, but at least she slept peacefully now. She wore a clean nightdress, and someone had plaited her long brown hair into a heavy braid that lay over one shoulder. Bethany shook her head, her eyes on the splint wrapped with strips of white linen around the girl's left wrist. What horrors had Michelle experienced at the hands of the Hacketts? She left quietly, knowing that the girl needed a long, undisturbed rest more than anything. Tomorrow, perhaps, they could try to communicate.

In the upstairs hallway again, Bethany leaned over the banister, watching a downstairs maid glide silently over the gleaming white and black tiles below. When the girl was lost from sight near the back of the house, Bethany descended the curving steps and stood before the library door. She took a deep breath, fighting her urge to find Peeto and flee again.

"Come in," said Luke's deep voice in answer to her timid knock, and Bethany turned the knob, hoping the man named Andrew would be there as well. He had seemed a friendly sort. At least he smiled a lot. Unfortunately, Luke Randall sat alone behind a long, cluttered desk.

Large unadorned windows stretched tall behind him, revealing a lovely view of the tree-lined avenue leading to the river levee, but Bethany stared instead at Luke, barely able to recognize him as he stood to greet her. He had shaved off his thick black beard, and gone as well were the fringed Indian garments he had worn since she had known him.

Now he had on a shirt of snow-white linen, unbuttoned at the throat, which made his bronzed skin ap-

pear as dark as teak. As he moved around the desk
and came toward her, she saw that tan riding breeches
molded his hard-muscled thighs, and his high brown
boots were shiny enough to reflect her own scuffed
and muddy shoes. He looked every bit like the rich
aristocrats of St. Louis and Natchez-Atop-the-Hill,
whom Bethany had seen so many times in their grand
carriages. All of a sudden, she felt shabby and awk-
ward and ill at ease in his presence.

When Luke smiled, the first smile she remembered
seeing from him, her gaze dropped from his strong
white teeth and penetrating jade-colored eyes.

"Good morning, Beth."

She looked up again, instinctively aware that something had changed between them. Last night had made
some kind of difference, at least to him. Hope trembled alive inside her.

"Please sit down," he said politely.

Bethany did so, and he moved around the desk
again, lounging in his big swiveling desk chair. There
was something unsettling in the piercing green of his
eyes, something she couldn't quite define. When he
continued to study her without speaking, she looked
down at her lap, growing hot with embarrassment.

"Would you care for some breakfast?"

She shook her head.

"Coffee or tea, perhaps?"

He even talked differently now, she thought. It was
as if, when he took off his buckskins, he shed every
other trace of his fur-trapping life, and that confused
her. How could he be two different people at the same
time? She didn't know the other Luke Randall well,
but she didn't know this tall, handsome stranger at
all!

She dared a quick look up at him through the veil of her long lashes, thinking he was acting awfully polite when she had just tried to steal his son again. He was treating her . . . well, almost like a lady, and she knew for an all-out fact that he didn't consider her one! What was he up to? She was suddenly very suspicious of him.

"How are you feeling today?" he asked with his newfound, unfamiliar solicitousness, and Bethany quickly covered her wrists with her fingers when she saw him looking at the bruises.

"I'm fine," she answered quickly. "And I'm surely grateful to you for coming for me." She looked away from those pure green eyes. His lashes were long and very black. That's what made his eyes appear so green, she thought irrelevantly. "I didn't think you would," she added.

"Why not?"

"Because I thought you wanted to put me in jail. You said you did, and I heard you send for the sheriff last night." Her finely arched brows drew down slightly. "I figured you'd be a mite angry with me. Why aren't you angry with me, anyways?"

Luke smiled again, and Bethany felt a ridiculous desire to smile, too, which she immediately stifled.

"I was perturbed at first," Luke admitted, "but I think you had already learned your lesson by the time I got to the Cabildo. You didn't need to run away last night, you know. I called the sheriff to put out an award on the Hacketts. It didn't have anything to do with you."

Bethany was relieved to hear that, but she looked down without answering.

"How old are you, Beth?"

Now, why did he want to know that all of a sudden? "I don't rightly know. Eighteen, I think."

"You don't know how old you are?"

A defensive note she couldn't help crept into her answer. "I can't help it if Pa didn't write it down, can I?"

It still hurt her even now to think about why her father hadn't cared enough to put her birthdate into his big black family Bible. He had wanted a boy; a girl didn't count enough to be written down.

"Your father's dead, I assume?"

"Yes, he got drownded. That's when I got put in the orphanage."

"That's where Anne found you, isn't that correct?"

Bethany nodded.

"Do you have any other kin?"

Why was he asking so many questions? "No."

"No one at all? No friends or distant relatives back on the Ohio? That's where you were born, is it not?"

Bethany hesitated. "Well, I have some friends. Valerie Goodrich and Captain Richmond. And especially Marcus Main. He's gone off to sea now. He said he's coming back, though, and he'd take care of Peeto and me."

Bethany was glad she could say that. She didn't want Luke Randall to think her totally unlovable, even if she was. She watched for a change in his expression, but there wasn't one.

"Indeed?" he murmured a moment later. "Where did you meet this man?"

"At the orphanage. He was an orphan, too."

"Was he your accomplice when you took Peeto?"

"He's not an accomplice. He's a friend," Bethany said, defending herself staunchly.

Luke stared at her until she felt obliged to drop her gaze.

"What are you going to do with me? Are you going to send me away?" she finally asked, suddenly tired of all the pointless questions. She wanted to know exactly where she stood with him.

Luke rose from his chair, pacing the few steps to the windows. Bethany watched nervously as he set his gaze on the distant river.

"Do you like it here, Beth?"

She was so startled by that out-of-the-blue question that for a moment she didn't know what to say.

"I guess so," she answered in confusion as he turned back to her. "We only just got here."

"Enough to live here with Pete?"

A great, numbing flood of relief spread over her. "You'll let me stay here with him?"

He was silent, taking his chair again. He steepled his fingers together as he leaned back. "Do you remember that first day we met, Beth, back in Natchez?"

She nodded, frowning slightly at the roundabout way he had of making conversation.

"You asked me then why I came back now after three years. Remember?"

She nodded again. He was doing an awful lot of talking and not saying anything, and he didn't usually do any talking at all.

"I came back because I learned that Anne had died, and I knew I had to see to my son's welfare. When I found him stolen away, I realized I didn't even know

him and that I might never get to know him if I didn't
find him.''

Bethany listened with new interest, still not sure
what he was trying to say.

"To get to the point," Luke went on, "I think
what Peeto needs is a mother, a real mother. Someone who will love him and take care of him in my
absence. Someone who won't ever leave him."

"You're leaving?"

Bethany sounded so pleased with the idea that
Luke's mouth twisted in a half smile.

"Yes. I plan to return to the mountains by the first
of the year. But before I go, I want Peeto's future
assured. He is my son, and the only child I'll ever
have. I owe him that much."

"Peeto's mother is dead, isn't she?" Bethany
asked. "He won't talk about her much, but I think he
remembers more than he tells me."

She watched Luke's face tighten like a patch of
parched soil. "His mother *is* dead, and nothing about
her needs to be discussed now or ever. I also think it
best if you discourage any talk of his Indian background. It'll be hard enough for him to survive in
New Orleans society without everyone knowing he's
half Sioux."

It was nothing less than a command, uttered in a
voice that was rock hard, and Bethany took heed of
it.

"In order to get him a suitable mother, I'll have to
marry again, of course, which is something I swore I
would never do," Luke went on calmly. "Of course,
it will strictly be a marriage of convenience, which is
common enough. No one will hold that suspect. And
another bank draft will keep Rachene quiet as to your

background," he added, as an afterthought to himself.

Bethany said nothing, wondering why he was going into all of this with her. It was enough to know he was going to let her stay at Cantigny and take care of Peeto.

"Then you agree?"

"Agree to what? To be Petie's nanny?"

"Of course not," Luke answered with a tinge of impatience. "To marry me."

"*Marry* you?" Bethany echoed in shock, rising unknowingly to her feet. "Marry *you?*"

Luke smiled grimly at her change of emphasis. "That's right. You're certainly the prime candidate since Pete already loves you like a mother. And you love him, too. I can see that now."

"Me? Me? You want me to marry you?"

"Sit down and calm yourself, Beth. It's not as if I'm asking you to share my bed, or my life. I'm just asking you to be Pete's mother."

"Share your—" She dropped back into her chair at that horrible thought.

Luke leaned forward to pour her some brandy from a crystal decanter. He pushed the goblet toward her, but she didn't touch it. She was still staring at him in stunned dismay.

"As I said, it's nothing more than a business arrangement. There are other women whom Pete could probably grow fond of, given time, but if I marry a Creole or anyone else hereabouts who is socially prominent enough to be suitable, it would mean a long, elaborate courtship, and frankly, I can't stomach the thought of that. Besides, it might prove difficult since I don't exactly possess a sterling reputation in these parts.''

"You don't? Why not?'' Bethany managed to say, feeling as if she were still upstairs in bed, having some kind of fantastic, nonsensical dream.

"Because,'' he answered with a sardonic twist of his lips, "I'm not exactly a sterling kind of man. What's more, I'm gone for long periods—years at a time, in fact—and any well-placed girl in Creole society might not take to that kind of abandonment, not to mention how her family would feel about it. You, on the other hand, wouldn't care if I never came back, would you?''

"No,'' Bethany answered truthfully, barely noticing the amused grin that appeared on Luke's dark face. "But this is all so crazy. I don't want to marry you. What if I find someone else, someone I really love?''

Luke's eyes grew shuttered. "Then you'll have to be discreet in your affairs, as I intend to be with mine. I won't allow Pete to be hurt by your dalliances.''

That last comment stopped Bethany as nothing else had. "No, no, this is all impossible. I can't do it.''

"Not even for Pete's sake? He loves you. You should have seen him last night when I brought you home. He was scared to death that he had lost you. That's when I decided this was the best thing to do.''

"But couldn't I just be his nanny, like before? There's no real need for us to get married, is there? I—''

"And have you run off with your accomplice, Marcus, or whatever his name is, when he returns from the sea? If that happens and I'm not here to prevent you, you'll either take Pete with you, robbing him of this plantation and his birthright, or you'll leave him behind and break his heart. I don't want either of those things to happen, and the only way to keep it from happening is to make you my legal wife and mistress of Cantigny.''

"Mistress of Cantigny?" Bethany repeated weakly.

"Of course. Think about it, Beth. You'll have everything you want here—servants, clothes, money, and you'll be Pete's mother. Where else could you have those things? You've been a servant all your life.''

Bethany bit her lip. "But what if I want to marry? What if I want a child of my own? I always wanted lots of children.''

"As I said, I don't expect you to share my bed. I won't even be here much." His jade eyes glinted. "But if you should ever decide you want your own children, I daresay I'll do my best to oblige you.''

His comment made her remember the way his muscular body had looked, naked and powerful in the firelight the night they had camped beside the river. The same sensation she had felt then, a thrill she didn't like, shot through her loins, bringing a blush to her cheeks.

"No, no," she assured him with embarrassed haste. "I'd never want that.''

She frowned, trying to think of more reasons to dissuade him from his absurd idea.

"But I couldn't be the mistress here. I don't know how to do things like that. I could never act like the grand lady.''

"Perhaps not right now, but you're clever enough to learn. You've certainly proven that. Andrew and I will help you, and Tante Chloe runs the household anyway. The girl upstairs, Michelle, can probably teach you a lot about the Creole way of life. Her father's probably one of them.''

''How do you know that?''

Luke ignored her question. ''And I assure you I won't return to the Rockies until you are completely accepted by the Creoles. As soon as you are, Pete will be, too.''

''But you said they didn't think much of you.''

''They don't, but I have twenty times more money now than all of them put together, and the trappers I have working for me in the Rockies are adding more to my wealth every day, not to mention the profits from this plantation. People will begin to like me more and more around here as time goes by, you can count on that. And Andy is very well thought of by both the Americans and the Creoles. Before I leave, we'll make sure everyone loves you and treats Pete as my legitimate heir.''

Bethany began to panic as he continued to outline her future as if he had given it a great deal of consideration. What was worse, she was running out of arguments. Luke watched her, his thoughts well hidden behind his handsome face, but somehow she intuitively knew he was anxious for her to accept his proposal. Perhaps he really loved Peeto after all.

''And what if I say no?'' she asked at last.

''If you say no, you'll still have to stay here because I had to sign an agreement to that effect last night to get you out of jail. You're in my custody until Hugh arrives and nullifies his St. Louis warrant.''

''Hugh's coming here?''

Luke recognized the fear in her silvery eyes, and

he wondered if she was afraid Hugh would put her in jail for striking him.

"He's coming, but he'll drop the charges against you if I tell him to. Now, what's your answer?"

"Can't I at least have some time to think about it?" Bethany cried. Everything was happening much too fast!

"Of course. Think about it all you want," Luke agreed amicably, and Bethany breathed easier until he qualified his statement. "Until tomorrow morning, when I intend to have your answer, one way or the other."

Chapter 6

When Bethany arose early the next morning, she was no more ready to accept Luke Randall's cold marriage proposal. She had spent the previous day hiding in her bedchamber with Peeto while she tried to decide what she should do. Luckily, Luke had left Cantigny for town just after their conversation in the library and hadn't returned, so she hadn't had to face him. Not yet.

The more she thought about his proposal, however, the more absurd it seemed. And Peeto kept looking at her with his big, trusting eyes, kept putting his thin arms around her. At those times she wavered alarmingly. If nothing else, Luke was right about Peeto needing a real mother, one who loved him and would always be there for him, especially if Luke didn't plan to linger long in Louisiana.

The fact that he planned a fake marriage so he could go away again without feeling guilty angered her, even though he made it sound very simple and reasonable. In truth, all he was doing was abandoning his son again. First, he had chosen his sister to take his place; now he was enticing Bethany herself with every inducement his wealth afforded him. Why was he like that? Why didn't he want to raise his son himself? Peeto was so young and sweet, with so much love to give. Why would a father want to give his own child over for others to raise?

She sighed heavily, watching Peeto playing on the floor with his miniature bow and arrows. Luke even wanted to take his Indian heritage away from him, but Bethany wasn't about to do that. Peeto had a right to know about his mother, even if she had been an Indian. If Luke was so ashamed of her, why had he gotten her with child in the first place?

She picked up the small suede satchel that Peeto had carried with him to the Younger mansion three years ago. Anne had given it to Bethany that first day with instructions to burn it, but when Bethany peeked inside the leather bag and found the little bow and arrows and the drawstring purse and headband worked with beads and quills, she hadn't been able to destroy them. Someone had painstakingly made Peeto's treasures for him, probably his unknown mother, and Bethany hadn't had the heart to strip away the only familiar possessions of a frightened and lonely three-year-old. She hid them instead, and let him play with them when no one else was around. Peeto kept them close to him even now, and no matter what Luke said, he was going to have them.

"You said we could go fishin' today?" Peeto reminded her, and Bethany smiled as she packed his bow and arrows in the bag, then hid them under her bed.

"That's right, I did. We'll go, but why don't we check on Michelle first? Then we'll ask Elise where we can get some fishing poles."

Michelle was awake, propped up against the plump satin pillows, and Bethany sat down beside her, picking up a bowl of clear chicken broth that Elise had just brought from the kitchen.

"This is warm and good for you, Michelle," Bethany said quietly, her eyes on the girl's swollen face. "You must try to eat a little of it. It'll make you strong again."

To her dismay, tears squeezed out of the octoroon's blackened eyes. "You are the one who saved me, *oui? Merci, merci.*"

Bethany was surprised to discover that Michelle spoke very good English, especially compared to that of Elise and the servants at Cantigny. She smiled. "I am so glad you speak English," she said, delighted to be able to converse with Michelle. "I didn't think you did. You spoke Creole French all the time on the river. My name's Bethany, and this is Peeto."

"I must thank you. If you hadn't come, they—"

Michelle had unusual eyes, a strange amber color, and as a terrible look of fear dawned in them, Bethany laid a comforting hand on the girl's arm.

"Don't think about them, Michelle. It's all over. You're safe here at Cantigny, and we won't let nobody hurt you again, I promise. You just rest up now, and get all well again, then we'll get to know each other better. Would you like me to feed you some broth?"

"*Non,*" Michelle murmured, shaking her head. Her eyes soon closed under the dose of laudanum the doctor had ordered for her pain, and Bethany left quietly, glad the girl was so much better. She would need a lot of support from them to forget the Hacketts, and Bethany would do everything she could to help her.

Bethany took Peeto's hand as they walked along the upstairs gallery. She looked out at the trees dotting the grassy lawns, the hanging moss swaying in the breeze. With so many different kinds of flowers blooming along the walkways and spilling out of the huge stone urns, it was hard to believe it was nearly October. Cantigny Plantation was beautiful, with its flaming hedges of poinsettias along the porticos and purple crape myrtle hugging the lower galleries.

After they reached the rear of the mansion, pausing to gaze into windows as they went, they descended a massive stairway of whitewashed brick that led to the rear columned entrance. Bethany looked out over the sweeping lawns to a good-sized red-brick building, which she assumed was the kitchen. Farther off, past a well-kept vegetable garden, she could see the small, whitewashed houses of the slave quarters.

Bethany led Peeto toward the kitchen building over a path of flagstones, but he stopped as the sound of talking and laughing filtered from the open door.

"What's the matter, Petie? Don't you want to go fishing?"

"I don't know nobody here."

In that moment Bethany knew she would marry Luke Randall. Peeto needed her, and if she didn't become his mother, Luke would find someone else who would, someone who might mistreat Peeto after Luke was gone. Bethany couldn't bear for that to happen. Peeto had always been so insecure and terrified of people, she couldn't abandon him, too. Not ever.

"But you know me, sweetie, and I'll stay with you the whole time."

Bethany kissed his cheek, then stepped over the threshold.

The Cantigny kitchen consisted of one large room flanked on either side by immense cooking hearths. Black kettles and pots hung suspended over the fires and were stirred and tended by several cooks, while at least a dozen scullery maids scrubbed dishes and cooking utensils at a table in one corner. Two long wooden tables stretched side by side down the middle of the brick floor, with more servants sitting around them and chopping vegetables or peeling apples. The moment Bethany and Peeto appeared, all activity stopped.

Bethany, a little intimidated by all the gazes fixed on them, felt very much the intruder. She was relieved when she saw the driver named Jemsy come to his feet from a bent-willow rocker beside one of the fires.

"Good morning," she greeted him. "We was just wanting some poles so we could go fishing."

"Oui, mamzelle," Jemsy said, obviously surprised by her request, but he hurried to fetch what she wanted.

Bethany smiled at the other servants, hoping they could be her friends like the servants in the Younger house, but her attention was soon captured by an absolutely huge Negress. Her skin was as black as ebony, and her bosoms were like great pillows. Bethany noticed at once that she was not dressed in the black-and-white uniform that the others wore but in a bright red-gingham skirt and blue blouse topped by a long, spotless, white apron. A massive yellow satin turban was wrapped around her head, and gold loop earrings hung from her ears.

"I be Tante Chloe, mamzelle. I teg kyah of dez 'ouse fo' marster."

"I'm Bethany Cole, and this is Petie," Bethany said. "I don't mean to be any trouble, but Petie hasn't had breakfast. Do you think we could get a leftover biscuit or something to take fishing with us?''

The servants exchanged glances, but a frown appeared on Tante Chloe's handsome round face. She snapped out a few orders in Creole French to a young maid, then looked apologetically at Bethany.

"Excusez-moi, mamzelle. 'Twas Delphine's job to serve de big 'ouse. She bring it to de dinin' hall, iv you pliz.''

Bethany thought of the long, formal dining table with its elaborate candelabras placed along its polished surface. When they had peeked through the windows of that luxurious chamber on their way past earlier, she had not dared think of eating at such a grand table.

''Couldn't we just sit out here with you? Jemsy will be back in a moment, I suspect. We're in a bit of a hurry anyways.''

Tante Chloe's eyes widened, then she frowned a warning to the younger maids who had gasped outright at Bethany's request. Another crisp command from Tante Chloe sent everyone back to work as Tante Chloe herself escorted Bethany and Peeto to the willow rockers in front of the fireplace. A small table was hurriedly placed between them, and moments later a gigantic pewter platter of fried ham, croissants, and griddle cakes was set before them. Bethany had never even seen so much food at one time, much less been expected to eat it, but Peeto delved into the delicious fare with all the appetite of a hungry boy, pouring far too much honey onto his griddle cakes.

Bethany was hungry, too, but she watched the servants, remembering how often she had helped out in the Youngers' kitchen when their Irish cook was shorthanded. She had helped occasionally with the cooking in her father's trading post, too, but some of the dishes Tante Chloe was supervising looked very alien to Bethany. Watching a man pour rice into some sort of soup, then add some kind of small fish to it, she thought Louisiana seemed like a whole different country, though she knew for a fact it was part of the United States and had been for seven years.

As her gaze swept the room, it stopped on a little Negro boy cleaning silverware on the floor by the fire not far from Peeto's chair. He looked a little older than Peeto, probably eight or nine, and he was a handsome little thing with coffee-colored skin and big, liquid jet eyes. He had been watching Peeto eat with a great deal of interest.

"What's your name?" Bethany asked with a smile.

"Raffy," he answered shyly.

"Do you like griddle cakes and honey, Raffy?"

"Oui, mamzelle," he answered with a quick bob of his close-cropped head.

"Rafael! Don zou bez bodderin' dem," scolded Tante Chloe from her place across the room before lapsing into French.

Raffy immediately scooted away, rubbing vigorously on the shiny silver coffee urn.

"Tante Chloe?" Bethany said. "Can Raffy come fishing with us? We don't know where to go. Maybe he could show us a good fishing hole? Would you like that, Raffy?"

"Oui, mamzelle. I's likes to fish."

"He bez as lazy as a hundred-year-old hound dog," Tante Chloe complained, but despite the gruffness of her tone, Bethany could tell that the old woman was fond of the boy. "But I guess it bez all right, iv zou wand."

"Do you know when the marster is coming back?" Bethany asked, feeling very strange to be calling Luke by that title, but the servants did and she supposed she should, too.

Tante Chloe nodded. "Marster Andrew say he bez back dis day."

"I meant Luke Randall," Bethany began, then paused, taken aback by the immediate hush that fell over the kitchen. She looked around, amazed to see fear on the faces of those around her.

"Le sauvage," came a shocked whisper from the corner, and Tante Chloe whirled, chastising the speaker with a sharp word in Creole.

Bethany was immediately curious about why Luke's name had caused such fright among the kitchen servants, but even more, she wanted to know what *le sauvage* meant in Creole.

Jemsy picked that moment to enter, carrying several cane poles, and Bethany accepted them from him. "Thank you very much, *merci,"* Bethany said, trying French for the first time on Tante Chloe.

At the door, she noticed a bucket of swarming crayfish and turned back. "Could we have some of those crawdads for bait?" she asked innocently, and was startled by the insulted look on the big housekeeper's face.

"For bait? Dad is fo' my gumbo dis night!"

For supper, Bethany thought in revulsion, remembering how often she had seen the crablike creatures scuttling into their mud holes along the riverbank. The thought of actually eating one was enough to turn her stomach. She escaped the kitchen with the two boys in tow.

Outside, she looked down at Raffy. "Do you know a good place to dig some worms, Raffy?"

"*Oui*, deys in de cane, mamzelle."

A horrible thought occurred to Bethany. "Tante Chloe doesn't ever cook worms, does she?" she asked Raffy, who grinned to show a wide gap between his front teeth. He shook his head.

"Good. Where should we go? Up on the levee?"

"Daz be a place, but it bez way oud dere," Raffy answered, pointing across the cane fields. "Ole Cricket tole me. He bez de chimney man at Ole Oaks acrost de river." He looked around, lowering his voice. "It bez a secret place."

Amused, Bethany lowered her own voice. "We won't tell, will we, Petie?"

Raffy scampered away, and Bethany followed at a more sedate pace as Peeto ran to catch up to the older boy. As they passed through the kitchen yards, two old black-and-tan hounds joined them, and not long after, so did a feisty white spaniel.

They stopped at the edge of a rippling canebrake where bare-backed field hands were hacking the sturdy stalks of sugarcane with big machetes. Peeto and Raffy dug in the rich black loam with pointed sticks until they had uncovered a great mass of wiggling black worms. Bethany laughed as Raffy promptly stuffed most of them into his clean shirt pocket. She had a distinct feeling that he might have earned himself a dose of Tante Chloe's displeasure.

The day was mild for the end of September, and Bethany studied their surroundings with interest as they moved away from the big house. Cantigny Plan-

tation was very different from other places she had
lived, flat and verdant, with no hills and lots of vines,
moss, and unfamiliar trees whose leaves didn't change
color at autumn. And there was water everywhere—
in small ponds and pools, and in sluggish, weed-
choked streams that Raffy called bayous. When they
passed an old, deserted building, Bethany asked Raffy
about it.

"Dat bez de ole sugar mill, but Marster Andrew,
he done gots a new one on de river. Dis bez de ole
madame's."

"The old madame?"

"*Oui*, she die and Marster Andrew buy Cantigny
and all its people, long time back, when I's bez little."

"I think he bought it for Luke to own," Bethany
said to herself, then noted the frightened look on Raffy's little face. "Are you afraid of Luke, Raffy?"

"I's no wand talk bad 'bout de marster. Tante
Chloe get me fo' dat."

"All right, don't say anything, just tell me what *le
sauvage* means."

Raffy looked around uncomfortably. "Dat mean de
savage, like de red injin."

"The savage? Why do they call him that?"

"Mimi, who work upstair in de big house, say de
madame she haz afore say he lived wid de injins,"
Raffy said, looking fearful, as if a band of Indians
might be lurking about on Cantigny itself.

Bethany glanced at Peeto. Though he didn't seem
offended in the least, she decided to drop the subject
before it did bother him. After all, he was half Indian.

As they walked on, Bethany stopped beneath an
ancient oak tree with great gnarled limbs, examining

the coarse gray moss that hung down to brush her
head as she passed. It was strange and a little creepy,
and she turned, looking back at the big columned
house across the distant fields. If she married Luke,
she would be mistress of this magnificent place, mistress over Tante Chloe and Elise, and Raffy and
Jemsy, and the dozens of other slaves and servants
who lived here. She couldn't even imagine it. She
couldn't imagine being Luke Randall's wife even if it
wasn't a real marriage. But she couldn't help thinking
how beautiful a place it was, how grand and spacious
and serene. It was much easier to think of Peeto
growing to manhood in such luxury, then someday
becoming the master of Cantigny Plantation. Indeed,
that idea pleased her a great deal.

"Dere, dere it bez," Raffy called from several
yards in front of her. "See dere, de sign dere, it says
de name of dis fishin' hole, Ole Cricket say so."

Bethany glanced at the white board sign at the edge
of the narrow bayou, wishing she could read it. All
her life she had looked at the mysterious markings
painted on shop windows and on the pages of books,
wanting more than anything to know what they meant.
She had begged her father to teach her to read, but
he had always said girls had no need of learning. And
at the orphanage, they said she was too old. Besides
that, she had always been too busy with the smaller
children to have time to learn.

The bayou did look like a good spot for fishing,
with its dark, brackish water and cypress stumps, and
she followed the children to a relatively clear part of
the bank. They sat down near an old gray log, half
hidden by water willows.

"All right, let me bait your hooks, then you can both sit right here by me."

The little boys hunkered down obediently, taking turns handling the writhing worms that Raffy retrieved from his pocket. Soon Bethany had their lines ready, and the worms fell with a double *kerplunk* into the murky water. All three settled back to wait for the first bite, while the three dogs lay down to scratch their fleas or snore softly in the sun.

It wasn't long before Peeto's cork floated into a thick rootwad. Bethany muttered impatient words as she tugged it a few times, trying to dislodge it with a flick of her wrist. It proved to be stuck fast, however, so she sat down to take off her boots and stockings. She waded out to untangle the line, not particularly thrilled about the way the cold, slimy mud on the bottom oozed up between her toes. A moment later, the line was free, but as she turned around to head back, she froze. The log just behind Peeto and Raffy began to move, and she realized it was some kind of reptile with slanted eyes and a long, rounded snout. As it turned toward the children, she screamed a warning. The boys jumped up, backing away as Bethany splashed back to shore. She nudged them safely behind her, swallowing hard as the strange beast swiveled its ugly yellow eyes to her.

"Now where the hell did they go?" Luke muttered under his breath as he sat astride the great black stallion he had chosen from the stables of Cantigny, peering out over the rippling field of unharvested sugarcane.

Tante Chloe had said they had gone fishing, and James Barclay, the overseer, had seen them heading through the trees toward the bayous. Luke hadn't seen a trace of them, and he didn't know the paths and winding bayous of Cantigny very well yet. Neither did Bethany. He thought it unlikely she had tried to leave with Peeto again, not after what had happened the last time, but if there was one thing he had learned about Bethany Cole, it was that trouble followed her as surely as thunder followed lightning.

He jerked around as a loud commotion started up not far away. It sounded like several excited children and a whole kennel of barking dogs, and he spurred Onyx in that direction, his mouth dropping as the stallion nosed its way through some willows, giving him a clear view of the melee.

Peeto and a little Negro boy were jumping up and down, waving their arms and yelling at the top of their lungs, while a whole pack of dogs ran in circles, growling and snapping at a large alligator, which Bethany was furiously hitting over the head with her fishing pole.

"Shoo, shoo, git, git," came her angry cries, and Luke jerked his pistol from his belt, terrified the creature might turn on her. As close as she was, the alligator could bite off her entire leg with one snap of its powerful jaws.

"Get out of the way!" he yelled, and Bethany jerked around at his shout, backing off as he took aim.

The bullet hit the big reptile between its ugly eyes. As it writhed about, flipping its long tail in the last throes of death, the dogs went into an absolute frenzy. Luke spurred the stallion toward the boys, but one look at the black anger on the face of *le sauvage* was all it took for little Rafael. He fled the bayou with flying feet, his eyes round and white in his dark face.

Bethany pulled Peeto away from the huge black horse, which pranced nervously at the smell of fresh blood, and Luke swung one leg over the saddle, sliding to the ground, his gun still smoking in his hand.

"Good God, are you out of your mind?" he shouted furiously. "An alligator that size could have killed you!"

"Alligator? Is that what it was? I've never seen—"

Luke grabbed her by the shoulders. "Don't you understand how much danger you were in? How much danger Pete was in?"

His rage intimidated her, to be sure, much more than the alligator had, but Bethany rose to her own defense. "He was big, I admit, but he moved as slow as molasses. Why, he could barely even turn himself around. He never could have caught me."

Exasperated, Luke ran a hand through his hair, then turned angry eyes back on her. "Caught you? They don't have to catch you. All they have to do is knock you down with their tail or get hold of you with their jaws so they can drag you under the water and eat you!"

Bethany's gray eyes widened slowly to the size of silver medallions. "Eat you?" she repeated weakly. "They eat people?"

Luke nodded, still furious with her, and Bethany took an involuntary step backward, her face mirroring such unadulterated horror that Luke's anger faded somewhat.

"My God, Beth, there's a sign right there in front of your nose. Can't you read?"

His cutting rebuke hit Bethany where she was most vulnerable, and she shook off her newfound fear of alligators, her eyes blazing silver fire.

"Of course, I saw the sign! But what's the name of this place got to do with alligators, just tell me that?"

"What's it got to do—" Luke repeated incredulously, then turned to the sign. "Alligator Bayou. Beware," he read slowly and succinctly. "Didn't that trigger any kind of alarm in that fool head of yours?"

Bethany stared at the writing on the board, filled with humiliation, then lifted her chin to gather what was left of her tattered pride.

"So I made a big mistake," she said, taking Peeto by the hand. "I'm sorry, but I don't see what you're getting so angry about. I made the boys stay behind me, so I was the only one in danger of getting eaten, and nothing happened to me, did it?"

Luke didn't answer, shaking his head as he reached down to lift Peeto into the saddle. He swung up behind his son, and Bethany picked up her shoes, ready to walk back to the house, when Luke's voice, hard with authority, stopped her in her tracks.

"You'll ride behind me, Beth."

He leaned down, catching her around the waist and pulling her up behind him just as easily as he had lifted his son. Bethany reluctantly clasped her arms around him as he set his heels to the big stallion, her cheeks flaming as she was forced to hold tightly to his lean, muscular waist, her breasts rubbing intimately against his broad back.

It wasn't long before the rest of her body, pressed so close against him, began to feel a certain warmth that appalled her. By the time they reached the rear portico of the house, her face was flushed beet-red and was hot to the touch.

Confused by what was going on in her own body, she slid to the ground as soon as the horse came to a stop. Luke lowered Peeto beside her, his eyes roaming over her face, which was now a becoming rosy hue.

"Have you made up your mind about being Pete's mother?" he asked conversationally.

Bethany hesitated, realizing from his expression that he had known all along that she would say yes and hating him for it. But Peeto was looking up at her, his eyes big and brimming with pleasure.

"Yes, I want to be his mother."

"Good. I've brought you the necessary clothes for the wedding. You'll find them on your bed. I'll have the priest here to marry us by the time you get ready."

Luke walked Onyx away, and Bethany stared after him until Peeto tugged on her hand.

"Are you really going to be my mother, Beth? Really?"

Bethany forgot Luke then, kneeling to take the child in her arms. "Yes, Petie, I'm going to be your mother."

Chapter 7

"How do you like Raffy?" Bethany asked Peeto from behind the damask dressing screen in her bedchamber as she slipped over her head the dainty pale pink chemise that Luke had chosen for her. She was surprised by his thoughtfulness, and the undergarment felt wonderful against her skin, the silk so soft and smooth. She had never had anything so fine as the lustrous fabric, with its beautiful lace and white satin ribbons.

"I like Raffy," Peeto admitted from his cross-legged position on the floor. "He knows lots about gators."

Peeto had decided right off that he liked the sound of that new word, *gators,* almost as much as he had liked helping Beth scare off the big lizard from the bayou. But even that wasn't as good as the idea of Bethany being his mother. He smiled to himself just thinking about it.

"Well, you and Raffy have to stay away from that bayou from now on," Bethany said, stepping into sight. "I got us in enough trouble with Luke by taking the two of you there, and besides that, those alligators are dangerous."

She considered the size of the one that had slid into

the water as they rode off. She hadn't even seen it until then! What if one had been lurking under the water when she waded out to the stump? Her swallow went down hard as she picked up the dress lying across the bed. It was made of fine white lace with short puffed sleeves and a low, square neckline. She turned it over, examining with distaste the long row of tiny pearl buttons.

"Will you help me fasten this, Petie? Look, there's about a hundred buttons on the back!"

Peeto bent to look, and Bethany stroked the fragile swirls of lace, thinking it was by far the most magnificent gown she had ever seen, which made her all the more reluctant to don it. She had only had one other dress in her life, a plain gray wool like the ones worn by the other Younger servants. She couldn't deny that she had dreamed about such a gown as this, especially in the orphanage when she had closed her eyes and imagined herself in a bridal dress of white lace. In those childhood visions, her friend, Marcus, had always been the groom, mainly because he was the only boy she knew who was close to her own age. That was before he had gone downriver with Captain Hosie to sign up on a sailing ship. Now Luke Randall, with his piercing green eyes that could look right through her would stand beside her.

She pulled the dress over her head, letting the flowing skirts settle to the floor with the rustle of expensive silk and lace. Then she turned around for Peeto to work on the buttons. He had no trouble with them until he reached those at the middle of her back.

"They won't go in," he said, bending over the task with a concentrated frown.

Bethany sucked in her breath so he could finish, then moved to the mirror, feeling like a pig stuffed in a keg.

"I can't wear this," she exclaimed in dismay, staring at the way the tight bodice pushed her breasts upward into soft mounds of bare flesh, more than noticeable above the delicate scalloped lace edging the low décolletage.

"Marster Luke bez waitin' for zou, Mamzelle Beth," piped Raffy's little voice from the doorway, then he beamed his wide, gap-toothed smile at Peeto. "Lookee here at what I's gots."

What he had was a big green bullfrog in a crock jar. Peeto immediately reached in and picked up the creature to examine its bumpy back under the nearest candle.

"He's a big'un," he admitted solemnly.

"Does Tante Chloe know you have that frog in the house?" Bethany asked, trying to tug her bodice up enough to hide her nearly naked bosom.

"*Oui,* mamzelle. She uses frog spit when she ma-gue her medicines and charms."

Bethany wrinkled her slim nose and made a solemn vow never to be sick enough to have to swallow any of Tante Chloe's remedies. Poor Michelle, she thought, recalling the spoonful of tonic that had been fed to her not an hour ago.

"What do you mean by charms, Raffy?" Bethany asked.

Raffy glanced around as if for invisible eavesdroppers. "Why, de hoodoo gris-gris, mamzelle. To keep away de evil ones and bring de luck. Like dis one." He held up a little cloth bag that was tied around his neck.

Bethany bent for a closer look. "Maybe that's what I need tonight," she murmured, more to herself than to the boys.

"Zou can wears mine," Raffy offered generously. "I's don't minds, iv zou promise to give it back afores I's goes to sleep."

Bethany looked at him quickly, but his offer had been quite serious. So was her answer. "Thank you kindly, Raffy, but I guess it wouldn't match my dress."

Both boys agreed with sage nods then turned to a more interesting subject as the frog gave a hoarse croak.

"Tante Chloe say I's could bez Marster Pete's boy, iv zou pliz," Raffy said to Bethany in an abrupt change of subject.

Bethany was somewhat startled by the designation he used for Peeto, but he was right. Peeto was the young master. Someday he would own Cantigny.

"That sounds pretty good, since you're already friends. What do you do if you're his boy?"

"I's jez gots to keep close to 'im and helps 'im gets his clothes on in de morning. And I's gets to sleep in his room at night."

The boys grinned at each other as they contemplated what that could mean.

"You wanna see how far he can jump?" suggested Peeto, still intrigued by the bullfrog's lumpy back.

Raffy nodded with enthusiasm, and Bethany smiled as they exited by the outside gallery. They were fast becoming good friends, exactly what Peeto needed. He had never had a friend his own age, had never been around other children. Already Peeto was coming out of his shell with Raffy. After all, they both liked frogs and gators. What else could she ask for?

"Are you quite sure you want to go through with this?"

At Andrew's question Luke looked up. "I explained my reasons to you once. I don't see any need to belabor them," he said, taking a drink from the snifter he held idly in his hand.

"A rather cold-blooded approach to marriage, I must say," Andrew pointed out. "Not that I ever expected you to marry again. You've certainly made a point to avoid commitments in the past."

"I'm doing it for the boy, as you well know. He loves her, and she'll take good care of him for me."

"So would Tante Chloe or any other Creole mammy, and from what little I've seen thus far, Bethany Cole's barely reached womanhood. She acts and dresses like a tomboy, yet you stand back, blithely expecting her to take over the reins of running a place like Cantigny?"

"With your help, she can do it. She's a bright girl—you'll find that out in time—and she's got guts, too. More than most men I've known. As far as her clothes go, I got her a dress to wear when I was in town this morning. More are being made right now."

"*You* got her a dress? How'd you manage that? The ladies I know need about a dozen fittings before they even get a bloody gown on."

"What the hell difference does it make?" Luke said, suddenly impatient with his brother's questions. "I just told Madame Josephine that Beth was little and boyish and stood almost to my shoulder, and she did the rest. Now why don't you go see if Père Demongeot has arrived yet? Beth should be down any minute now.''

Andrew shrugged, well acquainted since his boyhood with Luke's short temper, but he was more than convinced that his older brother was making a huge mistake. He rose to summon the priest, then stopped as Luke's tomboy bride appeared in the doorway. His eyes riveted on her in disbelief, then moved to Luke. His brother was staring at the diminutive beauty, his mouth slightly agape. Amused at his brother's expression, Andrew spoke so that only Luke could hear him. ''I think *boyish* was the word you used, brother.''

Andrew gave a slight bow in Bethany's direction, then strode off to see if he could find the priest.

Bethany watched him depart, feeling idiotic, especially when Luke Randall just stood there staring at her without saying a word. She was nervous enough, afraid she'd bust out of the bodice and tear the expensive lace, as tight and uncomfortable as it was. She stiffened as his gaze lowered to the immodest display of her breasts, and bit her lower lip as his regard lingered there long enough to send a flush creeping up her neck.

''I see that I underestimated you again. The dress is much too tight. Madame Josephine will have to alter it when she brings the others.''

''What others?''

''I ordered you a wardrobe suitable for the mistress of Cantigny. Once you're my wife, I can't have you running around looking like a river boatman. You look good in a dress,'' he added as an afterthought.

As he continued to appraise her, Bethany blushed,

feeling gawky and ill at ease. It didn't help her state of mind to know she would have to wear such clothes in the future. She preferred her old pants and shirts. But the gown was beautiful, and perhaps if the new ones weren't so tight, it wouldn't be so bad to wear them.

"The priest will marry us in the library," Luke told her, and Bethany tried to hide her shiver as his long fingers closed over her bare elbow.

Memories stirred to disconcert her even more, memories of the way she had felt when she had been pressed so close against Luke in the saddle. Feelings she didn't really understand but knew she shouldn't be having, feelings she didn't want. He had made it clear he only saw her as Peeto's new mother. He didn't want her in any other way, so she had nothing to worry about.

In the library, Père Demongeot awaited them with Andrew at his side. The priest was an old man with white hair and quick black eyes, and he smiled at Bethany as Luke led her forward. She stood quietly at Luke's side, venturing a surreptitious sidelong glance up at her husband-to-be, acutely aware of his great height and size, of his overwhelming virility, of the power over her life she was willingly giving him by agreeing to become his wife. More shivers came, rippling down her back beneath the long row of pearl buttons.

The priest began to speak in Creole, so she wasn't even sure what he was saying, which further unnerved her. She watched the aged man in his flowing black robe until he stopped speaking and awaited Luke's response.

"I will," came Luke's deep, calm voice from beside her.

Then it was her turn. After Père Demongeot had finished speaking, she agreed in a barely audible voice to honor and obey the tall, handsome stranger beside her, a man known as *le sauvage*.

To her surprise, Luke slipped a wide gold band on her finger. The ring was set with a large square emerald surrounded by diamonds, and it felt strange on her finger, heavy and binding and unnatural. A moment of pure terror welled up inside her. What in heaven's name was she doing marrying a dangerous, powerful man like Luke Randall?

When the priest smilingly blessed them as man and wife, Luke gave a mental sigh of relief. He had half expected Bethany to change her mind at the last minute. But she had gone through with it. Peeto had a mother.

"Now the signatures, monsieur and madame," Père Demongeot murmured, spreading the marriage certificate out on the desktop. Andrew leaned forward to sign his name as the witness, then Luke affixed his own signature at the bottom.

"Sign your full name, Beth," Luke instructed, handing her the plumed quill.

"Beth?" he said when she only stared at it. "You'll have to sign. I want everything to be legal and binding."

Bethany finally took the quill from him, wetting dry lips as humiliation ate into her like acid. She put the sharpened tip just beneath the beautiful flowing lines of Luke's well-educated script, then hastily drew a small *x*. She lay the quill down quickly and turned away, but not before Luke saw the dark flush of embarrassment that rose to stain her high cheek-bones.

At that moment, a good many things began to make sense to him, and he instantly regretted what he had said earlier that day at the bayou. *Can't you read?* he had demanded harshly, and it had never even occurred to him that she couldn't. No wonder the sign had meant nothing to her. She would have to learn to read, and to write, as soon as possible. Her spoken English could use some work, too.

Père Demongeot took his leave soon afterward. Bethany sat stiffly beside the fireplace in the dining room as Andrew and Luke saw the priest off in his coach. Luke had requested that she partake of the evening meal with them, and although she would have much preferred to join Peeto and Raffy and the frog upstairs, she had no choice but to agree. Especially not after hearing Luke's tone when he asked her.

"Are you ready?" he said a moment later.

Bethany rose and walked to the place he indicated for her, lifting her skirts as he stood back and held her chair politely until she sat down. She tried desperately to remember how Anne Younger had comported herself in her formal dining room when Bethany had helped serve the Youngers' guests. She looked down at the glittering array of crystal goblets and the fine white china rimmed with navy blue and etched with patterns of gold filigree. Several heavy silver spoons, and as many knives and forks, lay in shiny precision beside her plate, and she realized in one dreadful moment that she was about to show Luke and his brother just how ignorant she was about fine manners. She thought of pleading some horrible illness so she could flee the table, but that would be just too cowardly. Instead, she decided to watch the two men and do exactly what they did.

Several maids, one of whom Bethany had seen that morning in the kitchen, commenced serving the meal, beginning with some kind of thick soup in silver bowls. Bethany furtively eyed her dining companions. Luke had ignored the first course and was lifting his wineglass instead, but Andrew was watching her. His dark blue eyes twinkled, and he gave her a secret wink as he picked up the biggest of the spoons to show her, then dipped it carefully into Tante Chloe's crayfish gumbo.

Relieved and more than pleased with Andrew's help, Bethany followed his lead. Several courses proceeded in a similar fashion as the men talked about the sugar cane harvest and horses, which she soon learned was a passion with Andrew. When the entrée was finally placed in front of them, Bethany carefully cut a piece of the very white meat with her knife and fork, just as Andrew had done, and was about to place it in her mouth when Luke spoke directly to her.

"How do you like the alligator?"

Bethany looked at him, then down at the piece of meat on the prongs of her fork.

"In the bayou," she said in a totally revolted voice, quickly placing her fork back on her plate.

Luke's initial look of surprise changed to one of amusement, and he burst out laughing; bringing Andrew's eyes in his direction. Andrew was more impressed by Luke's hitherto unknown laughter than by Bethany's amusing quip. Any woman who could make his aloof, self-contained brother laugh with such abandon had to be special.

For the first time, Andrew really looked at Bethany. He saw soft blond hair falling in wispy ringlets over her shoulders and small, delicate features. She was really remarkably beautiful even though she had not bothered to apply lip rouge or any of the other artificial embellishments used by most of the fair ladies of New Orleans. Bethany Cole was an innocent beauty, so much so, in fact, that Luke wouldn't help but notice it eventually. That, Andrew decided, would be a most interesting day.

Luke was looking at him. "Andy? You didn't answer my question."

"I was admiring your wife's beauty."

Bethany blushed, and Luke looked at Andrew, then at his wife, and repeated his question without additional comment. "Are you pleading anyone's case at court at the moment?"

"I think I'm about to," Andrew replied with a curious expression that made Luke follow the direction of his brother's gaze back to Bethany. "Perhaps you will allow me to escort your lovely wife along the gallery?"

"Be my guest," Luke said. "I have some papers to go over in the library."

Andrew moved around the table, and Bethany placed her hand in his outstretched one, glad to be freed from the dining table but feeling very strange in the new role she was playing. Her spirits improved as she and her new brother-in-law moved into the night air. She breathed deeply as they strolled together down the wide stone gallery.

"Why did you marry my brother?" Andrew asked suddenly, stopping at the balustrade.

Bethany leaned her palms against the cool stone.

"Because I love Peeto. Didn't Luke tell you about our agreement?"

"He told me, but I have to say I was surprised. I've never claimed to know my brother well, but I would have laid a high wager that he would never marry again."

There were so many things Bethany wanted to ask him, but she was reluctant to do so for fear of alienating him. Luke said Andrew would help her run Cantigny after he left, so she didn't want to do or say anything to make him angry.

"I would have thought you would know your brother better than anyone," she said, curious about their relationship.

Andrew smiled as he leaned against a pillar. "I probably do, but that's not saying much."

It made Bethany feel a little better to know that even Andrew didn't understand Luke, although she could tell he was fond of his brother.

"Do you love Luke?" he asked bluntly.

"Of course not," Bethany answered quickly. "To be honest, I'm not even sure I like him much."

"Why?"

"Because he abandoned his son without a care, and now he's planning to do it again. Petie needs a father as much as he needs a mother."

Andrew perched a hip on the wall, gazing up at the stars twinkling far above, thousands strong in the dark sky.

"Luke's not like other men. He's had a hard time of it nearly all his life. He grew up with the Indians—did you know that?"

Bethany turned her head quickly, not sure she

wanted Andrew to know that she had asked the servants about Luke.

"How did that happen?" she asked.

"A band of Mandan Sioux attacked our farm just outside St. Louis. Nobody ever knew why they had wandered so far south. My father was able to save Anne and me—we were just babies then, Anne three, and me one—but Luke was five, and they took him and mother."

"How awful!"

"They murdered mother, and Luke didn't return to us until he was fifteen."

"Fifteen!" Bethany parroted in surprise. "He was with them that long!"

"For ten years. Then one day he just rode into St. Louis on an Indian pony. His hair was braided, and he was dressed like an Indian, but he never said why he came back, if he escaped or was set free, or anything else about those years with the Sioux. He refused to talk about it. I really shouldn't be telling you all this, I guess, but you are his wife now, and I don't think Luke will ever tell you."

What Andrew had related did make a difference in the way she thought about her new husband. It must have been horrible to have been kidnapped as a child, just as bad as it had been for little Peeto when he had been suddenly thrust into the white world.

"Luke still left his son with others without a thought to what would happen to him," she said a moment later.

"That's not true."

Andrew's remark drew her full attention. "He didn't?"

"No. As a matter of fact, the day he brought Pete

back to St. Louis to stay with Anne, he sent a letter to me here, where I was handling this end of our fur business, directing me to acquire a plantation and enough holdings in New Orleans to insure his son's future. When he was older, Pete was to come to me so he could grow up in a proper setting.''

''I see,'' Bethany murmured, though she didn't really. Luke was so strange. Apparently he did care for Peeto, but not enough to act like a real father. Why was he willing to arrange security and wealth for his son, yet refuse to raise the child himself? It didn't make sense.

The next morning Bethany sat alone, the long dining room table stretching out in front of her for twenty feet, elaborately set with linen and silver. It was a lonely place for a solitary person, but she was glad that neither Luke nor Andrew had joined her for breakfast. At least she didn't have to worry about making blunders in her table manners.

Actually, she probably wouldn't have been that uncomfortable with Andrew. He had been nice to her the night before, even walking her to her bedchamber door before bidding her good night. He was so much friendlier than Luke, it was hard to believe they were brothers. She knew now that their dissimilar experiences growing up had made them so different, and she was glad Andrew would be around to help her with Peeto and Cantigny after Luke left Louisiana.

Suddenly she wished she had insisted that Peeto come down to breakfast with her, but he had been eager to play in the garden with Raffy. She could hear them now, calling to each other as they tried to catch frogs among the lily pads of the fish pond. She lifted her hand, admiring the emerald ring. The diamonds winked and glittered in the sunlight slanting through the French doors, but Bethany didn't feel married at all. Her wedding night had been so strange, nothing like she had envisioned in her childhood dream of marrying Marcus. She gave a self-mocking smile, remembering the way she had locked her bed chamber door the night before and listened fearfully for Luke's footsteps, even though he had made it clear he did not expect her to share his bed.

Luke's voice sounded in the hall outside the dining room as he spoke to a servant, and she thrust her hand back into her lap, forcibly resisting an overpowering urge to flee onto the gallery.

Luke's tall frame appeared almost at once, making escape impossible. He had been riding, and she had to admit he looked superbly masculine in his dove-gray riding breeches and dark linen shirt.

"Good morning," he greeted her, placing his gloves on the sideboard as Jemsy hurried to pour him a cup of coffee. Luke drank his coffee plain, but Bethany had taken only one sip of the teeth-tightening chicory brew the Creoles called coffee before she had diluted it liberally with cream.

Luke lounged at the other end of the table, placing himself a good distance from her, but even so his green gaze made her want to squirm. She focused her attention on the trees outside the open doors.

"I've decided it's time for Pete to begin his lessons. Has he had any instruction at all?"

"No," Bethany answered, glad he was taking an interest in the boy's education. "Except that Mistress

Anne used to read to him sometimes, stories about the founding fathers and the rebellion.''

"I think it's time he learned to read and write for himself. He's old enough now.''

Hot color flowed up Bethany's neck to her chin, cheeks, and the roots of her hair, but Luke continued talking as if he didn't notice.

"I want to teach him myself, since most of the tutors hereabouts instruct in French. He'll have to know Creole eventually, of course, but that can wait.''

"Raffy's already teaching us some words,'' Bethany told him.

"Raffy?''

"He's one of the servants. He's about Peeto's age, and they're already friends.''

"I prefer that you don't call him by that name anymore.''

Bethany looked blankly at Luke. "What do you mean?''

"Call him Peter, or Pete, if you like, or even Petie, as I've heard you do. Drawing attention to his Indian background will only make it harder for him.''

"But that's his name! He's used to it—''

Luke placed his cup carefully in the saucer, the look in his eyes cutting off further argument. "He'll be called Peter or Pete, is that clear?''

Bethany was silent, but mentally she told herself she would call Peeto whatever she wanted, and Luke couldn't do anything about it.

"Since the boy still doesn't take to me much, I want you to sit in on the lessons with us,'' Luke continued. "He'll probably respond better with you there. Don't you agree?''

"He's very smart. He'll catch on fast whether I'm there or not."

"All right then, but I want you present. Fetch the boy so we can get started."

"Now?" Bethany asked in surprise.

"Do you have an objection to starting now?"

"No, but—"

"Then run, get him. I have to go into town later this morning. The schoolroom's up on the third floor. You shouldn't have any trouble finding it."

Peeto didn't prove to be particularly thrilled about beginning his studies, not with five newly captured frogs and one albino lizard in the gunny sack Raffy was holding. His face was long, indeed, as they mounted the steps that led to the attic schoolroom.

Luke had not yet arrived, and Bethany examined the large room with interest. The hardwood floors were as clean and polished as those in the rest of the house, a good example of Tante Chloe's regime, but the toys that lined the shelves against the walls looked worn and well used, as if some child had loved them very much. She touched a red wooden rocking horse with a white tail and mane made from real hair, making it rock, then looked up as Peeto cried out in delight and dug into a hinged wooden box full of gaily painted tin soldiers.

"This will be a good place for you and Raffy to play on rainy days," she said. "Just look at the toys!"

"Can I go tell Raffy?" Peeto asked, glancing longingly at the door.

"No, Luke wants to teach you to read. I know you want to play now, but just think, Petie, you'll be able to read anything you want!"

"I would just as soon go fishin'," Peeto answered

sullenly, not impressed with the prospect of book learning. "You're gonna stay here, ain't you, Beth?"

"Yes, but you have to pay attention and do what your father says."

"I don't like him," Peeto reminded her stubbornly.

Bethany gave him a stern look. "He won't be around much longer. He said he's leaving before the first of the year. Will you try to like him until he leaves? For me?"

Peeto gave a reluctant nod, and Bethany left him to play with the toy soldiers on the floor while she moved desultorily around the room, examining the slates and books and the pictures of cherubic children that were on the walls. She stopped in front of a cupboard with glass doors, her attention on a beautiful baby doll on the second shelf.

She took out the doll, smiling in delight at its fancy white dress and lacy bonnet. The head was made of delicate china, the face was painted with big blue eyes and a fragile rosebud mouth.

"What do you have there?"

Luke's unexpected question almost made her drop the doll. Never had she known anyone who could move so silently!

"It's a doll. I was just looking at it," she answered defensively. "I've never seen one before."

"Didn't you have one when you were little?"

"No," she answered, quickly placing the doll back on the shelf. "My pa didn't believe in toys. Peeto and I are ready for his lesson."

"Pete," Luke said, correcting her mildly. "Why don't you sit over there on the window seat?"

Bethany and Peeto sat down together where he had

indicated. Joining forces against him again, Luke thought, as he picked up two drawing slates.

"You better have one of these, too, just in case Pete needs some help," he said as he put a slate in Bethany's hands.

As Luke turned away to pick up a book, Bethany felt the purest joy bubble up inside her, and she wasted no time selecting a piece of chalk.

"All right," Luke began. "First, you have to learn the alphabet. There are twenty-six letters used in the English language, each with a different sound. Once you know them, you can put the sounds together to form words, and after that, reading is easy."

Bethany watched intently as he drew something on the slate, then held it up for them to see.

"This is an *A*. *A* is for"—he paused, giving Bethany a significant look—"alligator."

Bethany flushed, but nodded encouragement to Peeto as the little boy carefully copied the letter on his slate.

"Very good," Luke praised him. Then he smiled to himself, because out of the corner of his eye he could see Bethany bending diligently over her own slate, her delicate brows drawn together in concentration.

"Let's try another. This is a *B*. *B* is for bayou, and beware, and Bethany," he said with a grim smile. This time Bethany had to laugh as she attempted several copies of that letter on her slate.

Peeto, on the other hand, spent most of his time with wistful eyes on the windows facing the levee, where Raffy was playing with their new frogs.

At that point, Luke decided he would have much more trouble keeping his son motivated in his studies than he would his wife. Even now, Bethany obeyed his every directive with such eager, pleased anticipation that he had to smile. She would learn to read very quickly, he had no doubt. And she would learn to be the mistress of Cantigny with just as much ease, because he meant to help her in every way he could. She would have instructors for dancing and etiquette and every other subject she would be required to master in order to take her rightful place in Creole society. Luke would see to it himself, and as soon as possible.

Chapter 8

Luke reined up at the edge of the levee and looked out over the river. On the opposite shore, he could see the workers of the Fortier plantation burning the residual of their cane crop, as was being done on Cantigny. He had ridden out early to look over the fields and the rum distillery and had found all in order and working well. Andrew had been a good manager for him, with both his fur accounts and his other business holdings, and he would be for Pete as well.

It was hard to believe it was already mid-October, harder to believe that he had arrived at Cantigny little over a fortnight ago. Time was moving fast. As he gazed out at the low delta lands downriver—swampy, alligator-infested bayous and cypress forests for the most part—an intense longing for the Rockies enveloped him. It would be beautiful there now, with the brilliant yellow of the aspens and snow on the ground at the higher elevations. He wished he were there.

He sighed, turning his horse upriver toward the big house. Would it never change? Would he always be torn between two vastly different worlds? Each had its own merits—the great western plains with their gigantic herds of buffalo and magnificent snow-covered peaks, and New Orleans Society with its sophistication and civilized ways. The life of the Sioux was so simple compared with that of the whites. He remembered the summers of his youth spent hunting elk with Snow Blossom's brothers, or splashing and laughing with Snow Blossom herself in the cold mountain streams.

They had been young and innocent then, and life had been free and easy. Sometimes he wondered what his life would be like if he had not felt compelled to come back to St. Louis to seek out his white family. If he hadn't left the tribe in the first place, perhaps when he trapped alone in the pristine mountains with only redmen for companions, he wouldn't long for the warm summer breezes of New Orleans and the sophisticated white women dressed in pretty silks and satins. Yet now, when he rode along the muddy shore of the Mississippi River, it was the wilderness he craved, and the isolation of the Sioux villages.

Luke knew one world as intimately as the other, but he didn't fit into either one, not like other people. Thank God Peeto would never experience such a hell. Luke had made certain about that. Although at Peeto's birth, Luke had assumed the child would grow up with the Mandan Sioux, an ironic twist of fate had decided otherwise. Peeto would know only the ways of the white man.

Luke halted the stallion as he caught sight of Bethany on the levee, still a good distance upriver from him, sitting on a big blue-and-white quilt spread over the grass. He looked around for Michelle, the two boys, or the menagerie of stray dogs and cats that usually accompanied her.

For once, she appeared to be alone. He smiled, noting that she was poring over the *Louisiana Ga-*

zette, one of the New Orleans newspapers. Every time he came across her these days, she was trying to read something, either a book or a newspaper or the family Bible that was on the carved wooden stand in the drawing room. Pete had proved to be an intelligent boy, but Bethany was learning to read with a quickness that astounded Luke, despite his earlier prediction. He was even more impressed by her undisguised joy over her accomplishment.

While he watched her, wind whipped off the river, playing havoc with her newspaper. To his amusement, she rolled over onto her stomach and tucked the newspaper under her body to hold it in place, her apple-green skirts falling away to reveal shapely, naked legs that she bent at the knees, idly swinging her feet back and forth in the air. Not exactly a ladylike pose, he decided, then frowned as an unexpected, unwanted surge of desire sprang to his loins. He touched his heels to his mount, guiding the horse toward her.

At the sound of a horse, Bethany sat up quickly, hastening to pull down her dress when she saw Luke walking his big black stallion toward her. He wore buff breeches and black Hessian boots turned back at the cuff to reveal a doe-colored lining. A black leather vest covered his white shirt, and she wondered how she could ever have thought him to be a mere fur trapper.

She smiled uncertainly as he slid off the horse next to her, holding the reins idly in one hand. He returned her smile, looking so devastatingly handsome in that moment, with his white teeth and green eyes, that her heart skipped a beat. Could this big, virile man really be her husband? *Her* husband?

"What are you doing all alone so far from the house?" he asked.

"It's not so far," Bethany answered, realizing instantly that, despite his smile, he was in a bad mood. She had already learned to identify his tone of voice with a corresponding emotional state. "I just wanted to be by myself for a while," she added with a look that plainly indicated he was interfering with that wish.

Luke grinned. "Well, now you have company."

Bethany watched as he stretched out on the quilt beside her. He was so close she could smell the wonderfully masculine scents of leather, tobacco, and the faint essence of some cologne. It made her want to lean closer, a desire that made her uncomfortable. She watched him draw up one knee and rest his arm on it. He looked at the paper in her hand.

"What are you reading?"

"The newspaper."

"So I see," he said dryly. "Anything interesting?"

Bethany blushed guiltily. She had been trying to read a section in which she had found Luke's name, but much of it was in French, which had her pretty well stymied. *Le sauvage* had been mentioned twice, however. She wondered if he had read the article.

"Well?" Luke prompted.

"I was reading something about you."

"Oh? How boring. Let me see," he said, taking the paper from her. He read the article, then looked at her, his expression unfathomable.

"You shouldn't waste your time on gossip, Beth."

Now Bethany's curiosity was truly piqued. "Well, actually, I couldn't make out much of it, since it was mostly in French," she admitted. "Why don't you read it to me?"

"You shouldn't waste your time on gossip, Beth," Luke repeated pointedly.

But she wasn't ready to be put off. "Are they telling lies about you?"

Luke shifted his gaze out over the river. "If you must know, they have found out about you, and they are saying my child bride will rue the day she ever married a savage like me. There's more, but it all boils down to the same thing."

He had spoken without expression, and the very lack of emotion made Bethany wonder if he was hiding his feelings from her.

"You're not a savage," she said softly. "Why do they say you are?"

"How would you know if I am or not?" he asked, turning his green gaze back to her. A subtle note of anger threaded his next words. "You don't know me. You don't know where I've been or what I've done. Perhaps you should heed their warnings and not ask me so many questions."

"I know you grew up with the Indians, if that's what you're talking about."

She detected a flare of surprise in his eyes, then his face settled back into its usual impassive mask, so that she couldn't tell what he was thinking.

"I suppose Andrew told you. He talks more than he thinks."

"No, he doesn't," she said, quickly defending Andrew, whom she liked better every day.

Luke didn't answer as he idly tossed a piece of gravel into the water, and Bethany decided she would try to get him to talk to her. More than anything, she wanted to know about the circumstances of Peeto's birth and early years. The little boy deserved to know about his mother.

"Did you like it?" she asked him, bringing his attention back to her.

"Like what?"

"Living with the Indians."

Luke stared at her, then startled her by throwing back his head and laughing. But his amusement didn't last long.

"Leave it to you to be different from everyone else," he said. "Believe it or not, that's the first time anyone ever asked me that. Most people either express revulsion or, at best, pour out a shallow dose of sympathy, but no one except you ever wanted to know if I liked it."

"Well, did you?"

Luke was silent. "I got used to it after a time."

"Andy told me you went back again after you came home the first time. Was it because of Petie's mother?"

"Where is Pete, anyway?" Luke said with an intentional change of subject.

Bethany met his gaze, not daring to pursue the subject further at the moment. But that didn't mean she wouldn't do so at some other time, when Luke was in a more receptive frame of mind.

"When I left, he and Raffy were fishing on the dock with Jemsy and Michelle. She's much better, you know, though she's still afraid the Hacketts will come after her. They told her that if she ever tried to escape they would find her and kill her."

"Not if I find them first," Luke said, angry again at the mere thought of the men. "I offered a thousand dollars for them, dead or alive. Somebody will get greedy eventually.''

Silence prevailed until Bethany felt the need to alleviate it. "It's very different down here in Louisiana, isn't it, Luke? I was just thinking a moment ago how much I missed autumn, the way it is up north, I mean, when the leaves turn all gold and scarlet and fall to the ground. Michelle says it rarely gets very cold down here, and it never snows.''

Luke was amazed at how closely her thoughts paralleled his earlier musings. "Are you telling me you're too homesick to stay here?''

His question surprised Bethany. "I'll stay as long as Petie needs me.''

She said it with such sincerity that Luke had no doubt that his son came first with her. He stared at her, at the lovely, open way she was smiling at him. Before he could think to stop it, his hand moved toward her cheek.

Bethany stiffened as his fingers lightly traced the soft curve. "You can be so sweet sometimes,'' he said a little gruffly, and Bethany found herself caught spellbound by his warm eyes.

Her heart sped wildly as his thumb moved downward across her chin to caress her lower lip, making it tremble, and her mouth suddenly went dry. She wet her lips with the tip of her tongue with such provocative innocence that even the very experienced man with her felt its effect. His hand slid beneath the silky blond curls at her nape, and her eyes closed with a natural, womanly instinct as he pulled her forward.

His mouth came against hers, gentle, soft, undemanding, and her heart began to pound, harder and harder, until she knew he must surely feel it. If he did, it didn't stop him. His lips gradually began to demand more from her, molding her mouth to fit his own, pressing, tasting, caressing, until a low moan of pleasure escaped her.

His arm shifted suddenly, and without warning she was lying on her back, Luke bending over her, his mouth moving to the side of her throat. As his warm lips nuzzled her earlobe, sensations stirred deep inside her; no, they shuddered alive, provoking needs she had never before experienced. Instinctively she slid her arms around his neck as her mind began to reel and shiver, just like her heart.

"Oh, Luke," she murmured, and it was as if her voice was a signal that he had been waiting for. Before she knew what was happening, he was gone, striding a few steps away and staring out over the river. Bethany struggled up, feeling weak and confused as the lovely feelings his touch had engendered dwindled away.

"I'm sorry, Beth," he said, without looking at her. "I shouldn't have done that."

"Why did you, then?" she managed to say breathlessly, not understanding why he had stopped.

"It won't ever happen again, I promise."

"Not ever?" Bethany said with obvious disappointment, and Luke gave her a long look.

"I'm expecting a fur shipment, so I'll be spending the next few days in town. We have a house there on Toulouse Street. Your lessons are going well, but if you or Pete should need me, send a message with Jemsy." Then he was in the saddle, galloping along the levee toward the house.

Bethany watched him go, but it took her a long time to control the thunder in her heart.

* * *

On the east side of Cantigny, just off the gallery
beside the formal dining room, a curved flagstone
terrace overlooked a long, rectangular goldfish pond.
A breakfast table had been set there, its glass top
supported by handsomely made wrought iron in the
design of clustered grapes, and it was here that Bethany preferred to take her meals.

A week after Luke had kissed Bethany on the levee,
Michelle Benoist sat alone at the table and watched
Bethany and the boys playing blindman's bluff near
the pool. She wore one of Bethany's wide-brimmed
and beribboned straw hats to protect her face, which
had almost completely healed during the weeks she
had lived at Cantigny.

She sat quietly, her hands in her lap, but her mind
was filled with haunting memories and relentless fears
that kept her fingers laced together in a white-knuck-
led grip. What if Smiling Jack and Braid found her?
she though, the mindless panic beginning to rise once
again.

Jack Hackett's face appeared in her imagination,
smiling constantly as he hit her with his big fist. And
the horrible, dreadful smell of Braid when he had
done such terrible, unspeakable things to her . . .

She came to her feet, her body shuddering uncontrollably, her eyes darting around the columned porch
behind her. They had said they would find her and
cut out her heart if she ever ran away. They had said
they would come in the night when she slept and cut
off her head. And they would! She had seen them kill
people with their big knives, women and little children like Pete and Raffy. She had seen them kill
Etienne . . .

Tears welled, and Michelle sat down again as Bethany came running up the wide flagstone steps to the terrace. She owed Bethany her life, Michelle thought, tears burning in her eyes; she would do anything for her, anything she ever asked.

"Are you getting chilled out here?" Bethany asked, perching on the chair across from Michelle. "There's a bit of a breeze today."

"*Non*, I am fine. *Merci*," Michelle answered softly as Elise moved down the gallery behind them, carrying a tray of Tante Chloe's fancy petit fours and a silver pot of diluted coffee.

Michelle cast her gaze downward as the pretty Negro maid gave her a scornful sidelong look as she set the tray on the table.

Elise curtsied respectfully to Bethany, but as Bethany called out for the boys to join them, leaned close to Michelle. *"Na pas savon qui tace blanc pou blanchi vous la peau,"* she whispered viciously.

Michelle bit her lip, and Bethany looked up as Elise hurried away. "What did Elise say?" she asked when she saw the dark flush staining Michelle's creamy skin.

"It is nothing," Michelle answered quietly.

"Please, Michelle, it is terrible for me not to understand what people say. I am trying very hard to learn Creole so I can teach it to Petie."

"She said there is no soap strong enough to whiten my dark skin," Michelle said, very low.

"Oh, no. I am sorry, Michelle! Why would Elise be so hateful to you? She is usually so nice!"

"It does not matter. I am used to such sayings. The darker slaves have always hated the quadroons because of their pride and light skin."

Peeto and Raffy chose that moment to run up to the table and grab several of the small iced cakes. They took off again at once, and Bethany sighed, looking at Michelle. "There is so much I don't understand about New Orleans and the Creoles. Luke expects me to fit in as his wife, but I don't even understand who the Creoles are or why they are so important here. There aren't any in St. Louis, and New Orleans is an American city. Yet Andrew says the Americans worry constantly about what the Creoles are doing and saying."

"Perhaps I can help you," Michelle offered shyly. "I was born here."

"Would you, Michelle? Could you teach me the customs and such? Luke and Andrew said I will have to meet some of these Creole people at parties and receptions and places like that, and I don't know how to act around them."

"Oui, I will help you."

"What are Creoles, anyways—I mean, anyway?" Bethany amended, remembering how Luke had once corrected her.

Michelle smiled. "They are descendents of the French and Spanish who first came to this region. Their blood is pure."

"Is that all?"

"Oui, but they are very wealthy and powerful here, and they hate the *Américains* for coming as foreigners and trying to change their ways. The Creoles do not wish to speak *Anglais* and be *Américain.* My father will not even learn your language, but he insisted that I be taught, along with his white family and servants, so that we could interpret for him. He is very stubborn."

"Your father is living?" Bethany asked in surprise, having assumed that Michelle had no family in New Orleans because she had made no effort to contact anyone since her recovery.

Michelle nodded without comment.

"Then we must tell him at once that you are here! He must be very worried about you!"

Michelle's head dropped. *"Non,* I cannot. He would never agree to see me."

"But why? You are his daughter."

"I am the daughter of his quadroon mistress," Michelle said, very low. "Mamam died of the yellow jack two springs ago."

"But surely he would want to know you are all right."

"You do not understand, Bethany. It is different here in the Vieux Carré. I ran away with Etienne because I did not want to be kept in the way my mother was. My father treated us well and called us wife and daughter, but we weren't. He had a white wife and son whom he really loved."

"You mean he had two families at the same time?" Bethany said, scandalized. "Isn't that against the law or the Church or something?"

"Here, it is the way of the wealthy. Most Creole gentlemen own a quadroon mistress whom they keep in a different house. There are even balls given here on Thursday nights where the quadroons take their daughters. That's why I ran away with Etienne, so I wouldn't have to go there."

For the first time since Michelle had been well enough to be up and about, she let herself cry.

"Etienne was white and poor," she continued, "but he didn't care that I was a *femme de couleur.*

He was taking me up the river where we could marry, but the Hacketts just rode up to us on the Trace. They shot him, Beth, and left him on the road to die, and there was nothing I could do to help him."

Bethany put her arm around Michelle's trembling shoulders as the girl wept heartbrokenly. Bethany well remembered those terrible men at Old John's. She could almost smell the rank, fetid odor of the one called Braid.

"They'll pay for what they did to you and Etienne, Michelle. Luke's got a reward out on them. He told me."

Michelle's body went rigid, and she squeezed Bethany's hand between both of hers. "They did such awful things to me. Awful, awful things," the girl said, nearly choking on the words. "I had not known a man, not even Etienne, and it hurts so much to be used by a man."

Bethany felt a little sick, remembering how it felt to have a man want her like that. She shuddered to recall how she had been held down on the bed while hard fingers bit into her shoulders, hurting her so much. Her clothes had been torn, her body bruised, and just the thought of it made her cold with dread. What if Luke wanted to use her in such a way? He was so big and strong. She fought down those thoughts as Michelle pulled away, wiping her tears with her handkerchief.

"I think you should go see your father," Bethany said suddenly. "I think he will want to see you."

"But, Bethany, I said such horrible things to him before I left with Etienne! He surely hates me!"

"What if he doesn't? Didn't he take care of you and your mother when you were a little girl?"

"Oui, he was good to us." Michelle raised tearful amber eyes to Bethany's gray ones. "Do you really think he might want to see me after all I've done, after what those men did to me—"

"Hush now. None of that was your fault. Your father doesn't even have to know about it. We'll go to his house, and if he doesn't want to see you, then you can come back to Cantigny and live with me. Luke's leaving, and I will be the mistress here." It still sounded strange to say that, Bethany thought, pausing. "You can help me learn to waltz, since I'm having so much trouble understanding my instructor's Creole. He hardly speaks a word of English. You can help me with that, too—speaking French, I mean—and then you can help me teach the words to Petie. Don't you worry. I'll take care of everything."

Chapter 9

The fact that Luke remained in the city the following day gave Bethany the courage to give her first order as mistress of Cantigny. In response to her polite request to have a small carriage brought around to the river portico, Jemsy acted with as much promptness as if a command had been given by *le sauvage* himself. Clearly, Bethany's easy smile and courteous manner had already endeared her to each and every one of the servants.

She waited with Michelle at her side, hoping the gray dress she wore was suitable for a social call to a Creole home. Luke had said she would be expected to visit Creole families occasionally . . .

"Now, I want you and Raffy to behave yourselves while we're in town, do you hear me, Petie?"

Peeto nodded, but his green eyes searched her face. "You'll come back soon, won't you?"

"We'll be back later today, I promise. Stay close to the house and away from those bayous. Tante Chloe will be here if you need anything."

Leaning down, she gave him a quick hug and a kiss, then did the same for Raffy before she stood back, waiting for Michelle to step into the coach. But Michelle, who looked absolutely terrified, hung back.

Bethany patted the girl's arm. "Don't worry, everything's going to be all right. I know your father will want to see you again!"

Michelle glanced at Jemsy, who sat high on the driver's perch, but the black man looked pointedly away. Michelle stared at the ground, her words coming very softly.

"You don't understand. There are many laws here concerning quadroons. They are not allowed to ride in carriages. I once saw my cousin whipped publicly for doing so."

Bethany gasped in outrage. Her chin angled up in her characteristic gesture. "Well, I am not a Creole, thank goodness, and this is my carriage—or Luke's, I guess—and if I say you can ride in it, you can. Hurry, though, before Luke or Andrew comes back from town."

Michelle still seemed reluctant, but Bethany gave her a little push toward the open door. "No one will see you anyway if you stay away from the windows."

Michelle let herself be persuaded, but she hoped Bethany didn't get into trouble, not after all Bethany had already done for her. More than anything in the world, though, she wanted to see her father again. She wanted him to hold her in his arms and pat her hair as he had when she was a little girl and he had visited them in their cozy house on the Rue des Ramparts. She could still remember the scent of his fragrant tobacco and the peppermint candies he always kept for her in the inside pocket of his coat.

Bethany settled across from Michelle on the gold velvet seat, then leaned out to wave at Peeto and Raffy, who chased the coach until they were covered in dust. Jemsy took a route that led away from the levee, and the team of matched grays trotted down a narrow country lane dappled brightly with sunlight.

Cool breezes from the open window blew their hair, and though Michelle often put her hand up to neaten the tight chignon at her nape, Bethany didn't pay much mind to her blowing curls, not even when a good many of the silky tendrils escaped their pins and formed wisps around her nape and temples. As far as she was concerned, the breeze felt good.

It didn't seem long before they reached the narrow dirt streets at the outskirts of New Orleans. Bethany peered out the window with a good deal of interest. With its narrow buildings of pink or pale yellow stucco-covered brick, the town was very unlike St. Louis or Natchez. Here nearly every house had fancy iron galleries with decorative grillwork behind which stood long rows of tall, shuttered windows and doors.

"Do you know where we are now?" Bethany asked Michelle as the carriage rattled past one such building.

"*Oui*, we have just turned into the Rue Ste. Anne. I grew up not far from here."

Bethany heard the wistfulness in her friend's voice and hoped with all her heart that she was right about Monsieur Louis Benoist. She could not bear to think what it would do to Michelle's fragile state of mind if he refused to see her.

"Luke said he has a house on Toulouse Street," she told Michelle. "Is that far from here?"

"*Non*, but 'tis strange for *Américains* to live here in the Vieux Carré. Most live past the Rue de Canal," Michelle told her, then grew quiet as Jemsy brought their conveyance to a stop before Number 34 Rue de Dauphine.

Bethany climbed out first, gazing up at the narrow house with the same wide iron balconies overhanging the wooden sidewalk, called a banquette, along the edge of the street. All the houses were built with their entrances right on the street with no yard or porch, and all the shutters on the windows of the upper gallery were closed, making the house seem deserted and unopen to visitors.

A few steps away was a tall archway for carriages, the entrance blocked by two heavy wooden doors. A smaller door was cut into one of them for the use of pedestrians, a brass bell bolted to the bricks beside it. Bethany pulled the leather cord, smiling reassuringly to Michelle, who still hovered inside the coach.

"I shouldn't be here, Bethany," Michelle whispered. "This is the house of my father's white family. Mother never even allowed me to walk down this street."

"Wait there if you want. I'll talk to him first and find out if he wants to see you."

Michelle ducked back inside the carriage as the small door swung inward.

"*Bonjour,*" Bethany said to the Negro butler who stood in the opening. Since that was about the extent of her French Creole, she was forced to revert back to English. "I would like to see Monsieur Benoist."

"*Oui,* mamzelle," was the butler's answer, and Bethany followed him, relieved that he understood English. Apparently a good many people in New Orleans did not.

The archway led through a cool, dark tunnel to an open gate of iron bars. Bethany wondered at the age of the place as she was led across a large courtyard paved with uneven cobblestones. Masses of dark green foliage darkened the brick walls where more iron galleries faced the courtyard and the walled gardens that stretched for at least a block behind the house. The property was much more extensive than it had looked from the street. In the distance, she could see the stables and carriage house. Michelle had told her that the Benoist family had always raised horses.

Bethany saw an old man sitting in a brown wicker chair on one of the galleries overlooking the gardens. He was an elegant-looking gentleman with iron-gray hair and a long drooping mustache of the same hue. He was attired formally in a jacket of deep, rich brown, but he appeared very frail as he sat with one blue-veined hand braced on the top of a silver-headed cane. He turned to look at her as the servant led her forward, then rose stiffly with gentlemanly courtesy, inclining his head and speaking to her in rapid Creole, which Bethany couldn't begin to understand.

"Please tell him that I am here with news of his daughter, Michelle Benoist," she said to the servant.

At mention of Michelle's name, Louis Benoist started visibly, one hand moving to his heart.

"Michelle, ma cherie?" he cried.

The butler looked concerned at the excitement the old man was displaying and listened carefully to what he was saying. Bethany waited helplessly until the butler turned to her.

"He wand to know wad zou know of hez daughter?"

"She is in the coach. She would like to see him, if he will allow it."

The butler translated, and Louis immediately nodded, gesticulating wildly and sending the butler running toward the street entrance. Louis turned to Bethany then, speaking in quick, incomprehensible sentences.

"I'm sorry, I don't understand. No *parlez-vous francais,"* she added, remembering that phrase from Michelle.

Louis Benoist looked exasperated with her inability to answer his questions, then his eyes moved past her. He made a choked sound, his faded blue eyes filling with tears, and Bethany turned to find Michelle moving across the courtyard toward them. She backed away as father and daughter stared at each other, then Louis Benoist took a few feeble steps toward Michelle, leaning heavily on his cane.

"Michelle, ma petite, ma cherie—" he cried before Michelle ran into his outstretched arms.

Bethany smiled, touched by their reunion, suddenly glad she had insisted Michelle come. After all, why wouldn't Monsieur Benoist want his only daughter back? She was kind and gentle and beautiful, and she needed him. When father and daughter sat together on a small iron bench, speaking in Creole, Bethany moved away, wanting to give them some privacy.

Looking around, she decided to stroll toward the stables. She walked along a cool, shady path made of white shells. This would be a wonderful home for Michelle, so quiet and private and protected. Behind the tall brick walls and barred gates, she would feel safe from the Hacketts and after Luke left for the mountains again, Bethany would bring Peeto and Raffy here to visit her.

The thought of Luke troubled Bethany, and she sighed, wishing she understood him. He could be so kind at times, she had seen that, but it was almost as if he didn't want to be nice, as if the kind words slipped out of his mouth before he could stop them, then made him angry. Why in the world did he act that way?

Bethany closed her eyes, remembering how he had kissed her with such tenderness. But he didn't care about her, and he didn't want her to care about him. In fact, he had married her because she didn't like him. Now she didn't know how she felt about Luke. She didn't exactly dislike him.

A whinny sounded nearby, and she looked up to find a sleek white mare trotting restlessly back and forth along a low stone wall. Bethany stopped where she was, filled with admiration for the beautiful Arabian mare. It was the most magnificent animal she had ever seen, with its long, flowing white tail and braided mane. It galloped a short distance, arching its neck and swinging its tail with proud arrogance.

Fascinated, Bethany moved to the wall, tucking the hem of her gray skirt into the waistband so she could climb to the top. The spirited mare was wild and free and beautiful, and Bethany watched the horse for a few moments, then began to hum the soft, melodic tune that had always had a near-magical effect on the horses she had handled in the past. All her life she had had an unusual affinity for animals, especially horses, and never yet had she found one she couldn't ride.

She sat motionlessly until her song finally brought the mare nudging close, eyeing her hesitantly.

"You're a real beauty," she whispered, deciding in that moment that she had to ride the mare before she went home.

After a time, she reached out to stroke the mare's smooth back, and to her delight, the horse stood still for her as if hypnotized by her voice. Carefully, ever so gently, just as she had done so many times before when breaking horses for her father, she eased from the wall onto the animal's back, her fingers entwined in the thick mane.

Her slight weight made little impact on the mare, and Bethany smiled in triumph, leaning close to speak soothing words into the animal's quivering ear. The horse took a step forward along the wall, then at Bethany's gentle urging, broke into a slow trot down the length of the corral. She turned the mare with a gentle pressure of her knees, exhilarated at being astride again.

"Uh oh," she muttered beneath her breath as a young groom emerged from the nearby carriage house and saw her. He ran toward her at full speed, waving his arms, shouting at her in Creole. Bethany slowed the mare, who pranced nervously to one side as the boy continued to yell.

"No *parlez-vous francais,*" Bethany said for the second time that day, glad when she saw Michelle hurrying across the gardens toward them.

The groom immediately began to yell toward Michelle, who promptly blanched, turning terrified eyes on Bethany. "He says Osiris is dangerous! He says no one can ride her!"

"But I am already riding her," Bethany replied calmly.

The groom kept up his frantic gestures, and afraid the horse would be eventually spooked by the commotion, Bethany slid to the ground and climbed quickly over the wall. The mare galloped away with a contemptuous shake of her mane, and the groom stared at Bethany as she straightened her long skirts around her legs.

"Will your father be angry with me for riding Osiris? She was just so beautiful I couldn't resist."

"Oh, no, the horse does not even belong to Papa. Jean-Paul here says it is Philippe's horse. Philippe is Papa's son, but he is in Pensacola."

"Good," Bethany said, and Michelle hugged her.

"Oh, Bethany, how can I ever thank you! Papa wants me to stay here. He has been very ill for a long time now, and he needs me to nurse him."

"You see, I told you everything would be all right, didn't I?"

"*Oui*. But come, Papa insists that you dine with us. I have already told him how you saved my life, and he is very grateful to you and Monsieur Randall."

Bethany looped her arm through Michelle's as they walked back to the house. It was wonderful to see her friend so happy after all the tragedy she had experienced.

Before they left the garden, Bethany gave one last, lingering look back at Osiris.

Luke paced back and forth in the entry foyer of Cantigny, his jaw clenched tight. He still couldn't believe Bethany had been so brazen as to order the carriage and take off in it without a word to anyone about her destination. It was a good thing he had decided to come back to check on her and Pete, but now she had been gone all day, and it was already dark outside. Good Lord, would she never learn? The last time she had been out alone at night, she ended up chained to a wall in the calaboose! He couldn't believe she had run away again, though. Not with Peeto safe upstairs with Tante Chloe. But where the hell could she have gone? And was the stupid kiss he had given her the reason she had fled?

That thought raised more questions about why he had kissed her in the first place, something he had asked himself more than once in the last week spent away from her. Not really wanting to think about what had happened between them, he turned and went to the library.

Andrew looked up as Luke passed by him on his way to the liquor cabinet. "She'll be back," he said without much concern. "What are you so worried about?"

"Because I know Beth better than you do, and she attracts trouble like a bloody magnet."

Andrew smiled to himself. If nothing else, Luke's black scowl proved one thing—Bethany had managed to get under his skin. That in itself was an accomplishment for any woman.

At the sound of the foyer door opening, he looked toward the hall. Luke straightened, bottle still in hand. Their eyes locked as the sound of Bethany's laughter came to them. Luke set down his glass and moved out of the room with long, angry strides. Andrew followed, curious to find out where his pretty little sister-in-law had been all day and what Luke was going to say about it.

"Where the hell have you been?"

Bethany whirled to face Luke, startled to see him back at Cantigny, and even more surprised by his angry tone, especially when she saw Andrew standing behind him in the library doorway, almost as if they had been waiting for her.

"Why?" she asked. "Has something happened to Petie?"

"Dammit, nothing's happened to Pete! Where have you been? And where's Michelle?"

"I took her home to see her father, and he insisted she stay there with him. Isn't that wonderful?"

"Don't you know how dangerous it is for two women to be alone in town at night?" Luke demanded furiously, ignoring her news about the octoroon.

"I wasn't out alone. I was at Monsieur Benoist's house on Rue de Dauphine."

Bethany was beginning to feel annoyed at the way Luke was glowering at her, but at her last answer, Andrew spoke up. "Not Philippe Benoist?"

Luke looked at him as Bethany shook her head. "No, his father, Louis Benoist."

"And he asked her to stay with him?" Andrew asked, finding it hard to imagine. After all, Michelle was the illegitimate daughter of Benoist's quadroon mistress. Her presence in his home would create a huge scandal among the Creoles.

"Does Philippe know about her being there?"

"Not yet. He is away on business."

"Who the devil is Philippe Benoist?" Luke interjected angrily, furious at being talked around, especially when he was demanding an explanation.

"He's quite a rogue hereabouts, and a horse racing enthusiast as well. That's how I got to know him. It's said he's had quadroon mistresses since he was fourteen."

"Fourteen!" Bethany said, laughing.

"To hell with that!" Luke said through clenched jaws. "By going to a man's house unescorted like that you could have destroyed all the work Andy and I have done to make you look respectable! I'm taking you to the opera a week from Saturday for your debut appearance, and I don't want you leaving this house before then without my permission. Do you understand?"

"Is that an order?" Bethany asked coldly.

"You're damned right," Luke answered tightly. "And you better take heed of it."

Bethany's fingers curled in frustrated anger as Luke stalked back to the library. She looked helplessly at Andrew.

"He's impossible," she declared, her face flushed.

"True," Andrew replied with an unperturbed grin. "Would you care to join me in the drawing room for a glass of wine?"

Bethany hesitated, glancing up the stairs. "I really should see about Petie."

"He and his little shadow are sound asleep. Tante Chloe told me so not fifteen minutes ago."

"All right."

"You'll have to overlook Luke's behavior now and again," Andrew advised a few moments later in the drawing room. "Believe it or not, I think maybe he was worried about you."

Bethany finished tugging off her gloves before she accepted the glass he handed her. "Really? He certainly didn't seem worried."

"My brother's not one to show much emotion of any kind."

"But why? I don't understand him at all. One moment he's so nice, the next he's angry and saying cruel things.'' She blushed, remembering the gentleness of his one haunting kiss.

Andrew sat down beside her. ''He's a loner. He's always been like that since he came back from the Indians. It was hard for him then. I can remember how he wouldn't sleep in a bed for a long time or even stay in a crowded room. I think it makes him uncomfortable to be around people.''

''I can't imagine anyone wanting to be alone,'' Bethany said, thinking of her own early childhood, when her father had ignored her, and then about the orphanage, where she had been even lonelier.

''Me neither. I like people, but Luke always backs off when anyone gets too close. Like Camille.''

Andrew grimaced as Bethany regarded him with new interest. ''Camille? Who's she?''

''I really shouldn't be talking about all this with you. Luke wouldn't like it.'' That was an understatement, Andrew added to himself.

''Was she from New Orleans?'' Bethany prodded, curious about any woman to whom Luke had shown attention.

''Yes, from a wealthy Creole family. But I think you ought to let Luke tell you about it.''

''Oh, be sensible, Andrew. Do you really think he will?''

She sounded so exasperated that Andrew had to laugh. ''No, I suppose not. From what I understand, it was all a big mistake, but a scandal resulted anyway.''

''What mistake?''

''It happened after Luke returned from the Indians. He stayed with us in St. Louis for about five years. We were living with Hugh and his mother then. The

Widow Younger took us in after our father died. Then Luke decided to come down here for his education. That's when he met Camille. There was talk of a marriage, but apparently Luke backed out at the last minute to go west again with Captain Lewis and Captain Clark.''

Bethany frowned. ''I don't understand why that made everyone here hate him. Things like that happen all the time, don't they?''

Andrew looked uncomfortable. ''The Creoles take a breach of promise like that a bit more seriously. Here, it's an affront to the whole family. And the Dagoberts were influential in the Vieux Carré.'' He hesitated. ''The whole family moved back to France not long afterward, but the Creoles are a clannish lot, and they don't forget things like that very easily.''

Bethany stared at him, beginning to understand the situation a little better. ''Thank you for telling me, Andy,'' she said at length. ''I think I need to know all this. Poor Luke.''

Andrew watched her leave the room, thinking that Peeto was a lucky boy to have her. Although he didn't know it yet, so was Luke.

Chapter 10

Bethany barely recognized her own reflection as she gazed into the full-length mirror. The birdlike Creole hairdresser gave the finishing flourishes to Bethany's carefully arranged blond ringlets, which were swept up at the crown with ropes of pearls and left to cascade down her back. The small woman's name was Francine, and she chattered constantly in her own heavily accented French patois, which Bethany was actually growing to understand.

Smiling at all the flowery compliments the lady was giving her, Bethany turned to Peeto and Raffy for an honest opinion. They sat together on the blue velvet bench at the end of the testers, watching with fascinated gazes the spectacle of Bethany preparing for her debut at the opera.

"Do I look all right?" she asked as she nervously smoothed the azure-blue chiffon that draped gracefully from the wide satin ribbon beneath her bust in the elegant style inspired by Bonaparte's court. The rounded neckline dipped low, revealing a goodly amount of her white breasts, and Bethany frowned at the display, wondering if it was acceptable among the Creoles to be so immodest.

"*Oui*, madame, zou look like a glowin' angel

comin' down from de heavens,'' Raffy told her, his jet eyes rolling in wonder.

Bethany laughed, thinking that was surely one comparison Luke would never make. He certainly did not consider her anything closely akin to an angel. She waited for Peeto's reaction as she pulled on elbow-length white gloves. He frowned darkly at her, clearly not the least bit happy about her plans for the evening.

"I don't see why you have to go just because Luke says so. He ain't your boss."

"Isn't," Bethany corrected him, then had to correct herself. "Well, he is in a way, I guess, now that I'm his wife."

Peeto's scowl deepened. "I don't like it when you and him go off alone. He might hurt you like he hurt my mother."

Concerned by his unexpected words, Bethany sat down beside him, oblivious to the way Francine sucked in her breath in dismay as Bethany paid no heed to crumpling the back of her magnificent gown.

"What do you mean, Petie? How did Luke hurt her?"

Peeto was silent as he always was whenever his mother was mentioned, and Bethany sighed, wishing he and Luke could become closer.

"Luke won't hurt me," Bethany said finally, wanting to reassure him. "And I've never been to the opera house before, and I think it will be wonderful fun. I wish you could come with us, but you probably wouldn't like it even if you could, because Michelle says it's just a bunch of people singing in words nobody can understand. You'd much rather stay here and play with Raffy, wouldn't you? Or should I ask Luke if you can put on that new suit Madame Josephine made for you—the black velvet one with the ruffles on the necktie?''

Peeto shook his head quickly, but his handsome face remained glum. ''I don't want to go. I want you to stay here with Raffy and me. We could all play with the tin soldiers up in the schoolroom like we did last night.''

''We can do that tomorrow, or perhaps we'll go fishing. Or,'' Bethany added, resorting to a suggestion that she knew would appeal to him, ''maybe Luke will let us visit Michelle again like we did on Tuesday. You liked Monsieur Benoist, and you can feed apples to Osiris.''

Peeto's eyes lost their unhappy light, and he gave Bethany the bright, dimpled smile that she loved so much. ''Can Raffy come with us, too? And can I ride Osiris?''

''Of course, Raffy can come, but you're not old enough to ride yet, especially a horse like Osiris. Luke said he would teach you to ride someday soon.''

''He won't. He never does anything he says. He doesn't even see us much except for our lessons, and he's been gone for two whole days.''

''He's got business to attend to in town, you know that. Maybe he'll stay at Cantigny when he brings me home tonight,'' Bethany said, her spirits still high from Luke's message, instructing her to ready herself for their first public appearance as man and wife, which had come early that morning along with Francine, the hairdresser, and the filmy blue gown. Despite the brief formality of the note, Bethany had been thrilled by the fact that she could actually read it herself. Every word. Whatever else Luke had done, he had made that possible for her, and she wouldn't forget it.

"He's teaching us to read, isn't he?" she added in Luke's defense when Peeto's scowl remained in place.

"But that's dumb old book stuff. I want to ride Osiris like you do. Your hair blows out behind you in the wind, and I bet it feels real good."

"Yes, it does feel wonderful," Bethany had to admit, "but someday when you are master of Cantigny, you can have a horse like Osiris, if you want, and one for Raffy, too."

The little boys looked at each other, slow smiles brightening their expressions at that notion. Bethany hugged both of them.

"Now go find Tante Chloe and see if she'll give you some of that praline candy she's been making all day."

As the children ran off, the hairdresser knelt to artfully rearrange the folds of Bethany's azure skirt, then fussed with the pearl-encrusted short sleeves.

"*La magnifique,*" she murmured. "Monsieur will be pleased."

Bethany hoped she was right, because more than anything she wanted to please Luke on this night that was so important to him. In the last few days she had often considered what Andrew had told her about her husband, each time with a greater sense of compassion and understanding. Over and over she had tried to imagine what it must have been like for a five-year-old boy to be stolen from his home. How terrified he must have been!

Shivering, she remembered once long ago in Ohio when she had been very small and two Shawnee warriors had appeared suddenly from the surrounding forests with their feather headdresses and garishly painted bodies. Her father had made her hide in the stable while he spoke to them, eventually trading food and blankets for their beaver pelts. After they had gone, she had envisioned them sneaking back in the dark of night to steal her. She had lain awake in terror for hours, her eyes on the door of her tiny room behind the fireplace.

"Monsieur bez waitin', madame," Elise said from the doorway.

Bethany lifted the dainty white lace fan from the table, then draped an azure-blue satin cape that exactly matched her gown over her arm. More afraid than she had been since the night she married Luke, she lifted the hem of her long skirt the way Francine had showed her and made her way to the main staircase.

He was waiting below in the foyer, and Bethany stopped on the mezzanine to gaze down at him. He looked absolutely wonderful, so handsome and elegant in his black evening jacket and neatly folded white cravat. It was hard to imagine him now in the fringed buckskins, moccasins, and short black beard, though she well recalled how overpoweringly virile he had seemed then as well. With Luke, the garb didn't really matter.

He looked up suddenly as if sensing her presence, his eyes sweeping over her with a swift appraisal that made her stiffen self-consciously, until he flashed a smile so very much like Peeto's, his teeth white and even against his deep tan that her breath caught in the most delicious way. Luke didn't smile often, not at her, and not as he was now. She was inordinately pleased, so much so that she grew slightly alarmed.

But the first words he uttered only added to her burgeoning happiness.

"You will do me proud this night," he murmured, still smiling up at her as he moved to the bottom of the stairs to await her.

Three steps from the floor, she could look directly at him, giving rise to an uncanny sensation since she normally had to tilt back her head to gaze up into his face. His great height had always intimidated her, as it probably did anyone who met him.

Luke stared at her a long moment with an inscrutable expression, but when his gaze dropped to her low décolletage, a warm blush moved up her neck to tint her smooth, creamy skin a rosy hue.

"I was thinking how very different you look now than you did in Natchez," he said, and Bethany smiled.

"I was thinking the same about you," she admitted as he took her satin cape and drew it around her shoulders, his strong fingers fastening the silken frog at the throat.

Bethany glanced at the empty foyer. "Is Andrew not going with us?"

"He plans to join us at the opera house. Come along, the carriage is waiting."

Something in his tone suggested that her question might have annoyed him, and Bethany immediately regretted having asked it. She wanted so much for the night to be pleasant for both of them.

He stood back without touching her, allowing her to precede him outside into the cool night air, and Bethany could not help being affected by the feel of his hand on her bare arm as he assisted her into the coach. He settled on the gold squabs beside her, the small confines of the carriage playing havoc with his long legs. As the conveyance lurched forward, Bethany gave him a shy, sidelong glance.

"I have never attended the opera," she began hesitantly. "Is there anything special I should do or say? I wouldn't want to embarrass you . . ."

Her words faded weakly as he focused his vivid green eyes on her once more; they were glowing like emeralds in the lambent light of the carriage lantern. "You won't, not the way you look tonight. Any man would be proud to call you his own." He flashed his disarming smile again, one that cut deep grooves in either side of his mouth. He had dimples, just like his son!

"Don't worry so much," he advised her. "I'll be there to help you, and so will Andrew. No one can rival you, not in that dress."

Bethany looked down, but her heart fluttered like a trapped sparrow.

"We will be under the scrutiny of everyone in the house, however," he continued a moment later, "so we'll have to put on a pretty good act of caring about each other. I hope you're up to playing the part of a loving wife."

Acting, Bethany thought, both her heart and her high spirits dropping several degrees. It made her angry that he felt obliged to put on an act of affection for her. Her silvery eyes flashed.

"I will do my part as we agreed so that you can return to your mountains on schedule."

Something flickered in his eyes for a mere fraction of a second, something she couldn't read, as usual.

"Good girl" was his only comment, a nonchalant scrap of approval fit more for an obedient child than a grown woman. He probably thought of her that way, she realized, feeling insulted as she turned her gaze into the darkness.

The Theatre of Rue St. Philippe was a bees' nest of activity in the early evening hours, and Bethany was caught up in the excitement that permeated the crowded banquette as Luke assisted her from the coach. Great iron oil lamps, resplendent in their ornate holders, heralded the entrance to the theater, while the sounds of clopping hooves and rattling carriage wheels filled the night air.

A multitude of opera patrons vied for the seven hundred available seats in the new, splendidly appointed opera house. Bethany tried not to stare openly at the elegant Creole women with their carefully kept pale complexions and fine silk gowns.

"Surely every Creole family in town is here tonight, Luke!" Bethany said as he took her elbow to lead her toward the elegant front doors.

"They probably are, since this is the debut performance of *The Marriage of Figaro*," Luke told her. "After you've been in New Orleans a while you'll find that the opera is the Creole's favorite pastime, except perhaps for horse racing. That's why I chose tonight for our first appearance together."

As he led her across the gold-flecked marble floor of the lobby, Bethany was so caught up in the gaiety of the bright lights and chattering groups of people in the magnificent theater that she was hardly aware of heads turning to follow her every movement. But Luke saw the haughty Creole matriarchs eyeing Bethany with supercillious airs and whispering among themselves. No doubt they were thanking the Virgin

Mother that it was not a Creole daughter who had
been so foolhardy as to marry *le sauvage,* he thought
bitterly.

The young Creole gentlemen were regarding her
with quite different expressions, however, and as a
sudden mood of protective possession swept Luke, he
put his hand on Bethany's slim waist, guiding her toward the grand staircase. When she smiled up at him,
her gray eyes filled with wonder, clearly overwhelmed
in her naïveté by the gala atmosphere, Luke felt a
wave of pleasure to have been the one who had escorted her there. He realized he wasn't the least bit
immune to her soft, innocent beauty, or to the way
her breasts swelled above her bodice.

Bethany was startled when he suddenly lifted her
hand to his mouth, his lips touching the back with a
gentle caress. A streak of pure, fiery reaction shot
from where his mouth met her skin all the way to her
heart, and she fought her overpowering response to
him, painfully aware that his tender display was not
for her but for the Creoles watching them. He was
only playing his role, she told herself firmly.

Determined to do the same, she smiled up at him,
filling her eyes with as much warmth as she could,
then lifted her fingertips to stroke his lean, clean-
shaven cheek, her caress not as contrived as Luke's
had been. She had often wanted to touch the crease
etched there by his rare smiles.

To her surprise, Luke jerked his head back from
her touch as if it had burned him. In startled dismay
she wondered if she had inadvertently breached some
unwritten social etiquette. Michelle had told her
young Creole girls could not walk alone on the streets
or converse with a man without a family member's

presence, but surely a wife was permitted to touch her own husband in public, even in the strict, caste-conscious Creole society. Luckily for her, Andrew chose that moment to step between the crimson velvet drapes framing the doorway of his private box.

"Luke! There you are! Come on in, the lights will be going out soon," Andrew said, flashing a quick smile at Bethany. As Luke took the cape from her shoulders, Andrew stared openly at his brother's wife. "Good God, you look gorgeous tonight!"

Bethany blushed, Luke frowned, and Andrew grinned unrepentantly as he ushered them inside the box, which, he told Bethany, he had made sure closely overlooked the stage. He stood back, and Bethany sat down on the black velvet cushions of a graceful settee, looking around her with keen interest. Luke took his place beside her, smiling as she leaned forward, her gaze feasting on the sumptuous interior of the opera house. He followed her regard to the floor below, which was filled to capacity, conversation rising in a buzz as hundreds of people spoke at once. Above them, on the third floor, a second row of boxes stretched in a horseshoe shape around the curtained stage and just below the great, vaulted ceiling. He wondered briefly how many people were discussing the child bride of the *Américain* savage behind their plumed fans.

"You are not escorting anyone tonight?" he asked as Andrew sat down in a chair beside the settee.

Andrew grinned as he poured three goblets of golden French champagne from the magnum chilling in a silver bucket beside him. "Not until after the performance, when Miss Cynthia Ludlow will be free."

"The soprano?"

"Yes, and she's a beauty of the rarest kind."

"I didn't know you knew her," Luke remarked, sipping his wine. "Where did you meet?"

"I prosecuted a case against her brother the last time she played here. He's her manager, you know, and he took a bit more of the performance purse each night then he was entitled to. The theater owner turned him over to the authorities, but I got them to go easy on him. He had to stay in the calaboose for only ten days."

Luke turned to Bethany, who was sampling champagne for the first time in her life and finding the bubbly brew very much to her liking, though it tickled her nose.

"Didn't it upset Miss Ludlow when you got her brother thrown in jail?" Luke asked on a wry note.

"A little at first, I guess, but that was six months ago. They've been in Natchez since then—they have a home there—so she's had plenty of time to get over my part in her brother's trial. If not, maybe these will make her forget all about that little misunderstanding," Andrew said, his blue eyes alight with supreme confidence as he held up a gigantic bouquet of roses.

Luke shook his head, not at all sure Miss Ludlow would have forgotten or that she would think flowers adequate restitution for her brother's jail sentence. Bethany smiled when Andrew gave her a wink just as the lamps began to dim.

Bethany watched the people on the stage with great fascination, wishing she could understand the words they were singing. She took special interest in the object of Andrew's infatuation, in total agreement that Cynthia Ludlow was strikingly lovely with her black hair and flashing black eyes which made Bethany think of a Spaniard she had once met at Valerie Goodrich's house in Natchez. Cynthia's sweet, resonant voice made Bethany shiver.

By the time the intermission lamps flared, Bethany was enjoying herself immensely. All thoughts of the opera vanished instantly, however, when Luke draped his arm across the back of the settee and casually drew her closer to him.

"It's time for a performance of our own," he whispered, his warm lips moving against her ear. "Try to look as if you're enjoying this."

His mouth moved lower, along the sensitive cord of her throat, and Bethany's eyes drifted shut of their own accord, a small moan of pleasure escaping her parted lips.

"The moan was good," Luke said with a half smile, "except that I'm the only one who heard it."

Bethany wanted him to do it again, and was more than a little disappointed when he relaxed back into the chair, though he kept his arm around her. The chairs below them began to empty as Creoles and Americans alike began to make courtesy calls on friends and acquaintances milling about the glittering lobby or in their draped private boxes, more than a few gradually making their way toward the infamous *le sauvage* in this rare public appearance with his young wife.

Bethany sat quietly, sipping her glass of champagne, which Andrew kept filled to the brim. She smiled politely at each visitor to whom she was introduced, but all the while, she was powerfully affected by Luke's gestures of endearment, by his gentle stroking of her hand and the light kisses he dropped upon her temple. All of which left her in a burning, quivering state of she knew not what and made her feel almost as if Luke truly cared for her. It is only an act, an act, an act, she told herself over and over, but what a spine-rippling performance it was. Never had a man, any man, treated her as if she was actually desirable, as Luke was doing now. She was filled with a light-headed giddiness that made her feel gloriously happy. Or was that just the champagne?

"Good evening," Andrew was saying to another formally attired young gentleman who had entered their presence. His pale blue eyes went immediately to Bethany's flushed face. "Please allow me to introduce my older brother, Luke Randall," Andrew continued. "And this is his bride, Bethany. Luke, Beth, this is Monsieur Philippe Benoist."

Bethany's attention flew to the man. Though Luke knew Michelle was the reason for Bethany's interest, he did not particularly care for the familiar way Philippe Benoist returned her attention, especially when the Creole's gaze rested on her low-cut bodice long enough to be almost insulting. When Benoist shifted his gaze to meet Luke's hard stare, there was no sign of the hesitant, intimidated expression that had appeared in the eyes of so many of the young Creole rakes who had visited the Randall box that evening.

"My honor, madame, monsieur," Philippe said in perfect English. Bethany wanted very much to mention Michelle to him, but she knew better. The more she learned about New Orleans and the Creole way of life, the more she understood Michelle's reasons for fleeing its strict racial mores. It would be the worst possible affront to Philippe for Bethany to mention the daughter of his father's quadroon mistress.

"I heard you were to spend the winter in Pensacola, Benoist," Andrew said.

Philippe's blue gaze moved to him. "I returned only this morning on an important matter."

"The Métairie Race, perhaps?" Andrew inquired, and even Bethany could hear the subtle taunt underlying the question. She realized at once that there was more between her easygoing brother-in-law and Philippe Benoist than the polite words they were exchanging.

"*Oui*. I would not miss the most prestigious of the races."

"Will you be riding the Arabian then?" Andrew asked.

Philippe's mouth grew tighter. "If I do, you will no doubt find it a most unhappy day for your wagers, *mon ami*." He bowed stiffly, inclining his head toward Bethany, and was barely out of sight before Andrew chuckled.

"Poor Philippe. That mare of his has made him the laughing stock of the city."

"Oh? In what way?" Luke asked.

Andrew's smile was devilish. "He sent all the way to Egypt for prime horseflesh and paid a small fortune to boot, then, after constantly boasting he would win every race he entered, he found he couldn't even mount the mare."

"But whyever not?" Bethany had to ask, certain they were talking about Osiris. "Surely he can ride."

Andrew grinned. "Not without a saddle, he can't. No one can ride that mare, and believe me, Benoist's tried every known jockey within miles. Apparently, the Arabian was never broken to saddle in Egypt, and besides that, I hear the animal is so highly strung that no one has a prayer of ever sitting her. Even his own Creole cronies won't let Philippe forget his folly. I heard he fled for Pensacola just to get away from the ridicule.''

''But I—'' Bethany began, intending to tell Andrew that Philippe must be mistaken since she had ridden the Arabian, but just then the lamps began to dim and the house grew quiet as the opera resumed. A moment later, she saw Philippe Benoist enter a box just across from her. Their eyes met, and he nodded to her. She answered with a slight incline of her head, wondering if he really couldn't mount Osiris. She quickly looked at Luke, though, as his lips brushed the wispy blond curls at her temple.

''You're not supposed to exchange glances with other men quite so openly, at least not in plain view of your husband. I advise you to save your flirtations until after I have gone.''

Something in his tone arrested Bethany's full attention, and she was careful not to nod to any other man during the duration of the performance.

The curtain went down to thunderous applause, and Andrew's velvet-voiced beauty bowed and smiled amid dozens of falling flowers. Andrew stood and tossed down his own rather ostentatious floral offering with such accuracy that the beribboned bundle landed directly at the toes of the singer's dainty slippers.

Bethany watched as Miss Ludlow scooped up the flowers, obviously delighted and looked up to search out their donor. Andrew smiled down at her, bowing deeply from the waist. But upon recognition of her brother's prosecutor, the soprano's fair face did not reflect nearly so charitable a response.

Gasping, Bethany watched the woman raise her arm

and hurl the roses back up at Andrew with the same accuracy of aim with which he had dropped them to the stage. They hit him squarely in the chest. Luke gave a low laugh as the crowd applauded the singer's righteous indignation. Bethany felt sorry for Andrew until he turned, his imperturbable grin still in place.

"Didn't I tell you she had spirit?" he said to Luke. "Did you see the fire in those black eyes?"

"Enough to burn you alive, I'd say," Luke answered, but Andrew's gaze had already returned to the woman who had spurned him.

"I've always liked a challenge. She'll come around sooner or later, just wait and see."

Luke shook his head, eager to escort Bethany away from the gathering crowds so he wouldn't have to participate in the mindless chatter so enjoyed by the Creoles. He ushered her through the jostling crowd, stopping only when he was forced to do so by a friendly acquaintance. Once they were in the coach again, he was able to relax, glad the evening was over—and a success. As Jemsy commenced the drive home to Cantigny, Luke looked across at Bethany.

"You're very quiet. Did you have a good time?"

She smiled dreamily, leaning her curly head against the upholstered seat. "I was just wishing it could have lasted longer." The lamp glow made her eyes gleam like diamonds. A curious, vulnerable note crept into her voice. "Do you think I did all right, Luke?"

She waited, very much wanting him to tell her she had. He smiled, looking so big and handsome as he sat sprawled across from her that she couldn't take her eyes off him.

"You did very well, but it's only the first of many such evenings we'll have to spend together before you are fully accepted. As a matter of fact, there's a ball being given by Governor Claiborne, and several American soirees, which we'll be attending this week and next.''

There was a brief silence before Luke spoke again. ''Do you think you can enjoy your new role as a wife and a mother?''

''Oh, yes. I was very proud to be with you tonight.''

Her answer was so completely guileless that something moved deep inside Luke's heart, something dangerous that he had fought tooth and nail every day and night since he had rescued Bethany from the calaboose. He found himself wanting to reach out to her, to touch the creamy softness of her face just as she had touched him earlier at the opera house. He wanted to pull her into his arms, and most of all, he wanted to kiss those soft pink lips. She stared at him now, a quizzical expression on her face, and he turned away from her, thinking his own weakness the height of folly.

He had married Bethany Cole because she didn't like him and didn't make any bones about it, and because she didn't want anything from him. Now it was he who wanted to throw himself into the velvet trap she personified to any man with red blood in his veins. Even now, his hand trembled to touch her as she stole nervous glances at him.

''Stop acting afraid of me, dammit,'' he said, lashing out, angry at himself.

Bethany went rigid at his unexpected attack. ''I'm not afraid of you,'' she answered just as hotly, sitting forward. ''I just don't particularly like the way you—''

She got no further. Luke grabbed her shoulders and pulled her bodily across the space separating them, onto his lap, all the while waiting for her to fight against his intentions. To his surprise, she did not resist him. Instead, she put her arms around his neck and drew his mouth down to her own.

Bethany pressed herself eagerly against him, but was in no way prepared for the half-starved manner in which his mouth claimed hers. Demanding, relentless, wonderful, his arms tightened around her with the hard strength she had admired in him so often. It felt so good to be held and kissed, to hear his breath near her ear, as ragged and desperate as her own. Luke was her husband after all, and she was tired of pretending the affection she had come to feel for him was contrived. She did care about him, and it felt right and good to be held in his arms. Maybe they could love each other eventually; maybe they could have a life together, a real life in which Luke wouldn't leave and Peeto would have both a father and a mother.

Such thoughts assailed her as his lips burned across her cheeks and throat and shoulders, his hands sliding down to unfasten the row of tiny buttons of her bodice. He probed insistently at her mouth until her lips parted, and his tongue plunged to meet her own. Her entire body shuddered and came alive, and Luke forgot all caution, caught in the intoxication of Bethany's willing response, of the sweet fragrance of her silky hair and soft lips, of the satiny texture of the flesh he was finally able to taste and savor at will.

He pressed her back against the seat, his hands finding entrance beneath the folds of her gown. So caught up were they in their own passion they only vaguely heard Jemsy's shout of alarm as he tried to slow the carriage. Only when they came to a lurching stop did Luke return to awareness. He lifted his head, still holding Bethany tightly against him.

"Dey's a girl on de road, marster!" Jemsy cried from his perch outside. "I's done near ran her over in de dark!"

Luke released Bethany, and swung down from the carriage to help Jemsy lift a small cloaked figure from the side of the road. It wasn't until the glow of the driver's lamp illuminated her face that Luke recognized her.

"Michelle!" he breathed.

At the sound of her friend's name, Bethany pulled together her shattered composure and lifted her skirts to scramble down beside Luke.

"Is it really Michelle?" she cried. "Is she hurt?"

"*Non,* please, Bethany," Michelle cried. "I am sorry. I did not mean to cause more trouble, but I did not know where else to go." She began to weep. "I was all alone, and I was so afraid those men would find me again. I was so afraid . . ."

"Come, let's get her into the coach," Luke said, quickly assisting the two women inside. As he sat down across from them, Bethany searched Michelle's tearstained face.

"What has happened, Michelle? Is it your father? Is he ill again?"

A sob caught in the young woman's throat. *"Non, non.* It is Philippe. He came today and sent me away. Papa is too weak to protest. He's gotten so very much worse of late. He needs me, but Philippe said I can never see him again!"

"He can't do that!" Bethany cried angrily. "Luke! He can't do that, can he?"

"Yes, I'm afraid he can."

"But why? Louis Benoist wants Michelle with him! He loves her!"

"Philippe is the legal heir, and if his father is too sick to run his own affairs, Philippe is in control. There's nothing anyone can do about it."

At Bethany's distressed look, Luke added, "Michelle is welcome to stay at Cantigny, if you like."

Bethany was grateful for the offer. When they reached the portico, Luke descended first, then helped both women out, looking down at Bethany, still inwardly appalled at his own loss of control earlier in the carriage. What would have happened if Jemsy had not seen Michelle on the road? And what would happen if he himself decided to stay at Cantigny as he had originally planned?

Deciding it dangerous to find out, he said, "I'm returning to town tonight. I'll probably come home some time tomorrow."

Bethany couldn't hide her look of dismay as he reentered the coach and signaled Jemsy to proceed. She had hoped they could finish what they had started before they had seen Michelle, but already he was gone again and everything was as before.

"I'm sorry, Bethany. I have caused you trouble," Michelle murmured sadly.

"No, that's not true. You're my friend, and I want you to stay here. Come, I'll take you up to your bedchamber," Bethany added, shaking off her own disappointment over Luke's decision not to stay the night at Cantigny. "You'll feel better in the morning, just wait and see. We both will."

Chapter 11

The ball of the Honorable William C. C. Claiborne, the first American governor of Louisiana, took place in the spacious grandeur of the Theatre d'Orleans. When Bethany entered, her fingers lightly touching Luke's elegant black-clad arm, her whole being thrilled at the magnificence of the scene in front of her. Hundreds of people clustered about the cavernous ballroom in their jewel-bedecked dresses and matching plumes, fans and turbans, diamonds glittering from the creamy skin of many a Creole lady to reflect brilliantly in the gilt mirrors and polished oak floor.

Never in Bethany's life, not even in the fantastic imaginings of a lonely orphan girl, had she expected to attend an affair of such magnitude. It was a dream, a beautiful, incredible dream, one that Luke had given to her just as he had given her the lovely new gown she now wore, a gown of white crepe edged in silver and the necklace of sparkling diamonds clasped around her neck.

He had returned to Cantigny the day after the opera, acting as if nothing had happened between them though Bethany had relived his embrace a thousand times or more. She was glad for the social engagements they were obligated to attend, since they gave her an opportunity to be with a husband who almost seemed to avoid her.

She smiled up at him now with warmth born of a sincere pleasure to be with him, and was thrilled when he smiled back, showing the dimples that she loved.

"You didn't tell me your bride was such a beauty, my friend," said a masculine voice nearby. "No wonder you've kept her hidden at Cantigny all these weeks."

Bethany turned to find the governor himself standing there, a pleasant-faced man with regular features and bright eyes with a hint of purpose in them. Luke reached out to shake his hand, and Bethany noted with approval that the governor did not seem adversely affected by Luke's reputation as *le sauvage*. She had begun to suspect that Luke had no real friends other than his brother, but she hoped that was not the case with William Claiborne.

"I am hardly hiding her now," Luke was replying, his arm encircling her waist to bring her up against his long, hard side. Though she was sure the affectionate smile he bestowed on her was meant for William Claiborne to see, Bethany's heart melted. Luke's eyes could be so warm at times, and so incredibly green, like emeralds on fire.

"You're looking at me as if you really care," Luke commented, his tone slightly mocking as the governor moved away to rejoin his young Creole wife.

"Perhaps I do," she answered shyly as couples whirled gracefully past where they stood at the edge of the dance floor.

"Perhaps you shouldn't."

Bethany looked away from the cold expression that

overtook his tanned face. Her teeth caught at her lower lip, and she wished she hated him the way she had at first. But she didn't, not anymore. Somehow she had grown to care about him, though she knew that was exactly what he didn't want. He had told her so often enough.

Hot tears stung her eyes, but she fought her own searing emotions, appalled at herself. She couldn't cry, not here in front of all the people Luke was trying to convince of their wedded bliss. He would never forgive her. She looked around, letting cleansing anger replace her unhappiness, and saw Philippe Benoist threading his way through the crowd toward her. Their eyes met, and Bethany's gaze cut him like a silver dagger.

"*Bonsoir,* Madame Randall, Monsieur. How nice to meet you again," Philippe said, and after what he had done to her friend, Bethany could not affect even a remotely friendly expression, not even for Luke. An angry flush rose in her cheeks as Philippe Benoist stared at her with unabashed admiration.

"Good evening, Benoist," Luke said. "I understand your father is ailing. I hope he soon improves."

Bethany waited, knowing Michelle would want to hear everything she could find out about Louis Benoist's condition. Michelle had been mired in the lowest kind of melancholy since she returned to Cantigny, thanks to the detestable man now answering Luke's question.

"My father is still very weak, but the doctor seems to think he will improve with time," Philippe answered, his pale blue eyes straying again to Bethany. "May I have the honor of dancing with your lovely wife, monsieur?"

"If you wish," Luke answered politely, and Bethany was immediately vexed because Luke had given her over to him.

She did not smile as Philippe took her gloved elbow and led her out among the dancers who awaited the first strains from the stringed orchestra set up on a low balcony above the dance floor.

"You are even more beautiful tonight in white than you were in the blue gown you wore to the opera," Philippe said, smiling with practiced charm.

Bethany raised cold gray eyes to him. "I must tell you, Monsieur Benoist, that I do not like you, and if my husband had not given you permission to dance with me, I would have taken great pleasure in refusing you."

She could see that she had shocked him, and she was glad until he laughed down at her, as if delighted by her insult. Bethany decided he was a very strange man.

The music began, and she allowed him to put his hand on her waist, hoping she would remember how to waltz. Michelle had been working with her on the steps, but she had had very little practice in the arms of a man. She certainly didn't want to make a fool of herself in front of Philippe Benoist.

"I suppose this dislike you display toward me is a result of your friendship with my father's"—he hesitated, then finished distastefully—"indiscretion."

"Michelle is not an *indiscretion!* She is your half sister and my best friend, and she has suffered enough without you being cruel to her, too."

Bethany was getting angrier by the minute, and in her agitated state, she managed to tromp clumsily on Philippe's toe—and was glad she had!

Philippe only grinned. "You don't dance nearly as well as my groom tells me you can ride Osiris."

Bethany gritted her teeth. "Thank you very much. From what I hear, you don't ride Osiris nearly as well as you dance," she replied, then gave him a brilliant smile in case Luke was watching them.

Philippe laughed again. "I must say I find it hard to believe you can ride Osiris when no one else can. You must come visit us again and let me see it with my own eyes."

Bethany's gaze was icy. "Perhaps, if I can bring Michelle with me."

"I fear that is impossible. Then I suppose we will have to be satisfied with seeing each other at these social affairs."

"I intend to make every effort not to see you here or anywhere else," she answered furiously.

"I daresay your husband will be glad enough of that, but who could blame him for his jealousy?"

His compliment meant nothing to Bethany, unlike his remark about Luke. She looked over at her husband and found him, indeed, watching them. Could he really be jealous? she wondered, her hope rising. Did it bother him to see her dancing with another man? Perhaps that was the way to make him want her, to let him see that other men desired her. She knew so little about men and their ways. Luke wasn't like other men anyway.

"Do you really think he's jealous?" she asked Philippe, shedding her coldness long enough to look up into his face.

"I would be, if you were mine," he whispered intimately.

Despite Bethany's dislike for the man, she felt a

secret thrill at the thought that a tall, handsome Creole gentleman such as Philippe Benoist actually found her attractive enough to whisper such things in her ear. If he found her desirable, perhaps in time Luke would, too.

Such were Bethany's thoughts as the waltz came to an end. By the time Philippe had escorted her back to her husband's side, she had decided to see if Luke *did* care enough to be jealous. She smiled up at Philippe with all the warmth she could muster for such a disgusting excuse of a man. To her disappointment, though Luke's smile seemed rather stiff, he showed no sign of caring how she had acted with Philippe.

As the evening progressed and other gentlemen began to gather around Bethany, she began to gain more confidence. After all, they always did all the talking, usually a lot of compliments and such. All she had to do was smile and listen. She eagerly accepted one invitation to dance after another, while Luke stood back, speaking to the governor or to Andrew, who was still pursuing the elusive Miss Ludlow. The lady was still spurning him without mercy. Even now, the black-haired singer swept by the hapless Andrew on the arm of an American military officer.

As Bethany whirled around the floor for what seemed like the hundredth time, her partner a slender young Creole who barely spoke a word of English, she turned a surreptitious eye toward where Luke had been leaning against a pillar only moments ago. Now he was gone. Her first thought was that he might have left the ballroom, and she quickly scanned the spectators.

He stood nearly a head taller than most of the men in attendance, making it easy to spot him, and when she did, her heart beat frantically. He was dancing with a beautiful lady in a daringly low-cut golden gown, her flowing copper hair glinting in the candle-light as he whirled her around with all the elegant grace with which he did everything. She hadn't even known he could dance.

Bethany swallowed hard, missing a step and nearly stumbling, all the while fighting her overwhelming distress. She had never seen Luke with another woman. Her eyes sought him again just as he smiled down at his attentive partner. Bethany felt sick inside. She hadn't ever been jealous before, and if that's what she was feeling now, she hated it. Luke was certainly not the one with the heavy, suffocating pain in his heart that she had wanted him to feel. *She* was!

She danced with Andrew next, then with the governor himself, followed by three young Creoles, each of whom knew even less English than the one before. Luke didn't dance as often as she did, but when he did dance, it was always with the beautiful redhead. Bethany's high spirits were slowly sucked into the deepest morass of self-pity. She was so demoralized, she even agreed to dance with Philippe Benoist again. It wasn't until the strains of that waltz faded away that Luke approached her.

"I believe the next dance is mine," he said politely to Philippe, and Bethany was so relieved to have him back again that she didn't notice the look of dislike that passed between the two men.

"You have certainly become popular in a short time," Luke said conversationally as they circled the floor.

"I'm having a wonderful time," she said, lying

with a forced smile that she was finding increasingly hard to sustain.

"And making a mockery of our so-called happy marriage. If you continue to flaunt yourself at every man in this room, everything Andrew and I have done to get you accepted in the Vieux Carré will go up in smoke."

As on edge as Bethany had become, his biting rebuke, uttered with another aloof smile, cut her deeper than she could bear.

"Perhaps our marriage was all a mistake then. Perhaps you should forget it and give me an annulment so that I can have a real relationship with a man I care about and who cares about me," she said, wanting him to experience the same awful jealousy that wound in tight knots around her heart. "Jacques perhaps, or Antoine, or Jean-Paul—they were very nice to me."

His eyes lowered slowly to her face, and Bethany knew at once that she had gone too far. The music faded, and Luke gave a slight bow and escorted her back to a group of her admirers. He strode away without a word, and didn't return until the end of the last quadrille, and then only to escort her back to their carriage.

The ride home passed in a heavy, strained silence that Bethany dared not break. Once at Cantigny, she was subdued as she trailed Luke into the foyer, then lifted her skirts to follow him up the steps, by now very sorry for her behavior. To her surprise, he did not turn down the hall toward his own room as she had expected, but strode down the other wing toward Bethany's bedchamber.

Suddenly wary, she followed him, halting on the

threshold as he crossed the room in long, unhurried strides. He opened the big rosewood armoire with the curved top, lifting out an entire armload of her new gowns. He draped them across the bed carefully, so as not to wrinkle them, then lifted the lid of the enameled trunk in which her wardrobe had arrived from the dressmaker.

"What are you doing?" she asked in a small, fearful voice as he placed one of the dresses inside the trunk.

"Packing your things."

Realization dawned, with heartnumbing dismay close on its heels. Her hand went to her mouth. "You're sending me away."

"That's right."

"But where?"

Luke straightened, giving her a look that made gooseflesh ripple down her spine.

"I don't really care where you go. I don't like threats. You suggested we get an annulment and that's exactly what I'm going to do just as soon as I can arrange it. The idea of marrying you was a stupid mistake. Andrew said so from the beginning, and he was right."

Bethany stared at him, feeling as if her whole world was slowly sliding into a pit of quicksand. She put her hand on the wall for support.

"But what about Petie, Luke? I can't just leave him, you know I can't. He wouldn't understand."

"He's got Raffy and Tante Chloe and Andy now. He'll survive well enough, and so will you. It shouldn't take you long to latch on to a man. Most of your partners tonight would jump at the chance to keep you."

Luke didn't look at Bethany again as he stalked past her and down the long, carpeted corridor to his own bedchamber. He slammed the door, then leaned against it, shutting tired eyes. He was almost relieved that it was over. Bethany hadn't been able to go through with it. She had been the one who wanted out, and it was better that way for both of them. He remembered the way she had smiled up at Philippe Benoist and her other Creole partners, remembered how he had felt inside.

A muscle moved in his cheek, flexing hard for an instant. Damn her! Damn her for worming her way into his life. He hadn't let women get to him, only Snow Blossom, and Camille for a few weeks. But Bethany was so good at making him want her, with her soft innocent mouth and wide silver eyes. He wanted her away from him once and for all; he wanted her out of his life forever.

Deep inside, behind the bolted doors in his heart, a conflicting need rose, pushing hard to be free. Muttering a curse, he crossed the room and opened the French doors to the gallery. He stared into the night, still agitated with the feelings Bethany had dredged up inside him by taunting him with her masculine admirers. She had done it on purpose, perhaps looking for the very reaction she had forced out of him. But it was over now. He didn't have to think about it anymore; he didn't have to think about *her* anymore.

He turned as the door opened and closed. Bethany stood in front of him, looking like a small, beautiful, penitent angel in her flowing white-and-silver gown. Her eyes glittered with tears, one falling even as he watched and rolling down her cheek, wetting her lips.

"Please, Luke, please don't send me away. I don't want to go."

He couldn't find any words, so affected was he by her softly uttered plea and the sorrow on her face as she willingly humbled herself before him.

"I didn't mean it, I swear," she went on softly. "I don't want an annulment. I only want to be with you and Petie."

She came closer, stopping right in front of him, then rose on the tips of her toes and brushed her lips against his clean-shaven cheek.

"Please, Luke, let me be your wife. I won't do anything else to displease you, I promise."

At her softly beseeching words, her eyes filled with hurt and fear and perhaps even love, something brittle snapped inside Luke, some ancient shield he had erected long ago. Feelings he'd suppressed since a childhood of horror and pain flooded free to engulf him, numbing his mind, drowning his self-control. All he wanted was Beth in his arms.

He pulled her to him, buried his face in the softness of her sweet-smelling curls, his heart hammering out of control. He marveled at her willing surrender, at her weak sobs as his hands moved down her back, drawing her slender hips against his loins. He did want her, he did!

"Beth," came his husky whisper as he lifted her off her feet, turning with her held tightly against him. He lowered her to the bed, half laying on top of her as he cradled her face in his palms, kissing her with deep, relentless, hungry, demanding need.

All reason floated from Bethany's grasp, submerging her in an uncharted sea of pure bliss and unknown yearning as his fingers fumbled with her gown until her breasts swelled free for his pleasure. He swept away the remainder of her gown with a sharp rending of silk crepe, and for the first time since Luke had touched her, she felt her muscles begin to tense. The ripping of her dress brought back memories of a different night, the night she had been brutally mauled by a man. Terror began its slow rise inside her, fighting for release like a stifled scream.

Luke gripped her tightly, painfully, in his passion. As he jerked off his own clothes, eager to feel her silken body beneath his bare chest, Bethany was lost in a nightmare from her past.

"Please don't hurt me! Please, please!"

Her desperate cries brought Luke up short, shattering the enormous desire she had aroused in him. He stared down at her, reading the stark fear mirrored in her wide gray eyes. He gentled his hold, pulling her tenderly against him.

"It's all right, Beth," he whispered. "I won't hurt you."

Bethany wept against his chest as he stroked her back and hair, whispering soothing words.

"Tell me, what's wrong? Did I hurt you just now?"

"No," she muttered brokenly. "It . . ."

She couldn't say it, couldn't bring herself to talk about it.

"Sssh, now, it's all right," Luke murmured. "Forgive me. I shouldn't have been so rough with you this first time. I wasn't thinking."

Bethany clutched him tighter, her voice low and tortured. "But it doesn't have anything to do with you! I want to be here with you, but when you tore my dress, it made me remember something, another time when someone held me down and tore my shirt.

I was so scared then, because I thought I couldn't get away from him. Someone came and helped me, but he hurt me, he hurt me.''

''Who?'' Luke asked in a terrible, unnatural voice, his fingers flexing in her hair. ''Who did that to you?''

Bethany was quiet then, realizing she could not tell him, could never tell him. ''Please, I beg you, don't make me talk about it anymore! I can't bear it!''

Luke shut his eyes, sick to the depths of his soul. ''Did he rape you, Beth?'' he whispered hoarsely, needing to know for sure, his guts twisting with the desire to kill the man who had brutalized her.

Bethany shook her head where it lay against his chest, and Luke stroked her hair. ''Thank God,'' he muttered gruffly. He kissed her temple, raising her chin until he could look into her eyes.

''I don't want to hurt you, Beth. I won't ever touch you if you don't want me to. I only want to kiss you and hold you, but only when you're ready.''

Bethany closed her eyes as his lips settled against her forehead, his fingers wiping the wetness from her cheeks. He feathered slow kisses on her eyelids, and she felt new shivers racing over her flesh as his mouth pressed warm kisses on the tremulous pulse throbbing in her throat.

He no longer held her tightly, but tenderly, his touch so gentle it seemed impossible when she remembered how strong he was. Gradually she no longer thought of that other time, knew only the heat of Luke's mouth, burning, heating her naked flesh until she melted against his hard brown body pressing her down into the pillows.

She held him to her, awed by the feel of him, the smooth texture of his back as his bronzed muscles moved beneath her palms. She wanted to touch him as he was touching her, to explore the sinewy strength of his hard, masculine body.

"I love you, Luke, I love you," she whispered without knowing she had spoken. His lips stole her words away as his hands slid over her shoulders and cupped the softness of her breasts. His mouth followed, leaving a hot trail along her trembling flesh until she could only close her eyes and let herself experience the slowly awakening pleasures of being stroked and caressed and cherished by the man she loved. Slowly, lingeringly, expertly, Luke brought her to the brink of ecstasy, until she writhed for some unknown release her quivering body craved.

She moaned as his hips moved down to claim her as his wife and lover. She cried out at the sudden stab of pain, but his arms tightened reassuringly, his deep kisses distracting her until a warm, wonderful, velvet feeling spread through her aching loins, rendering her weak and pliant and dreamy as his mouth continued to taste and worship her, to erase the memories of the only other time a man had touched her.

Her last thought was that she loved Luke, loved him deeply. Then she was no longer capable of thought, or fear. She could only feel him moving on her, making them one as he held her close, whispering tender words as if he really loved her. She held him tighter as the exquisite sensations built until she felt she could not bear more of the shivering, shuddering spiral of pleasure. As she reached the heavens, she cried out, and felt the ultimate fulfillment, her fingers clenched tightly in Luke's thick black hair. He stiffened over her, his own groan of pleasure adding to her satisfaction.

Afterward, they lay unmoving together, Bethany still caught in breathless wonder as Luke held her tightly and tenderly, realizing how very different it had been with her. After a few moments, he turned onto his back, pulling her close. Bethany roused from the lovely lethargy that weighted her limbs long enough to speak.

"Do you love me, Luke, just a little?" she whispered against his strong neck.

He turned slightly so that he could smile down into her eyes. "You are my wife, sweet. You are here in my bed, in my arms, and you please me more than any woman I have ever know. Isn't that enough for you?"

Bethany gazed up into the rugged, beloved planes of his face and felt the gentleness of his fingers as he brushed a soft blond ringlet from her cheek.

"Yes," she murmured. "That's more than enough for me."

Luke smiled, and the tender kiss they shared soon flamed into much more.

Chapter 12

Bethany opened her eyes, sleepily watching the gauzy mosquito baire hanging from Luke's carved bed stir in the morning breeze. She let her long lashes drift together, vaguely hearing the faint chirping of a bluebird on the gallery. She drowsed contentedly for a moment longer, comfortable and warm, until a pair of burning lips touched her bare shoulder.

As Luke pulled her to face him, everything came spiraling back to her. Her heart thumped with an excruciating awareness of her own nakedness, but she was even more conscious of the big, hard muscles of her husband, who lay so close against her.

"Good morning," he said, nuzzling her cheek, the black stubble of his beard scraping her delicate skin.

"G—good morning," she replied stiffly, embarrassed by the nervous way she had stuttered.

Luke laughed softly, knowingly, drawing her body fully against his. "I like waking up with you in my bed," he whispered.

Bethany swallowed convulsively, not sure if *she* did or not. It was daylight outside, and the whole household would be astir soon. When he smiled again, his eyes warmer than the sun as he took her lips in a gentle kiss, she decided she liked waking up in his bed, after all.

Luke lingered over the kiss, in no hurry at all, his palm sliding slowly from her shoulders to her breasts, then over her ribs and lower. Bethany could not suppress her growing pleasure, or the inarticulate sounds being wrenched from her throat.

Her arms moved up to twine around his neck. She wanted to feel his mouth against hers again. Her lips parted willingly for his questing tongue, and darts of flame shot through her to her core.

An urgent knock on the door brought a muffled expletive from Luke, who sat up with barely time to draw the bed sheet over Bethany before Andrew burst into their presence.

"Luke, get up quick! Beth's gone! Her bed hasn't been slept in and Pete's scared—"

His worried words halted and his mouth dropped open at the sight of Luke's bed partner. His expression of shock soon turned into his usual good-natured grin.

"Well, I'll be damned. Sorry, brother, but it never occurred to me—"

Before he could finish his apology, Michelle and Tante Chloe rushed through the doorway, Peeto and Raffy close behind them.

"Good God, doesn't anybody in this house believe in a man's privacy!" Luke muttered furiously, pulling a sheet around him before he slid off the bed to face nearly the whole household of Cantigny, all of whom stared in open-mouthed astonishment at Bethany, who sat in the middle of the bed with tousled curls and kiss-reddened cheeks. Luke's anger faded as his eyes fell on Peeto. The little boy was staring at Bethany, a look of betrayal whitening his face.

"Petie, wait—" Bethany cried, but Peeto did not wait. He bolted from the room before anyone could move.

His departure, and the black glare Luke was giving them, prompted the other intruders to withdraw. Before the door had closed, Bethany was up, plunging her arms into Luke's black silk dressing gown.

"I have to find him!" she cried, rushing toward the door. Luke hastily pulled on a pair of trousers before he followed her barefooted down the hall.

Bethany had disappeared into Pete's bedchamber, and Luke pushed open the door, surprised to find her on her hands and knees beside the bed. Peeto must have hidden underneath it.

"Please, Petie, don't be angry with me," Bethany was pleading, unaware that Luke had moved into the room and stood near the foot of the bed. When Peeto refused to answer, she squirmed under the bed as well, to where he lay pressed against the wall, his face turned away from her.

Bethany felt like crying herself. Peeto hadn't reacted so fearfully since the very first days after Luke had left him with the Youngers. He had been tiny and terrified, and it had nearly broken her heart to see him cower under the bed then as he was doing now.

"What is it, Petie? Are you angry with me?"

When she reached out to touch his hair, he pushed closer to the wall, covering his head with his arms.

"Go away," came his muffled voice.

"I won't go away, because I love you, and I'm worried about you. I'm going to lie right here until you talk to me."

"You don't love me," came Peeto's small, tortured voice. "You love him. He took you away from me, just like he took my mother away from me. I hate him! I hate him!"

Pain squeezed Bethany's heart. "I do, too, love you, Petie, you know I do. The only reason I married Luke was so I could be your mother, and take care of you, you know that's true."

"But he'll kill you just like he killed my mother," Peeto whispered, his voice roughened by fear.

Bethany gasped at the little boy's words, and Luke's fingers tightened around the smooth bedpost until his knuckles showed white.

"Petie, that can't be true! Luke wouldn't ever do anything like that!"

"Yes, he did! I saw him! I saw him push her off the rocks! He killed her, he did!"

Luke shut his eyes, remembering that day, remembering the cold rain and Snow Blossom's screams, remembering the terrible, abrupt end as she hit the jagged rocks below the cliff. Bile rose bitter and caustic in the back of his throat, and he turned away from the bed, from the son who hated him, from Bethany. He moved blindly toward the door, then out of the room, where he wouldn't have to listen to his son's terrified accusations.

Under the bed, Bethany remained unaware of either Luke's presence or his departure. She put her arms around Peeto as he began to sob, pulling his head against her breast.

"Sssh, Petie, you mustn't say those things about Luke."

"He took me away and left me. Now he'll make

you love him more than me, and you'll go off with him when he leaves and I'll be here all alone.''

Peeto wept brokenheartedly against her, and tears welled in Bethany's eyes as well. ''I will never, ever, leave you, Peeto.'' Her voice caught. ''Do you hear me? Not as long as I live. Do you believe me?''

Peeto finally nodded, and his tight grip on Bethany's neck relaxed. But Bethany remained close beside him, stroking his unruly hair from his forehead in the way he had always found soothing.

''I love Luke, too, Petie. I didn't mean to love him, but it just happened. You can love two people at once, you know. You love Raffy and Michelle, don't you? And Tante Chloe?''

''But I'm scared of Luke.''

''I don't believe Luke would ever hurt you, or me, either. Has he ever done anything like that to either of us?'' Peeto shook his head, and Bethany continued. ''Then you mustn't worry about that anymore. I know you think you saw him hurt your mother, but it must have been an accident. We should ask Luke about it and see what he says. Remember how we always give each other a chance to explain things we do before we get angry? We have to do that with Luke, too. We're a family now, you know. You were very little when your mother died. Maybe you just didn't understand what happened.''

''I saw it,'' Peeto whispered stubbornly. ''It was the day he went away and left us.''

''You know what, Petie?'' Bethany said, trying to hide her own troubled emotions. ''You frightened Raffy when you ran away. I heard him crying when Tante Chloe made him go downstairs. You don't want your best friend to cry, do you?''

"No," Peeto replied, and Bethany wiped his tears away with the silk sleeve of Luke's robe.

"Then come on, you can help me get dressed, then we'll go find him. Luke, too."

But they didn't find Luke. He had already called for Onyx and ridden away without a word to anyone.

To Bethany's distress, Luke had still not returned by the time she tucked his son into bed that night. She bent down to kiss Peeto's cheek, knowing the little boy was still very upset, though her solemn promise that she would never leave with Luke seemed to help. She had never yet broken a promise to him, and he trusted her.

Bethany left a lamp burning very low near his bed, then went slowly to her own bedchamber. She heaved a deep sigh as she looked around the empty room. All day she had wondered how Luke would explain what Peeto had seen. How horrible that such a little boy had witnessed his own mother's death! No wonder he had been so frightened and withdrawn when he came to St. Louis. No wonder he had been terrified of his father.

Although she had questioned Peeto further about his mother's death, nearly all his childish mind could seem to remember of that day was the moment his mother fell. But Bethany didn't believe for a moment that Luke had intentionally killed her. He was a hard man at times, difficult to know and understand, and even though she thought him capable of taking a life when warranted, she could not believe he would murder the mother of his only child. She wanted him to tell her what had really happened. Trying to bide her time until Luke came home again, she soaked in the hot bath Jemsy had brought up, all the while listening for her husband's footfalls in the quiet corridors of the sleeping house. The bath did relax her a bit, and afterward she donned a pink nightdress and began to pace her bedchamber. Her thoughts turned to the night before, when Luke had held her so gently, to the way she had felt when his hands touched her with such tenderness. An erotic shiver coursed through her at the memory of all they had shared.

"Thinking of me, little Beth?"

Luke's voice came unexpectedly from the gallery door, and Bethany jumped up, alarmed by his sudden appearance. He hadn't shaved all day, and his shirt was rumpled and pulled from the waistband of his trousers. He smiled with no warmth as he moved into the room, carrying a whiskey bottle in one hand.

"You've been drinking," Bethany said accusingly, stepping back.

"You got that right," he replied, taking a swig directly from the bottle.

He was in an ugly mood, but he wasn't drunk— Bethany could tell that much—and she wasn't afraid of him.

"I've been worried about you, Luke. No one knew where you were."

"It's no one's business where I go or what I do. It's especially none of your business."

Luke wanted to fight with her, Bethany realized at once. He was intentionally trying to make her angry. She sat down on the edge of the bed, silently watching as he stripped his shirt over his head in one swift motion.

"Why are you drinking?" she asked quietly. "Is it because you're sorry you made love to me last night?"

"Maybe," Luke said, wanting to hurt her. But when that very reaction burned a flush onto Bethany's face, he was sorry he had caused it. He didn't know why he wanted to hurt her. He didn't even know why the hell he had come to her room. She probably hated him now, just like his son hated him, just like everyone else in New Orleans hated him.

"Well, I'm not sorry about it," Bethany said, trying to hide her pain by lifting her chin. "I hope I will have a child from last night. I want to have your baby."

Luke looked at her for a moment, wrestling with the desire still raging inside him. Why was he fighting it so hard? He wanted her. She was his wife, and she said she wanted him. He had never fought against bedding other women who appealed to him. And there she sat, waiting, so calm and serene with her big eyes and soft hair, so damned beautiful that it made him ache inside.

As Luke continued to stare at her, his dark face devoid of expression, Bethany felt a curious sorrow seep into her heart. He was just like Peeto, she thought sadly, except that he wasn't hiding under a bed. Luke was hiding behind the whiskey bottle he held and the strange, self-imposed aloofness he had strapped on his mind like some kind of mental armor. Her heart jerked. Why? Why did he do that to himself? She knew something of Peeto's problems, but what had Luke suffered to make him so hard to reach? What had the Sioux done to him when he was little?

"Don't you see, Luke?" she said, suddenly wanting to tell him the truth. "I love you, and I want to help you and get to know you better. I've told you things about myself, about the orphanage and my father, but you've never shared any stories about your childhood, or your mother, or anything else.''

"You wouldn't like my stories," he said with a twisted smile, and Bethany's gaze dropped to the ugly scar across his exposed chest. When he saw her looking at it, he turned away, sprawling into a chair. He tilted the bottle again.

"Tell me about that scar," she said, sure it had something to do with the Sioux.

"No."

"You aren't being fair at all! You take me as a wife, then you take me to bed, telling me how much I please you, then you shut yourself off from me and Petie like this. I don't know what to tell him when he asks me what happened to his mother! He thinks—''

"Shut up, Beth," Luke said tightly, but she wasn't about to leave the subject.

"No. Petie needs to know about his past and where he came from. He needs to know about you. Luke—''

Bethany jumped as Luke suddenly came out of the chair, sending the bottle shattering into the grate with a crash. She quailed as he crossed the room with great angry strides, catching her by the shoulders.

"All right, Beth," he said, his jaws clenched, his face close to hers. "Since you want to know all about me, I'll tell you some of my ugly boyhood stories. I got this pretty scar that fascinates you so much when I was twelve years old. An elder of the tribe held me down while another man pushed a sharpened buffalo bone up through my chest muscle. There were long rawhide cords attached to either end of the bone so they could hoist me up on the ceremonial pole. You see, my weight was supposed to pull the bone through my flesh until I dropped to the ground, but I didn't weigh enough. So I hung there by my chest in agony all night until one of the chiefs finally took pity on me and pulled on my legs until the embedded bone was ripped the rest of the way out of my body. Well, love, there it is. Are you happy now?''

Bethany shook her head, tears rolling down her face, unable to hide her horror and revulsion. ''No! No, I'm not happy! It makes me sad and sorry that you had to suffer!''

Luke stared down at her, his raw rage draining slowly away. ''Oh, God,'' he half groaned, gathering her close as he lay down on the bed, holding her tightly against him.

''I'm sorry, Luke,'' Bethany said, sobbing. ''I didn't know they tortured you.''

He shut his eyes. ''It wasn't torture, at least not in their eyes. It's called the *o-kee-pa*, or the sun dance. The Mandans believe it placates the spirits of the waters when young warriors offer their flesh to the gods. I did it because it made me a member of the tribe.''

''But it's so horrible, so cruel! You weren't much older than Petie.''

''That's why I brought him back after Snow Blossom died. So he would never have to go through it.''

Bethany wanted desperately to ask him more about Peeto's mother, about Snow Blossom, but she was afraid to, so she lay quietly, her ear against the awful scar of his boyhood as he idly stroked her back. His heart beat strong and steady, and after a while he spoke again.

''I heard what Pete told you today about his mother.'' He paused as if trying to find the right words. "It's not true. I didn't kill Snow Blossom. It was an accident, a terrible accident. I swear it, Beth."

She looked up into his face. "I never believed you pushed her, not for one minute," she murmured, stroking his cheek, then lowering her fingertips to trace the angry scar on his chest. "You must have been very brave when you were a little boy, just like Petie is."

Luke stared up at the pink hangings on her bed. "No. I wasn't brave. I was just a scared child. It took me a long time to adjust to the Sioux ways. I can't remember much about those first few months except that I was always afraid of everyone, that I was angry and alone."

Bethany's heart ached for him as he closed his eyes.

"I didn't know their language at first," he continued, "not until Snow Blossom taught me. She was around my age. It was better after I could understand them."

Bethany took his hand, lifting it to her lips. "I'm glad she was there for you. It must have been terrible."

"I didn't think of her as anything but a sister until I went back with Captain Lewis's expedition. We wintered with the Mandan, and that's when Snow Blossom and I married and when Peeto was conceived. But I didn't know about him for several years, not until I went back again to set up my trapping network." He sighed. "I stayed there for a long time, but when I wanted to come back to St. Louis, she insisted on coming with me. I knew she couldn't live with the whites. I had seen how they treated Indians, how they treated me for having grown up with the

Sioux. I didn't want her, or Peeto, subjected to that hatred and prejudice, so I left them behind.''

A muscle flexed in his cheek. ''For a couple of days, I didn't even know they were following me. Then I saw them as we were traveling through a high mountain pass. I went back and tried to make her return to her village, but she wouldn't go. She tried to run away from me.'' He stopped again, fighting the agony he felt each time he lived through it again. ''It was raining. God, I can see that place in my mind as clear as if I was standing there with her. She slipped on a stone, and it caused a rock slide. I managed to grab Peeto, but I couldn't catch her in time.''

''I'm sorry, Luke, so sorry.''

''I hoped Pete wouldn't remember any of it. He was so little, just a baby.''

''He's older now. He'll understand what really happened if you explain it to him.''

''Maybe,'' Luke said, searching her face, ''but people who love me always seem to get hurt. Snow Blossom and Pete, and there was another woman, named Camille. I thought if I married her I might be satisfied to live here in New Orleans like other white men, but even while she was planning for the wedding, all I could think about were the mountains and the Sioux and Snow Blossom. I left Camille, too, and I hurt her and humiliated her. But I don't want to hurt you, Beth. Don't you see? You'd be better off if you didn't love me.''

''It's too late for that,'' she murmured. ''I already do love you. You and Petie.''

Their eyes met, then their lips. Bethany let him lower her down to the pillows. He shifted until he lay half over her, his hands tangled in her hair, kissing her slowly and thoroughly, over and over again. Bethany lay enraptured by his mouth and hands as he worked his magic on her senses, caressing, arousing, bringing her to the brink of paradise until their love was sealed once more by a searing, lovely, indescribable flood of pleasure.

Much later, when Bethany lay content, close against his scarred chest, floating in the dreamy fringes of slumber, Luke's mouth touched her brow very gently. Then they both lay quiet until they slept.

Chapter 13

Close to the river levee of New Orleans, just beyond the Place d'Armes and the St. Louis Cathedral, was an open market that always bustled with activity. Not only was it a marketplace with stalls displaying every conceivable commodity, it was also a social center where the people of New Orleans from every walk of life, mingled to socialize over warm beignets and café au lait in the coffeehouses and cafés. Here, whispered gossip abounded: stories of the latest duel in the Oaks behind the cathedral; discussions of the virtues of the current opera, and exaggerated descriptions of the gentlemen smugglers, especially the infamous Lafitte brothers whose activities were condoned by everyone in the city—except, perhaps, by Governor Claiborne.

On a fine Thursday morning in November, Bethany strolled through the market with Michelle, Peeto and Raffy trailing behind them. Ever since the week before, when Luke had brought them from Cantigny to stay in the fine Randall townhouse on Toulouse Street, Bethany had been anxious to visit the famed market.

Until today, the social whirl that Luke deemed necessary had kept her busy, but since the night Luke had told her about the terrible *o-kee-pa*, in fact, ever since they had first made love, she felt much closer to him. It was as if he had let down some kind of self-imposed reserve and let her peek into his heart. She wanted to walk the rest of the way into his heart, but it was not to be, not yet. He had still not told her he loved her or that he would stay in New Orleans. But she was not about to give up hope. He just *had* to stay with her and Peeto!

Bethany strolled eagerly along the roofed arcade supported by heavy pillars, intrigued by the market with its colorful sights and exotic odors, so different from St. Louis. All around them was a cacophony of sounds—chickens squawking, parrots screaming, and shouts in a dozen different languages as Negroes, Creoles, and foreign seamen explored the exciting place.

Bethany took it all in as they passed tables of blue-gray fish, their scales shining in the sun, then vats of river shrimp, somnolent bayou crabs, and the belligerent-looking crayfish, all wriggling together. Piles of eggs wrapped in Spanish moss lay on one long table. The little group passed into the flower section, where Bethany bought a bouquet of petunias because they reminded her of those in Val Goodrich's front garden.

Later, she paused before a selection of prickly pineapples, dozens of the pineconelike fruit stacked in neat piles like the cannonballs at the military parade ground. But it was a strange, unknown, golden fruit that next drew Bethany's attention. She picked up one of the odd stalks, examining it curiously.

"What in the world is this, Michelle?"

"It's a banana. There are many such trees in the city, but most of these bananas are brought by ship from Martinique."

Bethany had never heard of bananas, and she turned the tough-skinned fruit in her hands. "Surely it cannot be eaten."

Michelle smiled, which she rarely did since Philippe had heartlessly cast her out of her father's house.

"You must peel them first, like this." She demonstrated, then broke off a piece for Bethany.

"Oh, I like that," Bethany admitted, thinking it had a very different taste and texture from any other fruit she had eaten. "Petie, you must try this! Here's one for you, too, Raffy."

The children tasted the bananas and wanted more, and Bethany decided she must take some home with her.

"I will take this whole branch," she said to the Negro vender standing behind the table. His eyes widened in astonishment, and Michelle smiled again at the enthusiasm that was so characteristic of Bethany.

"*Non,* Beth. They spoil quickly. You must buy them fresh every day or so."

"Oh, I see. I wonder if Luke likes them?" Bethany murmured, but she bought a good-sized bunch of the delectable fruit anyway, placing the bananas in the woven basket Raffy carried for their purchases.

"If you see anything you want or need, Michelle, you must tell me," Bethany told her friend as they moved along. "Luke gave me this whole purse full of coins just this morning. I certainly don't need it all!"

"I need nothing. You and your husband have been very generous. I wish I was able to repay your kind hospitality."

"Don't be silly. You help me all the time with Petie, and you're trying your best to teach me Creole, though I don't think I'll ever completely understand it!''

They ambled among the crowd, passing rich Creole ladies in their high-waisted, pastel morning gowns with their Negro menservants carrying fancy parasols to shield their fair complexions from the sun. Other wealthy households sent their black cooks, dressed in calico skirts and gingham headscarves called tignons, to haggle over the prices of foodstuffs with the vendors. One section of the market was filled with animals—exotically plumed parrots, ducks and geese from the swamps, and big river turtles—even an alligator, heavily secured, his long snout strapped together with ropes.

Bethany was quick to lead the boys away from that frightful creature toward a large bamboo crate in which a small monkey was cavorting for the amusement of passersby. As Peeto and Raffy crowded close to the bamboo bars, the little dark-faced animal swung from side to side, using its tail as much as its arms. The two boys laughed in delight, fascinated by its antics. Peeto jumped back, startled, when the monkey suddenly reached for the banana he held, swiping it from his hands before he could blink. Bethany laughed as the mischievous creature peeled it deftly and popped the fruit into his mouth, then sent the peel sailing back out at the boys. She turned quickly, however, as someone's fingers tightened around her arm. Her smile disintegrated when she saw Michelle's white face.

''Michelle! What is it?'' Bethany asked in alarm.

''I . . . I . . . I—'' Michelle began weakly, but words failed her as her eyes rolled back into her head.

Bethany barely had time to grab for her as the octo-roon fainted dead away.

Bethany lowered her to the ground as best she could while the boys gathered close. She looked frantically for help, her eyes stopping on the handsome face of Philippe Benoist, who was standing not a yard away.

"May I be of assistance, Madame Randall?" Philippe asked solicitously, going down on one knee beside her.

"No! It was probably the sight of you that made her faint!" Bethany snapped angrily. "Just go away and leave us alone!"

Philippe only smiled at her display of temper. "I am afraid I cannot take credit for her collapse, since she had already swooned when I saw you. I would like to be of service, since you appear to be here alone. My carriage can have you home in minutes. You are living on Rue de Toulouse, are you not?"

Bethany hesitated, wondering how he knew that, and not wanting to have anything to do with the man. Glancing around, she found no one else paying much attention to her plight, and it was a three-block walk up Toulouse Street to Andrew's galleried mansion.

"Merci," she said stiffly.

Philippe turned at once, speaking a word or two in French to his manservant. The slave bent and easily lifted Michelle into his strong arms. Bethany followed him through the marketplace, holding the little boys by the hand, while Philippe silently followed.

The ornate Benoist carriage waited on the corner of Rue St. Pierre and the Rue de Chartres, and as the slave lay Michelle's limp body carefully on one of the velvet seats, the boys climbed delightedly up to the high seat beside the driver.

Bethany took her place beside Michelle, supporting her friend's head on her lap as she worriedly fanned her face with a handkerchief.

"It could have been the sun," Philippe suggested from the other seat of the open carriage. "It affects many ladies in that way."

Bethany glanced at him, certain Michelle's fainting spell was in no way caused by the sun. It was the coolest day she had yet seen in the sultry region of Louisiana, and besides that, she had seen fear in Michelle's amber eyes just before she lost consciousness.

"She hasn't been well of late, but are you sure she didn't see you?" she asked Philippe with not a little suspicion.

Philippe chuckled. "I do hope I am not so distasteful in appearance as to make one faint dead away at the mere sight of me."

"You are to Michelle, and to me, too. You are despicable to keep her away from her father, especially when he's so ill!"

"It pains me sorely to have you harbor such ill feelings toward me."

"Good," replied Bethany.

Philippe gave a lazy smile. "But I was most pleased to catch sight of you today. It gives me the opportunity to tell you about my change of heart."

"What change of heart?"

"I have decided to let Michelle visit my father after all."

"Really?" Bethany said, her eyes narrowing. "Why?"

"Must I have an ulterior motive?"

"Don't you?"

Philippe gave an expressive shrug. "Alas, you are too perceptive, *chérie*. There is, indeed, one condition that I must ask."

"What does she have to do?"

"Michelle needs do nothing. My condition concerns you."

"Me?"

At a loss, Bethany searched the young Creole's good-looking face. His blue eyes openly roamed over her in a way she didn't particularly like. "The Métairie Race is on Saturday. I have wagered a great deal of money. I want you to ride Osiris for me."

Bethany stared at him, thinking he must be the one who'd been affected by the sun. "You can't be serious."

"Au contraire, I am most serious. You impressed my groom as well as my father. Obviously you are an expert equestrienne, with or without a saddle. Osiris will win with you atop her."

"But a woman would never be allowed to ride in the Métairie!"

"No one will know you're a woman if you dress like a man. I understand you've done so before," he said. At Bethany's quick look, he added, "I have made discreet inquiries about you."

"Luke would never let me ride in a public race."

"He need never know."

"You don't expect me to deceive him about it!" Bethany said indignantly.

"Non, but what he does not know will not bother him, and it will surely make your unfortunate friend there most happy." He gestured at Michelle.

"But what if someone tells him about it?"

"You are not well known here yet, and no one will recognize you if you wear a mask of some sort."

"A mask? Won't that appear strange?"

"Breeders often have their jockeys ride anonymously to keep the bettors off balance. No one will think anything of a masked rider."

Still amazed by his proposal, Bethany nevertheless realized he had thought out all his answers in advance. Anger rose in her at his gall. "I think you are contemptible to ask this of me. If you were any kind of gentleman, you would do the decent thing and let Michelle see her father without any conditions."

"True, but I've never been accused of being particularly decent, and I'm not much of a gentleman, either—at least not when it comes to horseracing."

How true, Bethany thought as the triple balconies of Andrew's townhouse appeared around the next corner. Except for Luke's not liking the idea, though, what harm could it do, especially if she hid her identity behind a mask? She looked down at poor Michelle. She had suffered so much at the hands of others, and now her own half brother tormented her. The only time Bethany had ever seen her happy were those few days when Michelle lived with her father.

"All right, I'll do it," she agreed reluctantly, "but not until I have your promise to let Michelle visit her father anytime she wants, for as long as she wants. Written down," she added. "In English."

"*Bien*. The Métairie is at noon on Saturday."

"I will come to your father's house at eleven o'clock," she told him as the carriage rolled to a stop.

One of the Randall's many servants immediately appeared from the arched portal. Bethany quickly instructed him to carry Michelle to her room, then helped the boys jump down before she moved toward the house without another word to Philippe Benoist.

By the time Michelle had been carried to her bed, she had regained consciousness, but she was filled with terror. The entire household staff stopped in their dusting of the gleaming mirrors of the entry hall and their polishing of silver trays in the dining room to look with frightened eyes toward the front staircase as the young woman's shrill, terrified screams echoed through the house.

Luke flung open the doors of the study, where he had been working on his fur trapping accounts, and took the stairs to the second floor three at a time. Thinking that the screams were coming from Bethany, he was relieved when he pushed through the handful of servants clustered outside Michelle's door and found his wife trying to calm her hysterical friend.

"What the devil's going on?" he demanded, coming up beside Bethany, who was sitting on the edge of the bed.

"I don't know. She fainted at the open market, and now she's so scared she can't tell me what's wrong."

"He's here! He's here! No, no, no!" Michelle was crying frantically, then lapsed into fast, erratic Creole.

Bethany watched intently as Luke suddenly frowned and leaned down to question Michelle in his flawless French. His quiet, compelling voice brought a degree of calm to Michelle as it had in Natchez, but her answers were punctuated with sobs. Bethany turned to Luke as he straightened.

"She says she saw Jack Hackett," he muttered, his expression somber.

"Oh, no!" Bethany cried. "Could he really be here, in the city?"

"He could, but it would be a stupid thing to do considering the reward I've posted on him and his brother. Did you see him?"

"No, but it was very crowded. Oh, Luke, what if they had gotten Michelle again? What if Philippe hadn't been there to help us?"

"Benoist? What's he got to do with it?"

"Michelle couldn't walk, so he brought us home in his carriage."

"I thought he wanted nothing to do with Michelle."

"He was kind enough today," Bethany answered uneasily, already uncomfortable with the idea of keeping something from Luke. She wasn't used to being secretive, and she toyed momentarily with the idea of asking his permission to ride Osiris. Before she could, however, Luke paced a few steps away, his brow furrowed.

"If Michelle did see Hackett, we'll have to take suitable precautions. I'll contact the sheriff. The Hacketts might be out for revenge since we killed their brother." He turned back to Bethany. "I don't want you or Michelle to go marketing alone again, or anywhere else. Not without Andrew or me or one of the male servants. And that goes double for Pete."

Seeing the frightened look on Bethany's face, he put an arm around her shoulders. "I don't think they'll try anything here in town, where they might be captured. They're cowards, both of them. They like their victims helpless like Michelle was when we found her."

But his words weren't all that comforting to Bethany, and although she spent the rest of the day endeavoring to calm Michelle's fears, she felt increasingly uneasy. Even the thought that the Hacketts were nearby, perhaps lurking outside the house, shook her to the marrow.

The same heavy foreboding pervaded her after dinner as she prepared for bed. With a shiver she closed the balcony doors that looked out over Toulouse Street and sat down in front of her dressing table. Two white candles glowed in their holders on either side of the mirror, and as she studied her reflection, she thought of Michelle's battered face the day they had met, so black and blue and grotesquely swollen. Michelle's life had been so tragic, yet she was so good and kind. She had never done an unkind thing to anyone! It was so unfair! All Michelle wanted now was to be with her father, and if Bethany rode Osiris for Philippe, Michelle would be granted her wish.

Bethany jumped a bit guiltily as Luke's hands settled on her shoulders, her flesh quivering as she met his dark gaze in the mirror. All other thoughts fled, as they were wont to do when he was near, and she was happily appalled at her reaction. His mere touch sent her into paroxysms of trembling anticipation.

"Are you ready for bed?" he asked, leaning down to press a kiss to her temple.

"I really should check on Petie and Michelle first."

"They're asleep. Come to bed."

As his arm moved under her knees, lifting her against his chest, she decided to take his word about Peeto and Michelle. She closed her eyes, looping her hands around his neck until he placed her gently on the bed. As he discarded his silk dressing gown, she took in his wide brown chest with its dark hair, hardly noticing the scar as his hard muscles touched her naked breasts, making her forget everything but him.

She lay still, her hands threaded in his soft black hair, luxuriating in his long, thorough, intoxicating kisses. It took a moment or two for Peeto's frightened wail to seep through the sweet lethargy she was feeling. When it did, however, she immediately struggled to sit up. But Luke held her gently in place.

"No, stay here," he murmured.

"But he's frightened! He's calling me! I have to go to him!"

"Let Tante Chloe take care of it," Luke insisted, but Bethany angrily twisted away, pulling on her robe as she ran into the next room, where she gathered Peeto into her arms.

"I had a bad dream," he sobbed hoarsely. "I thought the Hacketts got me again!"

"Sssh, it's all right now, sweetie. I'm here, and I'll stay here with you, if you like. I won't let anybody hurt you, I promise."

Luke watched from the hall doorway as she held his son, humming and rocking him. He returned to his own spacious bedchamber and poured himself a tumbler of brandy, smiling to himself. Bethany was a born mother, but things were getting a little out of control of late. She hovered not only over Pete, but also over Michelle and Raffy and Tante Chloe and every other bloody servant in the house. It gave Bethany very little time to spend taking care of his needs—except at night in bed, and he had to admit she did that very well.

He sat down in front of the fire to await her, thinking how good she felt in his arms, with her velvety skin and silky hair and soft lips. Maybe he should faint or have a nightmare or some other thing that would send her running to him, he thought whimsically. Then, still smiling at his own ridiculous thoughts, he got to his feet. Surely Pete was asleep by now.

Pete was asleep, but Bethany was nowhere to be found. Luke frowned, walking down the hall to her bedchamber. She hadn't slept there since he had brought her into town. He turned the knob, his jaw clenching when he found the door locked. Controlling his rush of annoyance, he tapped softly on the panel. A moment later, Bethany opened the door.

"Yes?" she asked.

"Yes?" repeated Luke, cocking one dark brow. "What the hell do you mean, 'yes'? Come back to bed."

"You want me?"

"You're damn right."

"And you need me?"

"Damn right," he repeated, grinning.

Bethany gave him a long, level look. "So did Petie, but you said Tante Chloe could take care of him," she said sweetly. "Perhaps she'll see to you, too."

Luke stood transfixed as the door shut in his face, then he gave an inward laugh. He turned the knob, expecting to find the door locked again, but it opened easily under his hand. Bethany sat propped against the pink satin pillows on the bed, her expression earnest.

"Don't you see, Luke? Petie needed me. He was scared and wanted his mother, not Tante Chloe. When you want me, you expect me to come. It's the same thing."

"Well, not quite the same thing," Luke conceded with a smile, sliding the bolt behind him. He stripped off his robe on the way to the bed and joined her under the satin sheets.

As he took her in his arms, Bethany reached up to stroke his face, very much wanting him to understand how she felt. "Really, Luke, it's part of being a mother or a father, to be there when your children need you. Don't you remember when you were little? How it felt when you wanted your mother and she wasn't there?"

Luke's smile faded, and she knew with a sinking feeling that her words had touched a raw spot inside him, even though he gathered her closer to him.

"Yes, I remember how that felt," he muttered, stroking her hair. "I won't stop you from going to Pete again."

Bethany pressed her lips against his chest, wondering how it had been between his mother and him. She wanted to ask him, and comfort him if need be, but intuition told her not to pursue the subject. He would tell her someday when he was ready. Now she would be content to lie warm and safe in his strong arms. She would always be there for him when he needed her, just as she would be for his son.

Chapter 14

The Saturday of the race dawned bright and beautiful, but Bethany was a bundle of nerves from the first moment she opened her eyes. As she sat in the small, cozy dining room of Andrew's Toulouse Street townhouse with its rose-and-cream brocade walls, she fidgeted nervously. Wanting something to do, she stirred more milk into her coffee, all the while watching Luke, who sat at the other end of the oval mahogany table. They were breakfasting alone since everyone else was busy with some errand or commitment, and Bethany stared at her husband, her eyes playing over his tanned, handsome face as he read the *Louisiana Gazette*. He rarely said anything at breakfast, but he liked her to be there with him. He was dressed for riding in snug black breeches and high, shiny, black Hessians with a loose white silk shirt. Even in casual attire he looked so elegantly attractive that Bethany was proud to be the one he had chosen to wed.

But recurrent anxieties rose like wraiths to dance in her mind—he would never have married her if it hadn't been for Peeto; he did not love her and did not deny it; he wanted her, but he had wanted other women in the past; and worst of all, he planned to leave her before the first of the year.

She watched his straight dark brows come together as if he was annoyed at something he had read, and Bethany felt a chill. His anger could be formidable, and she had no doubt she would be subjected to it if he ever found out she was going to ride Osiris for Philippe Benoist. He must never, ever know. She continued to watch him, waiting for an opportunity to put her plan into action. After a while, Luke looked up by chance and found Bethany's eyes fixed on him.

"What?" he asked.

She raised a quizzical brow. "What what?"

Luke smiled. "You have that look on your face, the one that means you're just about to do something you shouldn't."

Uh oh, Bethany thought, appalled that he found her so transparent, especially now, when she really did have something to hide.

"No, I was just noticing that you're wearing your riding clothes."

Luke waited, but Bethany only sipped her coffee without further comment. He folded his newspaper and laid it down beside his plate. "All right, you have my attention. What is it?"

Bethany fiddled with the handle of her cup, and Luke's gaze dropped to her nervous gestures, then returned to her lovely face. Her big silver-gray eyes met his green ones, and when she smiled—a smile made in heaven—he knew she would probably get whatever it was she wanted, even if she was having trouble asking for it. He waited.

"Well," she began at last, "quite a while ago you

promised Petie that you'd teach him to ride, and he thinks you aren't ever going to.''

Luke should have known her request would be in behalf of someone else. Unlike most women he had known, Bethany never asked for things for herself.

"Does he really want *me* to be the one to teach him?'' Luke found that a little hard to believe. His son didn't seem to enjoy his company particularly.

Bethany's gaze dropped for a mere instant. "He wants to learn," she answered evasively, "and since you're going riding anyway, I just thought it might be a good time. Tante Chloe has taken Raffy to the market with her, and Petie's all alone upstairs—''

"All right," Luke interrupted. "Get him ready and the three of us will go together.''

He stood, then paused, regarding Bethany questioningly as she continued to hesitate.

"What now?'' he asked.

"Michelle's still awfully afraid. I really hate to leave her here by herself, and you never have spent much time alone with Petie—''

Her eyes beseeched him again, and Luke couldn't refuse her, although he knew Michelle would be perfectly safe in the house with all the servants.

"All right, I'll take him out to Cantigny. Andrew's there today, and he can help me choose a suitable mount for the boy. It's time he had his own horse anyway.''

Relieved, Bethany hurried to get Peeto ready. Though the child would have preferred that she come along, the idea of having his own pony was too much of an enticement for him to drag his feet about going alone with his father.

Bethany waved them off, then gave Elise strict instructions to stay close to Michelle until she returned. Half an hour after Luke and Peeto left for Cantigny, she donned a pair of Raffy's trousers and a plain linen shirt and left the house. The masculine attire felt strange now that she had grown accustomed to wearing gowns and petticoats, but she kept her long cloak tucked carefully around her as she walked the short distance through the narrow thoroughfares of the Vieux Carré to the walled courtyard of the Benoist home.

Philippe was pacing impatiently beside his black carriage, behind which Osiris stood tethered. He smiled in relief as Bethany appeared. She didn't return his smile.

"I was afraid you'd change your mind," he said, his eyes flicking down to her tight black breeches.

"I just want to hurry up and get this over with. Do you have the agreement?"

He produced a parchment from his inside coat pocket. Bethany read it slowly and carefully, chagrined when some of the big words gave her trouble, but the agreement seemed in good order. Nevertheless, she was careful to watch him sign it.

"You're a *petit* bit suspicious, aren't you?" Philippe asked with not a little sarcasm.

Bethany gave him a cold look. "With you, I am."

"I sincerely hope you'll change your mind about me one day. Maybe when your husband returns to his savage friends?"

"Whether Luke is here or not, nothing could make me like you," Bethany told him, then changed the subject, not wanting to discuss her marriage with him. "Did you bring a mask for me?"

"Oui," he answered, holding up a black velvet mask. "No one will suspect you're a woman in those clothes."

Bethany examined the mask, which was designed to cover the top half of her face. With the old wool cap she had brought with her, it should disguise her well enough. She waited until they were inside the closed coach and on their way before she stuffed her curly hair into the cap, but as they approached Métairie, where the race was to take place, she began to wonder if she was doing the right thing. Luke would kill her if he found out. Maybe she shouldn't, she thought, then she remembered poor Michelle, lying trembling in her bed. Yes, she had to ride.

As they drove across the grassy fields surrounding the track, she looked out at the dozens of carriages and coaches parked around them, their slave drivers congregated in small groups to pass the time.

"You didn't tell me it was such a big race!" Bethany said accusingly, her eyes on the long viewing stand at the far side of the field. It was filled to capacity with enthusiastic horseracing fans.

"It's the biggest race of the year, that's why it's so important for me to win it," Philippe replied, admiring Bethany's flushed face. Even in the black cap and masculine clothes she looked every bit a woman. He certainly hoped the rumor that Luke Randall would be returning soon to the western mountains was a true one, since his absence would leave his beautiful new bride fair game for pursuit.

"You better put on the mask. I need to fill you in on the route. There are several hedge jumps and three ditches—"

"It's a steeplechase?" Bethany asked in surprise.

"*Oui*. It goes through the woods yonder, then across a narrow wooden bridge. The water traps are in the last stretch before the grandstand."

"That's even better. No one will get a good look at me," Bethany murmured. She had often jumped horses bareback at her father's place, and Osiris was strong. Swift as well, according to Philippe. She couldn't imagine another horse outclassing the magnificent mare.

Bethany arranged the half mask before she stepped down, patting Osiris's neck as Philippe methodically outlined the different obstacles she would face. She listened dutifully as Philippe laced his fingers to boost her onto Osiris's back. She had ridden several of her father's horses in local races when she was only twelve. She had won all of them. Those had been some of the few times her father had seemed proud of her.

"You really should have ridden the course a few times in advance," Philippe said, "just to acquaint yourself with the traps. All the other riders have."

"Stop worrying about me. I know what I'm doing. But don't expect me to tarry long afterward. I don't intend to let anyone recognize me."

The insistent, hollow clanging of a bell drifted out over the field, summoning the riders into position. Bethany kept a tight rein on Osiris. The mare sidestepped a bit, keyed up by the shouts of the crowd and the neighing of the other horses, but the Arabian responded beautifully to Bethany's whispered commands and to the pressure of her knees. Bethany's confidence grew as she urged her mount forward to the starting line, positioning herself as far away from the spectators as she could. Even so, several people pointed excitedly at her, recognizing Philippe Benoist's spirited white Arabian. Bethany kept her face averted from their curious stares.

Gold and royal blue pennants on the red grandstand poles snapped and fluttered in the brisk wind, and the excited drone of the onlookers filled the air. Bethany nosed the mare into line, glad the other riders were too intent on calming their own steeds or listening to last-minute instructions from the horses' owners to pay much attention to her. She adjusted her black leather gloves and the mask as the man with the starting horn raised his right hand. Bethany bent close to the mare's quivering ear, suddenly filled with excitement.

"Come on, Osiris, all you have to do is run," she whispered. "You're the best! Show them what you can do!"

She leaned low over Osiris's neck, drawing her knees high in the way her father had taught her. As the starting horn blared, she felt the mare's sleek, powerful muscles jump beneath her thighs. They lunged forward as one, barely aware of the great roar that rose from the viewing stand.

Osiris took the lead almost at once as they galloped across the first level, grassy stretch. Bethany kept as low as she could, feeling an unrivaled exhilaration as the wind rushed past her ears, thrilled to be riding such a magnificent animal. She urged the mare to an even greater pace as they left the open field for the track that cut between huge cypress trees. She could hear the muffled thunder of hooves behind her, but a quick backward glance told her Osiris had outdis-

tanced the pack, except for one big black stallion that
was perhaps three lengths behind her.

Bethany hugged Osiris's neck, trying to cut down
the wind on her face as a wide, wooden bridge loomed
in front of her. Osiris's hooves beat a rapid, hollow
cadence across the planks then they entered the field
of final obstacles. Great, ground-devouring strides
took them to the first ditch and over it with surefooted
ease. A hedgerow was next, and the mare took it in
stride. As they came down on the other side, however, the ribbon on Bethany's mask snapped, and she
gasped as the fluttering velvet blinded her for a moment. Osiris must have sensed a difference in the reins
as Bethany tried to catch the mask, and the Arabian
slowed slightly as they approached the second hedge.
But the mare soon regained her footing, and they flew
over it.

The momentary lapse in speed, however, had
brought the black stallion to a half-length behind her,
and Bethany urged Osiris on with renewed vigor.
They were in the last stretch now, with only one jump
ahead; but it was the most dangerous one, she realized at once, as she saw the deep water ditch hugging
the far side of the barrier. Once over that, it would
be a fifty-yard dash to the finish line. She frowned as
the black horse moved slowly abreast of her.

Andrew turned slightly as Onyx finally gained on
the fast Arabian, then he froze in the saddle when he
saw Bethany's face. She was equally shocked at the
sight of her brother-in-law, but was forced to jerk her
attention back to the track as they approached the last
jump. Osiris landed cleanly on the other side and
raced like the wind along the home stretch.

Bethany had no idea that Onyx's back legs had

caught the top of the barrier, sending Andrew flying out of the saddle to land in a sprawl on the muddy edge of the ditch.

Luke came to his feet in the viewing stands as his brother fell, rolled, and lay still. Then Luke started toward him at a run, with Pete just behind him. He paid no attention to the great cheer that went up as the white Arabian won the race. He reached Andrew before the attending physicians could arrive and dragged him bodily out of the track just before several other horses thundered past them.

"Andy! Are you all right?"

"Yes," Andrew said shakily, groaning as he tried to sit up. "It's my leg. I think it's broken."

"Don't move. Thank God it wasn't your neck," Luke said, breathing heavily, then stepped back to make way for the stretcher. He missed Pete then, and turned to find the boy running toward the crowd at the finish line. He caught the boy in three strides, raising him high in the air.

"It's Beth, it's Beth, didn't you see her?" Pete cried, trying to twist loose.

Luke frowned. "Beth? Where?"

"Riding Osiris! She won the race, didn't you see?"

Luke examined the crowd surrounding the victorious white horse just as someone pulled the black cap off the victor and released a tumble of blond ringlets.

"Stay here with Andrew, Pete," Luke said with steel in his voice. "I'll take care of Beth."

Bethany was upset to have been caught in the midst of the excited Creoles, especially after having lost her mask and cap, but she no longer cared about being recognized. Her eyes were on Andrew, who lay sur-

rounded by doctors. Philippe fought his way over to
where she still sat on Osiris, a triumphant grin on his
face. His shouts in French momentarily quieted the
young men congratulating Bethany. Then, at that ex-
act moment, Bethany saw an enraged Luke coming
toward her with long, pounding strides, his face black
with fury, and all she could think about was getting
away.

"You've got to get me out of here, Philippe!" she
cried, but the jostling crowd of well-wishers pressing
in around Osiris made escape impossible.

Luke paid even less attention to the shouting men.
He pushed his way through them, his fists clenched,
his eyes full of fire.

"What the hell do you think you're doing?" he
demanded furiously, reaching up to get a tight grip
on her arm.

"Wait, Luke, please. I can explain—" Bethany began, but he paid no heed to her entreaty, pulling her
off Osiris and then after him through the onlookers
without a whit of regard for Philippe Benoist or his
Creole friends.

Those Creole gentlemen, however, were apparently
incensed to see their courageous young winner being
manhandled, especially by one of the crude *Américains* who had invaded their city and tried to impose
their will upon French ways.

"Unhand her, monsieur," cried a fair-haired young
man as Luke dragged his wife past. To Bethany's horror, the Creole fop pulled a lace-edged handkerchief
from his velvet sleeve and whipped it sharply across
Luke's dark, lean cheek.

If Luke was surprised by the sudden challenge, he
didn't show it. Instead, he gave a low growl and,

taking hold of the young man's frilly cravat with one hand, he lifted Bethany's hapless champion off the ground and shoved him backward hard enough to send the poor man in a somersault before he lay still on the grass. Luke's act immediately engendered a fresh onslaught of anger among the shocked Creoles, and at least seven challenges were spit out in vituperative French. Luke ignored them all, holding tight to Bethany's arm as he pushed his way through the angry mob.

"Leave them. He is her husband," Philippe yelled to his insulted friends. "He is *le sauvage!*"

More than one of the challengers blanched, appalled to learn the identity of the man they had so recklessly challenged, and not one among them attempted to follow the big, black-haired *Américain* as he headed back toward his injured brother.

As Luke knelt beside Andrew, Bethany hugged Peeto. Never had she felt so terrible about anything, and she was even more upset when she heard that Andrew's right leg was fractured. How could everything have gone so wrong? she thought miserably as several men hoisted Andrew on a stretcher and carried him to the hospital wagon.

Luke gave her a look that sent a flush of shame to her cheekbones. Saying nothing, he took her arm again, not pulling her as before, but keeping her at his side, while Peeto held tightly to her other hand. Jemsy sat waiting at the Randall coach, and Luke turned to Bethany, his face rigid with control.

"Take Pete back to Cantigny. There will be enough talk and scandal over this without us going back to the house in the Vieux Carré. I'm going with Andy."

Bethany watched him turn away from her, her heart full of fear. The fragile, tenuous threads with which she had labored so diligently to bind their hearts together had snapped in twain, and she wasn't sure Luke would ever forgive her.

Chapter 15

Cantigny was as quiet as a tomb the following morning, when Bethany finally found the courage to venture out of her bedchamber. Even the servants kept to the kitchens for fear of encountering *le sauvage*, and Bethany was relieved to meet Michelle on the grand staircase.

"Oh, Michelle, I'm so glad to see you!"

"Tante Chloe sent Jemsy for me," Michelle answered. "He told me what happened. Are you all right?"

Bethany nodded, looking away from Michelle's worried amber eyes. "Have you seen Luke this morning?" she asked.

Michelle shook her head. "No, but Jemsy told me he was in the library all last night and is still there now."

A stricken look entered Bethany's eyes. "Andy broke his leg, Michelle, and it's all my fault."

"*Non*," she answered sadly. "The blame is mine. You only rode Osiris for me."

"You know about that?"

"*Oui*. Philippe came to Toulouse Street early this morning to ask about you. He said that since you won, I can now see father any time I want." Michelle clasped Bethany's hand warmly. "I can never thank you enough for all you have done for me. I will go to my father today, but I couldn't leave without first seeing how you were."

Though Bethany tried her best to smile, her expression faltered when she realized she would soon have to answer to Luke.

"Would you look in on Petie and Raffy for me, Michelle? They're playing in Petie's bedchamber."

Michelle nodded, and Bethany watched her friend move down the upstairs hall before she descended to the tiled foyer. The door to the library was closed, and Bethany was relieved, since she was not yet ready to face Luke. She didn't blame him for being angry with her, though. Not the way things had turned out.

She went to the dining room, halting abruptly when she saw Andrew at the table, his injured leg propped up on a chair. Afraid that he would be as angry with her as Luke was, she hesitated in the doorway, but Andrew saw her almost at once.

"Beth! Come in! I need more whiskey, and Elise is nowhere to be found, as usual."

Bethany hurried to oblige him, amazed at his good spirits, but wanting desperately to make up for her part in his accident. She poured the golden liquid into his glass, and Andrew smiled as he sipped it.

"Where'd you learn to ride like that, woman? You made me look bad."

"Oh, Andy, I'm so sorry about what happened!" Bethany's words rushed out in a guilty flood. "I didn't mean for you to get hurt! I didn't even know you were going to ride. I only did it because Philippe Benoist—"

"I know. Philippe's already been here to see Luke.

He seemed willing enough to assume the blame, and as far as I'm concerned, he was nearly blackmailing you. You couldn't have known I was riding Onyx. I didn't decide to enter until the last minute.''

He grimaced as he shifted his leg, and Bethany bit her lip.

"Is it very painful?" she asked with a heavy heart.

"Some, but don't worry. I have another leg right here." He grinned, patting his good leg.

Bethany's smile was wan.

"Anyway," Andrew continued, lifting his glass of whiskey, "it gives me a good excuse to drink at breakfast. Who knows, maybe it will even make Miss Ludlow come back from her troupe's theater up in Natchez to see about me. It broke my heart when she left without a word.''

Bethany shook her head, unable to summon up a response to his jokes.

"Luke hates me now, doesn't he?" she said in a forlorn tone.

"Luke hasn't said much this morning," Andrew answered with a smile. "He's too busy reading all the apologies from those impulsive young Creole gents who challenged him to duels.''

"They apologized to him?" Bethany asked, surprised but even more relieved to hear that there would be no fighting.

"I figured they would when they found out who he was. According to legend around here, no one faces *le sauvage* and lives to talk about it.''

His grin was contagious, but Bethany felt so bad inside that hot tears welled up and fell down her cheeks, despite her attempts to stop them.

Andrew leaned over, handing her one of the fine

white linen napkins from the table, and Bethany wiped her eyes, feeling so low and disheartened that she began to tell Andrew things she wouldn't have ordinarily uttered to anyone.

"I only wanted Luke to love me and Petie, and now he hates me and he's going to leave us. I know he always said he was going to, but I didn't want to believe it. I tried not to love him, Andy, because he said he wouldn't ever love me and that I shouldn't expect it, but when he took me to bed and was so gentle and tender, I thought—"

Bethany suddenly remembered herself with a hot blush, appalled that she had mentioned such personal matters, but Andrew only shook his head.

"Luke can be so blind sometimes, Beth, but let me talk to him for you. Maybe I can shake down that brick wall he keeps building around him."

Andrew left Bethany dabbing at her tears in the dining room, wincing with each step as he hobbled painfully across the hall on his crutches. He leaned on one to open the library door and entered without knocking.

"You're not supposed to be walking yet," Luke said from behind his desk. Papers were strewn before him in many piles, as if he had been working on several different projects at once, and his jacket was slung over the back of his chair. "How's the pain?"

"Just like any other pain. It hurts like bloody hell," Andrew answered, easing himself into an armchair near the desk. "Beth's a little upset, too, if you have a mind to care."

Luke gave him a level look. "I don't have a mind to care," he said, going back to work.

Andrew frowned, leaning forward to lift his splinted leg to a small hassock.

"What are you doing?" he asked Luke sourly. "Writing Beth out of your will?"

It was Luke's turn to frown blackly. "Not that it's any of your business, but I'm getting things in order for you. I'm leaving you in charge of everything when I'm gone, and I hope you'll keep tabs on Beth and Pete, too. God knows she's going to need it now that she's ruined the good reputation you and I worked so hard to establish for her."

Andrew glared at his brother. "How long are you going to be gone, if I might ask? A mere decade this time, or are you going to wait until your grandchildren are born, so you'll only have to make one trip back."

"What the hell's your problem?" Luke asked mildly. "I told you I was leaving in January. Why the devil are you making such a big issue out of it now?"

"Because you have a wife now, and a little boy who needs you, for God's sake."

Luke shuffled papers into a neat stack, seemingly unperturbed by Andrew's angry outburst. "They'll do just fine. Beth always lands on her feet, and Pete can't stand me anyway."

Andrew heard it then, lurking subtly beneath the words, an underlying, uncharacteristic vulnerability. Luke wasn't made of stone after all, he thought in triumph, and now all he had to do was make his stubborn brother admit it. And he knew exactly how to do it. He leaned back, gazing at Luke over his steepled fingers.

"You thought you had it all figured out, didn't you, big brother? You thought you'd marry poor little tomboy Beth so she would take care of your son and you could escape back to the mountains without having to make any kind of commitment to your son, or to your wife, or to anybody else.''

Luke's quill pen stilled, his jade-colored eyes coming up to lock with his younger brother's blue ones. ''Shut up, Andy. It's none of your business.''

''What's worse,'' Andrew continued, disregarding Luke's warning, ''you found you were actually human enough to start feeling something toward them. You, the cold, unfeeling *le sauvage*—you actually fell in love with your little made-over-to-order tomboy bride, and now you don't know how to handle it. Isn't that right, Luke?''

Luke's palms hit the desktop with a hard double thud. His eyes blazed. ''Damn you, I said to shut up!''

Andrew watched silently as Luke stalked out of the room with a face like frozen granite, then he leaned back, his laugh loud in the quiet room.

''Well, I'll be damned if I wasn't right. Luke is doomed.''

Andrew rose then and made his way slowly back to the dining room, where Bethany was helping Peeto with his breakfast. When she looked up, Andrew's face split into a wide grin.

''You have nothing to worry about, Beth. He's so in love with you he can't see straight.''

Bethany's smile was tentative, and more than a little doubtful, but Andrew didn't give her time to question him. ''I just put the first burr under his blanket,'' he said, ''and together, my dear, we'll plant enough of them to make him buck like a stallion. Trust me.''

* * *

The next day they put Andrew's plan into action. But as Bethany sat in the garden surrounded by a half dozen of Andrew's young gentlemen friends, both Americans and Creoles, she wasn't at all sure her brother-in-law knew what he was doing. She kept a bright smile on her face as Andrew had instructed, listening attentively to the young men's compliments and glowing accounts of her win at Métairie. But she felt as empty as a dry sponge.

She hadn't even seen Luke since the race, and she missed him. She missed his strong arms around her in bed at night, his hungry kisses, his low, sensuous laugh when she was the one to lead him to their bed. How could she bear it if he returned to the Rockies?

She couldn't help but think that Andrew was wrong. He thought Luke would care if other men called on her, but clearly Luke didn't care what she did. Hadn't he been in the library all morning long without coming outside, even though Andrew had arranged for her to meet her gentlemen callers just under the open windows behind Luke's desk? Even their laughter and loud talk had not appeared to faze him. It was useless. Everything they did was useless, because Andrew couldn't make Luke love her any more than she had been able to.

"Smile, Beth, stop looking like you've lost your only friend," came Andrew's whisper from where he sat beside her. Bethany obediently put a smile on her lips, knowing full well that it must look terribly false. She wondered why the men around her continued to linger.

"*Voilé,*" Andrew murmured under his breath, and Bethany's heart leaped into flight as Luke appeared suddenly on the garden path in front of them.

He was dressed immaculately in a jacket of claret velvet over a black waistcoat and trousers, and she drank in every facet of his bronzed, rugged face as he strode toward them, then sat down on a bench a short distance away. He proceeded to present each male visitor in turn with an intense, unwavering stare that radiated hostility.

For a while, Bethany's guests made a concerted effort to ignore his silent regard, but in truth, little time elapsed before the animated conversation began to wane followed by long, uncomfortable lulls. One by one, Andrew's friends began self-consciously clearing their throats and claimed they had just remembered previous urgent engagements. Even the most determined of Bethany's admirers were no match for the hard green eyes that were riveted unblinkingly on their flushed faces. Soon the last of them bowed graciously in front of Bethany's outstretched hand and nodded apologetically to Andrew before scurrying away with a great show of relief.

"You'd think I had the plague," said Luke with a sarcastic smile.

"Poor Luke," Andrew murmured as he watched his brother depart for the house. "He's got it worse than I thought. His days are numbered, for sure."

Seeing Bethany's glum expression, he squeezed her hand. "Trust me, you'll see."

"Mon Dieu! I nod ever see de lag of dis entertainin'," Tante Chloé muttered as she pulled a baking tin from the brick oven. Wiping sweat from her ebony brow with the hem of her long white apron, she focused her eagle-keen gaze on the three kitchen maids who stood at the table and frosted fresh-baked petit

fours with Tante Chloe's special butter icing. Peeto
and Raffy stood at the table as well, nearly drooling
over the large silver tray filled with the miniature
cakes.

"Go on den, teg wad you wand, but you godd to
ead dem oud dere on de poach, heah?" Tante Chloe
told the two small boys.

The children hastily helped themselves before the
big woman changed her mind, and Tante Chloe made
sure to look the other way so they could steal a second
handful. Her gaze rested on Bethany, who sat in a
rocker beside the fire, still sunk in the low spirits that
had wrapped her in gloom since she found disfavor in
the eyes of her husband nearly a week before. Tante
Chloe's broad forehead wrinkled. She hated to see her
sweet, fair-haired mistress so morose.

"It'd be dat *le sauvage* dat be doin' all dis to my
lil' girl. He bez de debil," she grumbled under her
breath, causing Bethany to look up.

"Please don't talk about Luke like that. He's not a
savage. He says Indians aren't all that bad anyway,
once you get used to their ways." To Bethany's dismay, the tears she had been suppressing for days began to flow, and she lowered her face into her palms.
"Oh, Tante Chloe, I'm so miserable without him. All
I want is for him to love me, and I'm so tired of
sitting around with Andrew and his friends, and now
Luke hardly ever comes home at all."

"Iz dat why you bez hidin' in here all de mornin',
so you don godd to see all doz Creole mens?"

Bethany nodded. Tante Chloe watched her dry her
eyes, then she shooed the maids out of her domain,
shutting the big oak door behind them. She wiped her

big hands on her apron, then pulled one of the cane-bottomed chairs up close beside Bethany.

''Bez you shore you wand dat man to love you?'' she whispered, her sharp black eyes searching Bethany's tearstained face.

Bethany nodded, glad she could finally express all the hurt she felt. Tante Chloe was gentle and caring, despite her dictatorial ways, and Bethany was tired of disguising her grief behind a facade of happiness.

''Wad you knows 'bout hoodoo, madame?''

Bethany looked blankly at Tante Chloe, wondering why the Negress's voice had lowered to a conspiratorial tone.

''Hoodoo?'' she repeated. ''Like Raffy's gris-gris, you mean?''

''*Oui*. Id bez magic, chile, an' I can mague dat black-hair, green-eye debil love you iv you wand him to. But I nod sayin' you wand do dad,'' she added quickly, hoping her low opinion of the ominous master of Cantigny might bear some weight with Madame Bethany. Unfortunately, Madame Bethany looked more than a little interested.

''Can you, really? How?''

''Wid a love gris-gris. I mague dem for de udder girls in de quaders when dey's got dere heart set on a body. Id work, fo' shore.''

Bethany stared at Tante Chloe, not sure she could put any credence in such talk, but wanting very much to believe a gris-gris could help her. She had come to the conclusion that it would take magic to make Luke love her the way she loved him.

''How does it work?'' she asked, hiding her skepticism.

"Id bez a charm yous puts under you pillow. Id mague him come to you, *mais certainement.*"

"Will you make me one?" Bethany asked, ready to give anything a try. Tante Chloe nodded, but when Andrew appeared at the threshold of the kitchen, the big Negress rose quickly to return to her baking.

"So there you are," Andrew said to Bethany, leaning heavily on his cane. "Come on. Luke's expected out here sometime today, and I want you surrounded by men when he arrives."

Bethany went with him, but it didn't take Andrew long to notice her melancholy disposition.

"Now, Beth, you're not going to give up on him so soon, are you? We've hardly begun. Luke's not an easy nut to crack, but we'll get him eventually."

"But don't you see, Andy? I don't feel right doing this to him. He's my husband, after all, and I don't want him to think I'd be unfaithful with your friends. I want him to think I love him and want him. I feel . . . well, I feel disloyal being with all these other men, and it's not fair to them either, because everything I say and do is so fake."

Andrew looked down at Bethany's sad, beautiful face, thinking of Luke's less-than-discreet appearances of late in the Vieux Carré with a certain redhead. Thank goodness Bethany didn't know. It would devastate her.

"All right," he said, "but promise me you won't give up on him. I know he loves you, and I'll think of some way to make him admit it."

The next day Bethany tried to keep Andrew's words in mind as she sat on her bed, turning over in her hands the strange charm that Tante Chloe had brought up to her the night before. The gris-gris consisted of a small burlap bag hanging from a leather thong. Inside were several black feathers and a curious green stone the color of Luke's eyes. Depressed because Luke hadn't come yesterday when expected, Bethany didn't believe for a moment that the gris-gris would work for her. Nevertheless, she replaced it under her pillow, not willing to pass up any chance to win Luke back.

When she opened the sliding wooden doors of the downstairs dining room, however, and found Luke sitting at his place at the head of the table, she was suddenly much more hopeful that Tante Chloe's love gris-gris might, indeed, work.

"Good morning," he said politely, though he didn't rise to help her with her chair.

Bethany moved to her place, unable to take her eyes off him. He had been in town for a week, and she was so happy to see him that she sat down without filling her plate at the sideboard.

"Aren't you going to eat?" he asked solicitously, and Bethany shook her head, the thought of food furthermost from her mind. "Coffee, then?"

"Yes, please."

He raised his hand slightly to signal the dining room maid to pour for her, then went back to reading his newspaper. Bethany sipped the strong chicory brew to which she was finally growing accustomed. She wanted to ask him why he had come back and, more important, if he intended to stay at Cantigny with them. She didn't dare, however, her primary fear being that he would get up and walk out again. Instead, she picked up the copy of the *Daily Picayune* laying beside her plate. Luke's name nearly jumped off the page at her, and she leaned over it with interest, slowing making out the words. Though she didn't know a few of the French expressions, she could read enough to learn that Luke had escorted a redheaded actress to the opera.

A stabbing pain knifed through her heart, only to be replaced by raw, agonizing jealousy. She struggled with it, trying desperately to control the overwhelming anger she felt. How dare he do such a thing, then come home and flaunt the news in her face.

Another thought struck her, a realization that sent her initial fury dwindling appreciably. He had wanted her to know; he had intentionally laid the paper out for her to see. That probably meant he intended to either hurt her or make her jealous. If he wanted to hurt her, that probably meant she had hurt him by riding in the Métairie, and if he wanted to make her jealous, he probably wasn't sure she really loved him. Hope rose on the ashes of her jealous wrath. Maybe Andrew's plots had not been in vain, after all.

"I see here that you've been seen with another woman," she said quietly, carefully refolding the newspaper.

Unperturbed, Luke sipped his coffee, his eyes watching her above the rim of the cup. "That's what I get for teaching you to read."

Bethany ignored the comment which she knew was intended to rile her. "How else would I know what my husband has been doing with his time," she answered calmly, "since he doesn't come home anymore?"

"Everything I do is exaggerated in the newspapers. You know that."

"You didn't take her to the opera, then?"

"I didn't say that," he responded, and their gazes held for a moment.

"It doesn't matter," Bethany said. "It doesn't change the way I feel."

"No. I don't suspect it does, since we agreed from the beginning to go our separate ways, as long as we were discreet."

"That's not it at all," she said, smiling sweetly. "I will still love you, even if you are seen with a hundred different women."

Luke's coffee cup paused halfway to his mouth.

"Indeed," he murmured at last. "A hundred different women? It seems I have my work cut out for me, doesn't it?"

Bethany gritted her teeth as he rose and left the room. He was impossible! Impossible to know, to understand, to talk to! Why did she love him so much? Now he would probably go out and make love to a hundred different women just to spite her! Surprisingly, that idea amused her, and she laughed aloud, then quickly looked around to make sure no one had heard her. He was surely driving her "crezzie" as Tante Chloe would say. Bethany shook her head.

Later that evening, when Luke appeared again to join Bethany and Michelle for the evening meal, Bethany felt sure she had been right earlier to honestly express her feelings, but the fact that Luke was dressed in formal attire, his ruby cravat pin glittering in the candlelight, did little to reassure her.

"Are you going into town tonight?" she asked casually as the maids cleared away the dessert dishes.

"Yes," he answered. "I'll be spending the night at the townhouse, so don't bother to wait up."

He went so far as to press a kiss on Bethany's flushed cheek before he left. Michelle looked down in embarrassment, as if feeling sorry for her dear friend.

Bethany was more angry than hurt at the moment, however, and the instant Luke's carriage rattled away from the river portico, she stood, her face set with determination. She'd put up with enough! It was her turn to be less than discreet.

"Come on, Michelle, we're going into town, too. I will not sit here another night while Luke goes about with a hundred different women!"

"But where are we going?" Michelle asked, non-plussed by Bethany's remark.

"To Monsieur Girardeau's costume ball. His man brought the invitation last week, and I feel certain that is exactly where Luke is going. Hurry! We have to change!"

"But I will not be admitted," Michelle protested.

Bethany hardly heard her. "Yes, you will, if you're with me."

Bethany hurried upstairs without waiting for Michelle's answer, then took special care with her toilette, applying more lip rouge and powder than she normally did. She wanted to look her best so Luke would be sorry he wasn't with her. She chose a royal blue gown that glistened with a band of pearls around the square neckline and hem, because Luke had told her once he thought it particularly becoming with her fair hair. She placed a matching nine-strand choker of pearls around her neck and stared at her reflection. She would not sit home alone any more, nor would she degrade herself by entertaining other men. From now on, wherever Luke went with his paramour,

Bethany would be there as well. She would smile and act as if nothing was amiss. Perhaps she would even join them!

Her plans went abruptly awry when her carriage drew up in front of the Girardeau house on Rue de Royale and the black-liveried servant at the door looked down his nose at Michelle.

"Femmes de couleur are not permitted here, madame,'' he said in his haughtiest voice. ''Perhaps she can find entertainment there, across the way.''

Bethany's teeth clamped hard as she looked down the street to where he had pointed. The brightly lit galleried building was abustle with activity, and her eyes sharpened as she saw the small black coach of Cantigny parked just across the street from its entrance.

''That Luke's coach,'' she cried. ''What is that place, Michelle?''

Michelle lowered her eyes, looking distinctly uncomfortable.

Bethany frowned. ''Tell me, please.''

''It's the quadroon ballroom upstairs, and below there are gambling rooms for the gentlemen.''

''Then you would be allowed there! Come, we'll go find Luke.''

Bethany took hold of Michelle's arm, but the young woman held back. ''I am sorry, but we cannot go there. You will not be allowed inside. No white women are.''

''I don't understand. Why not?''

''Because it is where the Creoles choose their mistresses,'' Michelle informed her friend reluctantly. ''That is where my father met my mother.''

"No wonder Creole men are always smiling," Bethany muttered grimly, then looked again at Luke's carriage across the way. If Luke had gone to the quadroon ballroom to choose himself a mistress, he would get some help that he wasn't expecting.

"Come on, Michelle, we're going. I have a mask. No one will know I'm white."

She ignored Michelle's dismayed protestations, pulling her down the wooden banquette, mingling with the crowd entering the famed quadroon masquerade ball.

Chapter 16

Luke leaned against the red velvet cushions of his chair, paying little heed to the other patrons milling around the smoke-filled gambling hall. His cheroot lay smoking on a silver tray in front of him, alongside his substantial pile of winnings. Four other men sat at the green-baize-topped table with him, and four pairs of eyes watched his dark, impassive face for some clue to the cards he was holding in his hand. They saw only the same calm green gaze and the relaxed, self-confident posture Luke had displayed during the many other long evenings of gambling since he decided it wise to distance himself from Bethany. He won more than he lost, much more, but losing never bothered him. Indeed, nothing much seemed to bother him since Bethany had seen fit to ally herself publicly at the Métairie race with a womanizer such as Philippe Benoist.

A coin clinked against the stack of money in the center of the table, and Luke idly reached out to turn over his winning hand.

"Merci, messieurs," he murmured, pulling the pot toward him, not bothering to stack it.

While more cards were being dealt, he listened to the lilting strains of a waltz filtering down from the upstairs ballroom. He briefly considered going up to look over the batch of lovely *femmes de couleur* being peddled there by their mothers, but he dismissed the idea. He had never particularly cared for that Creole custom, especially once he knew the tragic life Michelle Benoist had suffered as the result of the Creole caste system.

Thoughts of Michelle brought Bethany's small, exquisite face burning into his brain, and once again her words reverberated in the deepest recesses of his mind. "I will still love you, even if you are seen with a hundred different women." He wondered if that was true, remembering the shuddering sense of betrayal he had felt when he realized she had been secretly consorting with another man behind his back.

If she really did love him so much, she shouldn't. He didn't want her to love him, just as he didn't want to love her. Already she had made him feel things no other woman had ever come close to making him feel. Other women no longer appealed to him, especially the silly actress with the red hair and insipid conversation with whom he had spent an interminable time at the opera. He had taken her home at the intermission just to get rid of her.

But Bethany was different. It would have been hard to leave her if she had not shown him how easy it would be for her to forget him once he was gone. The Creoles had courted her like a queen ever since she won the Métairie. In a fortnight, he would be gone anyway. He had lingered too long in New Orleans this time, and he hungered to see the Rockies again, to breathe the clean, crisp air. Bethany would land on her feet, just as he had told Andrew.

Luke's frown, though brief, gave encouragement to

the young Creole across from him, and Monsieur Betancourt promptly bet a larger amount than he normally would have, especially against one as lucky as *le sauvage*.

Betancourt scowled at his own stupidity a moment later, when Luke added yet more coins to his growing stack of wealth. Luke paid no attention to the young man as Andrew entered from the street door, looking worried.

"I guess that's all for me, messieurs," Luke said, casually gathering together the small fortune lying in front of him. The other players gave a collective sigh of relief as Luke strode off toward his brother to find out what woman was giving Andrew trouble now that Miss Ludlow had left the city. Andrew's first words were hardly what Luke expected.

"Luke, I think Beth's upstairs with Michelle!"

"What?"

For once, Luke was shaken from his self-imposed aloofness, and Andrew let himself be pulled out of the gambling rooms into the cool night air.

"What makes you think she's up there?" Luke asked grimly as soon as they reached the interior courtyard.

"Jemsy's outside in the rig, and he said she went in wearing a mask."

"Good God," Luke said, taking the outside stairs to the ballroom with Andrew at his heels.

Bethany found the famous quadroon ballroom much smaller than the spacious halls where the whites hosted similar parties. The room was very crowded, and the atmosphere was gay and festive—much more so, in fact, than Governor Claiborne's ball had been. As she searched the throng for her husband, she especially noticed the relaxed mien and air of informality displayed by the wealthy Creole men. Their laughter echoed often as they moved among the lovely, creamy-skinned young quadroons clothed in rich silks and satins who sat demurely along the walls, chaperoned by their turbaned mothers. Most of the mothers were light-complected themselves, though occasionally a darker face could be seen.

While Michelle took a chair by the door, staring at her lap, Bethany watched an elderly Creole gentleman escort a particularly beautiful young woman, who looked to be about fifteen, back to her velvet chair. He lifted her hand to his lips, and she smiled shyly at him as he gestured her beaming mother to one side. Bethany realized he was probably whispering an offer for her daughter. If it was accepted, the pretty girl would become his mistress.

What if Luke was even now making such an offer? Bethany thought, a sick feeling in the pit of her stomach. But surely he wouldn't do that, not Luke. The practice was so ugly—buying innocent young girls for the amusement of rich men as if they weren't people at all but some kind of thoroughbred horse!

The musicians near the balcony doors that overlooked the Rue de Royale began the next waltz, and Bethany continued to hover along the perimeter of the dance floor, searching for Luke and praying she wouldn't find him. During one such sweep of the dancers, her gaze fell again on Michelle.

Bethany stiffened when she saw Philippe Benoist bending low to speak to his half sister. His eyes came immediately to Bethany's masked face, a horrified expression overcoming his features. He left Michelle, coming straight to Bethany.

"Are you crazy, *chérie?*" he demanded softly, his fingers tightening around her arm to draw her outside onto the balcony.

"Philippe, let go. I can't leave Michelle in there alone!"

"Mon Dieu, don't you know what would happen if anyone recognized you here?"

His urgent tone gave Bethany pause. "No one will recognize me with this mask, but even if they did, what could happen?"

"Mon Dieu, Beth, this is a *quadroon* ball. Everyone forgave you for riding at Métairie because you won, but a white woman found here would cause a scandal that would never be forgotten! It would ruin your husband's business here, and Andrew's law practice, and the social standing of everyone connected with you!"

Bethany regarded him in dismay. "Oh, no! I never meant to do anything like that—"

She got no further. Philippe suddenly took her in his arms, shielding her with his body as someone emerged from the ballroom.

"Sssh," he warned. "Wait until they go back inside, then I'll get you out of here."

"I hate to interrupt your seduction of my wife, Benoist, but it's time for Beth to leave."

At Luke's voice, both Philippe and Bethany stepped back, horrified to see him.

"Now, wait a minute, Randall," Philippe began hastily. "It's not what you think."

"What I think is that you haven't been particularly discreet."

Luke remained half hidden in the shadows, and his words held no trace of anger.

"I was only trying to keep anyone from seeing Beth. You know as well as I do that she shouldn't have come here. Nothing inopportune has happened between us, I assure you. The last thing I want is to cause her more trouble after what happened at the race."

"Perhaps you should have taken that into consideration before now," Luke said calmly. "But if you'll excuse us, we really should be going."

Bethany looked up fearfully at Luke as they moved away, leaving Philippe to stare helplessly after them, but her husband said not a word as he took her arm and led her toward the spiral iron stairway and down into the courtyard.

"Wait, Luke, Michelle's inside. We can't just leave her!"

"Andrew's taking Michelle to the townhouse, but I'm surprised you even care. Didn't it occur to you how degrading it would be for Michelle to come here tonight? She originally left New Orleans to avoid this place."

Bethany was deeply appalled by his words. She *hadn't* considered Michelle's feelings when she dragged her into the quadroon ballroom. She had thought only of herself and her need to find Luke. Deep shame filled her as Luke handed her into his carriage, then followed her inside, calling for the driver to proceed to Cantigny.

Bethany fidgeted with the ribbons of her mask, feeling an awful need to explain everything to him.

He didn't appear angry in the least, as if he hardly cared what she had done, and that made her perversely resentful.

"I only went there to find you," she admitted, wanting him to know the truth. "I know now I shouldn't have gone."

"It doesn't matter. Just be more discreet next time you meet Benoist," was his offhanded answer, which sent Bethany's ire spiraling out of control.

"I will, believe me," she retorted. "I'll wait until you leave, and I hope that's soon, then I'll meet Philippe or whoever else strikes my fancy somewhere nice and private, perhaps at their apartments. Or maybe Marcus will come back for me like he said he would, and I'll let him make love to me in our bed at Cantigny, after everyone is asleep, if that's *discreet* enough for you—"

Luke moved so fast that Bethany gasped as his fingers bit into her arms. "Don't push me, Beth. I'm not in a good mood." He had ground out the words from between clenched teeth, and Bethany realized with some joy that he *was* angry—very, very angry. Never, ever had she thought she would be so thrilled to be the subject of Luke's formidable rage. She settled back when he let go of her, not ready to push him any farther. She had gotten the response she wanted. He *did* care about her!

By the time they reached Cantigny, the household was long asleep. Bethany nearly had to run to keep up with Luke's long steps as he pulled her after him up the staircase and down the hall to his bedchamber. He flung her inside and shut the door behind them, then turned on her, jerking loose his cravat in an angry motion. By now, however, Bethany was calm and

more than willing to meet his intentions, especially
if they included a night spent in his bed. More than
anything, though, she was pleased to see him finally
shaken loose from the awful, exasperating armor of
indifference he usually kept around him.

"I think we ought to have a proper good-bye, don't
you? Since I'm leaving soon," he said with a half
sneer, continuing to undress.

Meeting his challenge, Bethany tugged off her white
lace gloves, for once the unruffled party. "Oh yes, I
definitely think we should," she agreed affably, "because I do love you, you know, and I did all of this
tonight just to make you jealous. It was childish of
me, but you're being childish, too, by going around
town with that other woman just so you won't have to
admit that you love me as much as I love you."

Her words and the sweet smile that followed were
unexpected enough to bring Luke to a standstill, the
look of surprise on his handsome face almost comi-
cal.

"I'm going to love you, Luke, no matter what you
do," Bethany continued matter-of-factly, slipping her
dress off her shoulders and letting it slide down over
her slim hips with a faint whisper of silk. "So you
might as well accept that and enjoy the time we have
left together."

Luke was momentarily distracted by the sight of
her soft, creamy flesh beneath the black lace chemise
she wore, but Bethany pressed on, loosening her hair
from the chignon at her nape and shaking her head
until the silky blond ringlets fell over her shoulders
in glorious splendor.

"So do what you will to me, and it won't matter."

Luke's mouth went dry as she lifted one shapely

leg to a stool and slowly unrolled her black silk stocking. He gritted his teeth.

"I suppose you'd still love me if I decide to keep a mistress. A quadroon, perhaps?" he said.

Another stocking floated gently to the floor. "Oh, yes, it would make no difference at all."

"And if she gave me a child?"

Bethany smiled, nodding, her fingers tugging loose the ribbons that held her chemise over her breasts.

"And if I tell you I'm leaving in a week or so and might never come back?"

"Yes, yes, yes!" Bethany exploded at him, that pronouncement harder to ignore than the others. She was suddenly tired of his verbal taunts, his attempts to make her hate him. "I'd love you if you were the devil himself!"

Her words momentarily shocked them both, and Bethany was immediately appalled at having spoken them.

"Well, maybe I wouldn't if you were really the devil," she amended lamely.

Luke stared at her with incredulous eyes, then to Bethany's surprise, he laughed. "A lot of people think that's exactly who I am."

"I'm not a lot of people, Luke. I'm your wife, and I do love you. No matter what you think or say or do, I always will."

Luke stared at her for another moment, then pulled her against him, holding her tight in his arms, his voice gruff. "Why do you have to love me? I have to leave, and I'll hurt you."

Bethany laid her head on his chest, her own voice broken with emotion.

"I can't help it, Luke. You made me love you when

you came back for Petie, and when you saved Michelle from the Hacketts, and when you came for me in jail when I was so afraid. And when you taught me to read and when you let me be your wife. You make me feel beautiful, like a real lady.''

Luke shut his eyes, then lifted her, one hand tangled in her hair, one clamping her against him.

''I swore a long time ago that I would never love a woman again,'' he muttered against her hair, ''and I tried like hell not to love you, Beth. I thought if I stayed away from you these last weeks it would be easy to leave you, that you would want me gone and out of your life. Don't you see? I can't stay with you. I'll always have to go back west; it's something inside me, something I can't help.''

''Take us with you. I'll go anywhere with you,'' Bethany whispered.

''Beth, Beth, I can't. It's too wild and dangerous and full of hardship. I don't want you and Pete to have to suffer through it. Don't ask me why I have to go. I don't even know myself.''

''Then all I ask is for you to come back to us,'' Bethany murmured breathlessly.

She pulled him down onto the bed, wrapping her fingers in his thick curls, wanting him so much, loving him so deeply. He rose to strip off the rest of his clothes, and when he lay beside her, Bethany pressed up against his dark-haired chest, her arms around his neck, craving his touch, his mouth, his strength. She had missed the way his hands moved over her skin, sometimes with caresses so soft and gentle that she quivered uncontrollably, sometimes fiercely and possessively, as if he thought she would disappear unless he thoroughly claimed her. She luxuriated in the feel of his hard muscles contracting beneath her kneading fingers as they touched and kissed and loved.

Luke held her as tightly as he could, giving full rein to the yearnings he had forced himself to contain, to the hungry, all-encompassing need of her that had been ripping him apart for days.

He wanted her, needed her, and as hard as he had fought his own traitorous feelings, he knew he loved her. He loved her as he had never loved anyone. There was no one like Bethany, no other woman who could make him laugh the way she could, or make him ache with desire the way she could. Lying with her, touching her, was like being in a safe, warm haven. Her silky flesh against him was a balm to heal the loneliness of his soul. Yet he knew he would leave her.

They moved as one, bodies entangled, lips burning with long-starved desire until ecstasy took hold of them, hurtling them through dark skies among spar-kling, swirling constellations as they reached the bliss they sought, crying out together, clutching each other so that it would not end. When it did end, they lay contentedly side by side, drained and sated, and one as never before.

During the next week, Bethany tried hard not to think about Luke's impending departure. She banished such thoughts from her mind, unwilling to ruin their last days together.

He remained at Cantigny with her and made love to her often, slowly, lingeringly, with a tenderness that she cherished. She knew in her heart that these would be the memories she would hug to her after he was gone. She savored each smile, each caress, each murmured endearment, storing them away for when she lay alone in her bed beneath the filmy white baire.

But the day of departure eventually arrived with Andrew riding in early from town, then disappearing with Luke into the library. Agony tore at Bethany's heart as she sat with Peeto on the gallery facing the river, determined to see her husband off without the clinging, possessive display of emotion that she knew he dreaded. It was something she had to do for him, for herself, and for Peeto. She didn't understand why Luke felt he must return to his mountains, and in truth, she wasn't sure he understood it himself. It was something he felt he had to do or he wouldn't be going. She had no choice but to accept it.

Peeto and Luke had been getting along much better lately, ever since Luke had given the boy a pony and taken time to teach him how to ride. But Luke had not yet been willing to broach the subject of Peeto's mother with his son, though Bethany had made sure Peeto knew her death had been an awful accident. Luke should have reassured Peeto of that himself, and told him more about his mother and her life with her tribe. But now, just when they were nearing a point where they could start to build a close father-and-son relationship, Luke was leaving, and Peeto would feel abandoned by him again.

Bethany put her arm around the child, looking over his dark head to where Onyx, the great stallion, stood saddled and ready for the long journey along the Mississippi River, then over the vast plains that Luke had described to her with such glowing eyes, to the mountains where he had grown to manhood. Be brave,

Bethany told herself sternly. Luke will admire you for that. But he's leaving us, her mind countered with horrible bleakness.

"He'll come back," Bethany said beneath her breath, and when Peeto looked up at her with big green eyes, so solemn and sad, she forced a smile. "I know he will."

Peeto didn't answer, and they sat silently together until Luke appeared at the end of the gallery. Bethany's throat tightened. He was wearing his buckskins, the soft tan leather molding his thighs, the long, beaded fringe moving as he walked. He looked as he had when she first saw him in Natchez, so big and strong and virile.

Overpowering emotions rocked through her as she watched him walk toward them, and she tried desperately to memorize every part of him, the vertical line in his cheeks that deepened into grooves when he smiled, the wayward lock of hair that always fell over his forehead, his long silent strides. She let her thoughts caress him as her fingertips had the night before in their bed, when she had traced the strong angle of his jaw and his fine, straight profile. Her heart clenched like a fist when she remembered how his lips had closed around her fingertip as she had moved it over his mouth.

Luke stopped in front of them, and no one could find words until Bethany forced herself to smile. "Are you ready? Did you get everything we packed for you?"

Luke nodded, his eyes shifting to Peeto, who refused to look at him. He placed his palm on the top of his son's dark head, then squatted down beside him. He lifted Peeto's chin with his fingers until the boy was forced to meet his gaze.

"You be a good boy while I'm gone, you hear. Take care of Beth for me until I get back."

Peeto's head dipped in a single nod, and Bethany bit her lip as the boy leaned forward and threw his arms around Luke's neck for a brief moment before he bolted away, running down the porch and disappearing around the corner.

Luke watched the place where his son had disappeared, as if he was reluctant to turn to Bethany.

"He'll be all right," she said softly. "I'll take good care of him for you."

Luke turned to her. "I know," he murmured, reaching out to pull her into his embrace, and Bethany closed her eyes, not sure she could bear the pain twisting her heart.

"I don't think I'll be much good without you," she whispered in a choked voice as Luke sat down, setting her on his lap. He stroked her hair gently, as if wanting to remember its fine, silky texture.

"If you need or want anything, Andrew will always be here to help you. I mean *anything* you ever want. All I have is yours."

I want you, I want you, nothing else, Bethany thought over and over.

"Andy will handle Hugh when he arrives," Luke continued. "He'll make sure the charges are dropped, but I want you to promise me that you'll be careful. It's unlikely the Hacketts are around anymore; no one's seen them, but you must take every precaution as if they were. All of you, you hear me?"

Bethany listened, her dry eyes burning with her desire to weep, wondering how he could be thinking of so many trivial, businesslike details when she was obsessed with the fact that he was leaving. Why couldn't she look at it the way he did? Why was her heart breaking in two?

"When will you be back?" she murmured, her face hidden in his shoulder.

Luke hesitated, then his own voice came with a trace of gruffness. "A year, two at the most."

"I'll be here, waiting for you," Bethany whispered, and Luke's arms tightened around her for another moment before he released her and strode away with long steps then swung up into the saddle. He looked back at her, and Bethany waved, swallowing hard as he turned Onyx toward the levee road.

Her pent-up tears began to fall as he galloped away, and a sob escaped when he reined up a good distance down the avenue of oaks and lifted his arm in a last farewell. Bethany dabbed her eyes with a handkerchief, angry at herself for shedding tears. He would be back. He would. And right now, Peeto needed her. He understood Luke's need to return west even less than Bethany did.

She climbed the stairs to the second floor, her steps weary and dispirited, glad no servants were around to see her anguish. She felt she couldn't bear for even one person to express sympathy. Not yet. The wound was too fresh.

She went straight to Peeto's room, fairly certain she would find him beneath his bed. To her surprise, he sat huddled in the loose cushions of the window seat, crying his eyes out. Bethany went to him, sitting close beside him as she wordlessly put her arms around him. Peeto buried his face in her shoulder, and she patted his back, fingering his raven-colored curls in the same way she had so often caressed Luke's dark hair.

"I thought I'd be glad when he went away," Peeto muttered with a broken sob. "But I'm not glad. I don't want him to go."

"I know, Petie. I don't either."

She rocked to and fro with him held tight in her arms, her own tears rolling down her cheeks. After a while, Peeto's weeping calmed to a quiet sniffling.

"Why did he have to leave us, Beth? Doesn't he love us at all?"

"Yes, he loves us, but sometimes people have to do things that other people don't understand. We just have to let him be himself and love him anyway, just like we do each other."

"But I don't understand why he has to go away for so long!"

Bethany leaned her head against the wall, staring out the open window toward the river. Sunlight glittered on the surface of the water, and she could see a tall mast moving past Cantigny's landing toward the sea.

"Remember when you first came to St. Louis, Petie? When you were very little and afraid?"

His head moved up and down against her breast.

"Remember how you didn't like me to shut your door? You never could sleep if your bedchamber door was closed all the way." She stopped, then went on softly, "That's how Luke feels, I think. He needs to have a door open somewhere, so he doesn't feel all trapped inside. If we give him that door and let him go when he wants, I think he'll come back to us. Do you see what I mean?"

"But doesn't he care how we feel?" Peeto asked, more tears oozing from beneath his long black lashes.

Bethany wiped them away with gentle fingers. "Of course, he does. But he knows we have each other to love until he comes back."

She kept her eyes on the neverending flow of the mighty river, determined to believe her own reassuring words. But a year without Luke seemed an eternity of lonely torture, and it had only just begun.

Chapter 17

Almost a fortnight after Luke left, Louis Benoist died peacefully in his sleep. Bethany and Andrew accompanied Michelle to the old St. Louis Cemetery on Ramparts Street to pay their final respects to the old Creole gentleman. As the funeral bell tolled slowly and mournfully, Bethany kept her arm around her bereaved friend, who wept openly beneath her heavy black veil. Michelle had not been allowed to join the funeral procession a short distance away where Philippe stood, surrounded by many black-clad Creole friends and acquaintances.

Umbrellas were unfurled against the drizzling cold rain, and Bethany was disquieted by the spongy, soggy ground that sunk beneath their boots. The whole place seemed bizarre and foreboding to her, nothing like the peaceful graveyards in St. Louis with their grassy lawns and shady poplar trees. In New Orleans, where underground water lay only feet below the surface, the burial grounds were crowded mazes of tall marble tombs and crypts of white-washed brick, the flat tops overgrown with grass and weeds. Most strange to Bethany were the ovens, stacked casketlike crypts, often five or six atop each other, built against the outside walls of the cemetery.

Andrew had told her that many were only rented: oftentimes the bones of one corpse were swept out and burned to make room for the next.

Bethany shivered. It was like a city for the dead, with each of the deceased encased in his or her own small stone house, and Bethany felt a strange and awful presentiment of doom. She tried to shake such macabre musings as the priest droned on with his lengthy eulogy, but the dark skies and ominous rumblings of thunder only added to her uneasiness.

What if something had happened to Luke? Even the idea filled her with dread, and she realized if he should ever be hurt or killed, she would probably never know. She would wait and wait, never sure if he was dead or alive. She mustn't let herself think that way, she told herself firmly. Luke would be back. But the last two weeks had been the longest, most miserable she had ever experienced. As each day passed, she wondered how much longer she could stand it, how much longer she could put on the brave, cheerful mask that Peeto needed so desperately to see.

Bethany looked up as the casket was pushed inside the small opening of the six-foot-high white marble crypt. The iron doors were closed and secured with a turn of a heavy metal bolt, and the mourners began to file away. When only Philippe was left near the tomb, Andrew led Michelle forward. Bethany and Peeto followed, standing back as Michelle placed a single gardenia in a brass urn among the other flowers.

"I'm very sorry about your father," Bethany told Philippe.

He looked toward where Michelle still knelt in front

of their father's grave. "I'm only glad I let him see Michelle before it was too late."

"Michelle will miss him."

"As will I," Philippe said, his blue eyes searching Bethany's face. "I'm truly sorry for getting you involved in the race and all that. I guess I've been pretty selfish."

Bethany was too polite to agree with his assessment of his behavior, but she didn't disagree, either.

"I'm going back to Pensacola for a time," Philippe said then, "but if there's anything I can do for you, please let me know."

"Thank you, but Luke has provided for us until his return. I'm glad Michelle is coming back to Cantigny with us. Petie and I need her now."

Michelle did come to Cantigny, but even her presence could not lessen Bethany's growing distress about Luke's absence. One mild afternoon, as Bethany and Michelle strolled along the levee, Bethany's thoughts seemed to reach a low point. They sat together on the grass, and Bethany sighed, her eyes on the small sailing craft making its way upriver toward the city.

Michelle looked at her friend, knowing full well the extent of her suffering, although Bethany rarely expressed her feelings aloud.

"Perhaps Luke will change his mind and return," she suggested softly.

Bethany's second sigh was heavy. "I've been praying for that, but it's so hard, Michelle. It hurts so bad, almost as if he took my heart away with him."

"Perhaps he did."

Bethany smiled a little, grateful for her friend's quiet, comforting presence, thinking about all they

DREAMSONG

had been through together in the last few months. It seemed strange to think that just a year ago Bethany hadn't even known Michelle, or Luke, existed.

"I'm sorry, Michelle, about that night at the quadroon ballroom," Bethany said suddenly. "I knew you ran away with Etienne so you wouldn't have to go there, yet I didn't even think how awful it would be for you until Luke made me see."

Michelle reached out to touch Bethany's arm. "It was so little for me to do, after all you've done for me. I should never have left New Orleans and Papa in the first place, and I suffered for it. I think that now I am able to accept my place here. I am an octoroon by birth. There's nothing I can do about it. Running away certainly won't change it."

Bethany smiled. "There will always be a place for you here at Cantigny. I need you, you know. You always make me feel better."

Later that night, Bethany paced the carpeted floor of her bedchamber. It was always worse after dark, when everyone else was abed. The loneliness would rush in like a spring flood on the river, rising and rising until Bethany thought she was drowning.

Throughout each and every day, she labored to be brave, to smile until she thought her face would crack, but when she looked at the big empty four-poster bed where she had lain so close and intimate in Luke's strong arms, her false cheer crumbled away like dry mortar, stripping her emotions bare, raw, and bleeding.

Thunder gave an ominous rumble somewhere far downriver, sounding as hollow as her heart, and Bethany moved to the open French doors. Rain fell steadily, and she closed her eyes as the storm-cooled wind lifted her loosened ringlets, molding her pale blue silk nightdress to her slender legs. It was a strange kind of winter, with no snow or frost. She wondered if it was snowing in St. Louis, or wherever Luke was.

A bolt of lightning lit the dark sky, the brief flash illuminating the blowing trees for a mere second. A loud crack of thunder sounded, and Bethany hurried across the room, afraid it might have awakened Peeto. The little child lay fast asleep in his bed, however, his best friend, Raffy, breathing evenly on a small cot nearby. Bethany closed the gallery doors against the blowing rain, then leaned her cheek against the smooth wood of the bedpost and gazed down at Luke's son.

Peeto looked so much like his father, more every day, she thought with a curious mingling of pride and pain. She smoothed back his hair from his forehead, remembering how she had done the same thing for Luke as he slept the night before he left. Her heart tightened into a knot of despair.

Before tears could fall again, she hurried back to her own room and climbed into bed, where she sat cross-legged, staring into the fire. A moment later, she slid her hand beneath the lace-edged, satin pillows to retrieve the love gris-gris Tante Chloe had made for her. She clutched it tightly in her hand, and finally let the tears come. But they lasted only briefly as her misery slowly turned to anger.

She swung her slim legs over the bed steps, then ran to the hearth. She hurled the charm into the dancing flames. It wasn't working anyway! Luke was gone, and he wasn't coming back, not for months! And there was nothing she could do about it, nothing! For all she knew, he might never come back! He might stay in his beloved mountains forever!

That thought was more than she could bear, and she wept brokenheartedly into her palms with utter, devastating hopelessness. Most of all, she hated that her own happiness depended so totally on someone else, on a man like Luke who could abandon her so easily. She wished she could hate him!

Bethany lay prostrate in front of the fire for a long time, sobbing out her loneliness, and felt much better afterward. She had needed a good, long cry. She sat upright on the rug, blowing her nose, then drawing her knees in against her chest and staring dully into the flickering fire.

Thunder continued its sporadic rumbling, the gusting winds banging the shutters and filling her bedchamber with the fresh, wet smell of rain. The steady drumming of raindrops on the stone balcony was soothing somehow, but when a different sound interrupted the dripping, she turned toward the open doors.

Luke stood between the billowing white curtains, framed by the dark, stormy night, his tan buckskins soaked to a darker shade, his black hair plastered against his forehead. In that first instant, Bethany was afraid to believe her own eyes for fear this was yet another one of the dreams that plagued her nights.

Their eyes held. Then, at Luke's first step into the room, Bethany was up and flying into his arms with unabashed joy. She wept with pure happiness as his strong arms closed around her, her cheek against the wet roughness of his shoulder, the manly scent of damp leather filling her senses.

Luke held her for a long time, his eyes shut tight,

his emotions torn by the feel of her soft body and silky hair. Then he lifted her with one arm, bringing her up until his mouth found hers in a long, hungry kiss that left them both breathless and wanting more.

"Every time I closed my eyes, I saw your face," he muttered hoarsely against her soft cheek.

Bethany's arms tightened around his neck. "I love you so much," she said brokenly. "I've missed you so."

After a moment, he released her, turning to close the doors against the storm, and Bethany reached out once again to touch him, still half afraid to close her eyes for fear he would vanish. He smiled tenderly down at her, but Bethany saw the tired lines around his eyes and mouth, and realized he was unbelievably weary.

"You look so tired, Luke. Are you all right?"

"Now I am."

Bethany felt as if she had died and gone to heaven. An inexplicable rush of tears came unbidden. She held them back, not about to waste her time crying, not with Luke beside her. Her fingers went to the laces of his tunic, pulling them loose.

"You're so wet. You'll get the fever," she whispered. "Come to bed where it's warm. I'll help you."

Luke let her undress him, his eyes feasting on the face that had haunted his days and nights, robbing him of sleep and peace of mind. When at last they lay together between the smooth, clean-smelling sheets, his small, beautiful wife pressed against his side, warm and soft and loving, just the way he had remembered and craved and desired each moment away from her, he stroked the satin-soft skin of her back and hip, breathed in the flowery sweetness of her gilt-edged hair, unable to stop smiling.

"God knows I've missed you," he said, very low. "The day came when I couldn't take another step further away from you."

"Oh, Luke," Bethany murmured, enraptured. His mouth came again, so hungry yet so softly, gently, and strangely without passion, instead, with a deep, abiding love that transcended the desire of their bodies and fulfilled the most profound need of their hearts.

Bethany lay against him in the purest contentment of her life, leaning her head into his palm as his fingers caressed her silky hair.

"When I lived with the Sioux," he said very softly, his deep voice rough with emotion in a way Bethany had never heard it, "they told me that every man receives a gift from the gods one time in his life. They called it a dreamsong." He paused, holding her tighter. "You're mine, Beth. You're my dreamsong."

Bethany smiled, a new kind of warmth filling her heart with tenderness. She traced his strong, bewhiskered jaw with loving fingers, realizing that her every prayer, every wish and hope and dream, had been fulfilled with his words. It was she who had received the dreamsong Luke spoke of.

They were silent then, holding each other tightly, stroking and touching and enjoying the feel of each other, until Luke's weary muscles began to relax and exhaustion took him in its grasp.

"I love you," he murmured for the first time in his life, and then he slept.

Bethany lay quietly in his arms, listening to the soft sound of his breathing, turning over in her mind each word of love he had uttered, so she could place them forever in a special shrine in her heart and soul.

Much later, when the storm outside had abated to a lazy dripping from the eaves, Bethany reluctantly disentangled herself from Luke's heavy arms and tip-toed to the fireplace where the flames had died to a mere glow of embers. She dug into the ashes with the poker until she found the charred stone that was all that was left of the jade-green amulet, smiling as she wiped it clean with the hem of her gown. She took it back to the bed with her, carefully positioning it be-neath her pillow. Satisfied, she cuddled close to her big, handsome husband, pressing her lips softly against his whiskered jaw before she fell into her own deep and contented sleep.

Andrew rode up the long, tree-lined entry road to Cantigny, the thick-boled live oaks dripping Spanish moss high above his head. He smiled as he spied Raffy darting out from between the columns of the river portico to help him with his horse.

"Marster Luke bez back!" were the first words out of the little boy's mouth.

Andrew jerked his head around in shock, and Raffy gave his usual impish, toothless grin, which was nonetheless full of delight. Andrew threw back his head and gave a deep, knowing laugh.

"Poor old Luke. Where the hell is he?"

"In de dinin' parlor. I's bez waden fo' Marster Pete. We's bez gwine crayfish trappin'!"

Andrew dismounted and handed Raffy his reins be-fore he limped up the steps, leaning on his cane, his wide grin still in place. The dining room was deserted except for Peeto, who was piling a good portion of the leftover beignets into a large linen table napkin.

"Still a mite hungry, eh, Pete?" Andrew said with a smile, and Peeto looked around guiltily, relieved that it was only his good-natured Uncle Andy who had caught him stealing food from the table.

"These here are for Raffy. He likes 'em plenty, and Tante Chloe don't let him have any."

"He's outside waiting for you," Andrew told the boy, pulling off his gloves. "He said your father's come back." Andrew watched Peeto carefully, happy to see the pleased look that registered on the boy's face.

"Yes, sir, he came back last night while we was all sleeping, just in time for Christmas! He woke me up real early this morning and took me back to his and Beth's bed. He hadn't ever done that before. He said he wasn't ever going to leave us again!"

Peeto's wide smile warmed Andrew's heart. "That's wonderful, Pete. I told you he wouldn't stay gone long, didn't I?"

"Yes, sir, and you was right."

Raffy's voice calling for Peeto interrupted their conversation, and Andrew patted the boy's shoulder.

"We're going crawdad hunting," Peeto informed him, edging toward the door. "Luke said we could."

"Just watch out for the gators," Andrew called after him.

"Yes, sir," Peeto said, tightly clutching his bundle of food. Andrew watched the boy run across the gallery to join his friend. Maybe Luke was finally going to break down and let himself have a real family after all, he thought.

At the door of the library, Andrew paused, peeking

inside just in time to see Luke pull Bethany down on his lap and kiss her in a way that left no doubt of his intentions. Andrew began to feel a little warm in the face as Bethany reacted with an eager display that was nothing less than wanton. Swallowing hard, Andrew stepped back, deciding that Luke was even luckier than he had first thought.

He grinned to himself, making a loud display of stomping down the hall, hurting his splinted leg in the process.

"Luke!" he yelled loudly. "Where are you?"

When he entered the library a moment later, Bethany was standing primly at Luke's side, her face rosy and her bodice buttoned up wrong. Luke looked not a little annoyed at Andrew's intrusion. Andrew couldn't resist an impulse to tease his stony-faced brother.

"What happened, Luke? Get up the trail a ways and realize you forgot something?"

Luke gave him a tight smile. "You could say that," he replied, lifting Bethany's small hand to his lips.

Bethany colored with delicious pleasure, and although Andrew was surprised at Luke's uncharacteristic display of affection, he was just as pleased to see the happiness on Bethany's face. He hadn't seen her smile since Luke's departure. It seemed to him that things between them were going very well, indeed.

"What can we do for you, Andy, that can't wait until tomorrow?" Luke asked bluntly.

Andrew gave a good-humored grin. "I just dropped in to make sure Bethany and Pete were doing all right, but now that you're back, I can deliver Hugh's letter to you."

Luke felt Bethany flinch at the mere mention of Hugh Younger, and he put his arm around her.

"I need to speak to Tante Chloe about supper," she said quickly. Though Luke was reluctant to let her out of his sight, he released her hand and watched her until the door clicked behind her.

Andrew maneuvered his splinted leg carefully in front of him and sank down in a chair. Smiling, he leaned back without speaking as Luke took a narrow cheroot from the silver box on the desktop. Luke lit one for himself, then held it between strong white teeth as he retrieved another for his brother. Andrew took it, still grinning.

"All right, Andy, go ahead and say it. You're dying to."

"Me? What on earth would I have to say to you?"

"I told you so?" Luke suggested.

"Well, I did, and actually you lasted about a week longer than I thought you would. If it makes you feel any better, most men married to a woman like Bethany wouldn't have lasted nearly that long."

"What did Hugh say in his letter?" Luke asked, intentionally changing the subject.

Andrew's smile faded. "I doubt you'll like it. You'd better read it yourself."

Andrew retrieved a single piece of folded parchment from the inside pocket of his tan suede frock coat and handed it across the desk. Luke took it, and Andrew watched his brother's face deepen into a massive frown.

"He's lying when he says he didn't mistreat Pete," Luke said finally. "Bethany wouldn't lie to me."

"He's pretty adamant about it."

"That's because he's afraid I'll give him the thrashing he deserves for abusing my son, and I just might do it.''

''According to this, he'll be arriving soon to nullify the warrant. How do you intend to deal with him?''

Luke refolded the paper and laid it aside before he met Andrew's gaze. ''I want Beth and Pete to forget it ever happened. We'll have to receive him here, at least until he rescinds the warrant for Beth. I don't want that hanging over her head any longer. After that, he can go back to St. Louis, where Beth and Pete won't have to look at him. Beth cringes every time she hears his name.''

''He must have treated them very badly,'' Andrew remarked, ''for both of them to fear him so much. I never would have thought Hugh capable of such cowardly behavior. Anne would be heartbroken if she knew he had abused Pete.''

Luke nodded as he stood, not really listening any longer. He stubbed out his cheroot in the ashtray. ''Sorry, Andy, but I've been gone a long while, and I intend to find my wife and make up for lost time.''

Andrew laughed, but before he could make a teasing remark, Luke was already gone.

Chapter 18

Several days after Christmas, Bethany stood in the spacious brick kitchen of Cantigny, carefully placing a covered basket of honey-glazed chicken into a large wicker picnic hamper. On top of that went several portions of Tante Chloe's spoonbread, still warm from the oven, and a dozen of the crisp apple tarts covered in cinnamon sugar that Peeto liked so much. She secured the lid and handed the hamper over to Peeto, who waited eagerly at her side. Outside, Michelle and Raffy were waiting to accompany them on a fishing trip and picnic on the levee, something Bethany had promised them Christmas morning.

She smiled as she remembered that joyous day when the rooms of Cantigny rang with warmth and love and laughter. It had been the best Christmas she had ever known, and it had been almost sinful the way Luke had showered them all with expensive gifts. She shook her head as she went outside to join the others, who were carrying cane poles and standing beneath the spreading limbs of a pecan tree near the kitchen door.

"I guess we're ready now," she said, but a pleased smile lit her face as she caught sight of Luke coming toward them with his long, pantherish strides.

"Where are you going?" he asked, his eyes lowering to her lips with that hungry look which had not lessened since his return, the erotic invitation never failing to send Bethany's pulse into a race with her heart.

"On a picnic," she answered, breathless, as she thought of the night before in their bed and all the delicious things that had happened there. All of a sudden, she was heartlessly ready to send the children on ahead with Michelle so she could stay home with her handsome husband.

"And I wasn't invited?"

Bethany's face registered surprise, then delight. "But you've never wanted to go with us before. We just assumed—" she began, then hastily amended for fear he might think himself unwelcome. "Please, come with us! We'd love for you to!"

She smiled, taking his hand to draw him after the others, who had already started down the avenue of oaks. Luke laced his fingers through hers as they strolled under the towering trees toward the river. Bethany felt the most wonderful exhilaration of spirit, and the smile that rarely left her face of late settled into place again.

She looked up at Luke, and on impulse, stopped him, leading him by the hand behind the nearest tree so she could loop her arms around his strong neck. She pulled his head down to her lips, and he obliged with not a little pleasure, lifting her off the ground, his mouth moving over hers in that slow, caressing way that melted her heart and weakened her knees.

"Maybe we should save this for tonight," Luke murmured into her ear, but he didn't release his tight grip on her, and after another moment of particularly arousing endeavors, he gave a self-mocking grin. "Then again, maybe we shouldn't save it for tonight."

He released her, intending to take her back to the house with him and let the picnic wait, but Peeto's excited shouts from the top of the levee negated that idea.

"Tonight, without a doubt," Bethany whispered, and Luke agreed, with every intention of making it an early evening, just as they had done every evening since his return. He smiled, remembering Beth's deep blush each time they excused themselves to escape upstairs.

By the time they reached the dirt path that wound up to the grassy top of the embankment, they learned the reason for Peeto and Raffy's excitement. A long, cumbersome flatboat was edging its bow slowly toward the landing wharf of Cantigny. Luke and Bethany proceeded down the wooden walkway to where Peeto and the others stood and watched the boat's approach. Luke put one hand on his son's shoulder as he peered toward the man in the bow of the heavily laden craft.

"It's Hugh," he told Bethany, and was appalled as her face paled to a sickly shade of white, her eyes going wide with fear. She was not the only one affected by Hugh's arrival, for Peeto ran at once to stand protectively in front of her. Luke frowned as the boat bumped against the pilings, and Hugh hailed them.

"Luke! God, I'm glad to finally get here!"

Luke watched his brother-in-law climb out of the flatboat, but as Hugh's boot touched the dock, both

Bethany and Peeto stepped backward. Hugh paused when he saw Bethany.

"You lied to Luke," he accused her. "Why?"

Bethany stared at Hugh. In his neat traveling attire and clean-shaven cheeks, he looked different than he had on the last night when his clothes had been rumpled and stained and his whiskered face twisted with cruelty. When she couldn't form an answer, Luke put an arm around her.

"My wife doesn't lie to me," he said in a cold, measured warning.

"Wife?" Hugh repeated dumbly. "You didn't marry her, did you? Good God, why would you do such a thing?"

His appalled questions stopped abruptly as Luke's dangerous gaze bored down on him.

"Insults to my wife are insults to me," he said tightly, but he stopped there as Bethany suddenly bolted from beside him, lifting her skirts and fleeing up the dock toward the house. Peeto followed her at a run.

"I never touched that boy in anger, I swear it, Luke," Hugh said quickly as Luke gazed after his wife and son, a concerned frown drawing his dark brows together.

"Michelle will show you to the house," Luke told him before he turned to follow Bethany's flight.

Upon reaching the house, Luke methodically searched the lower floor for Bethany and Peeto, but it was in his own bedchamber that he found them, huddled together on the bed, crying and clutching each other. His frown deepened, and he shut the door quietly, at a loss to understand the violence of their reaction to Hugh.

"What is it, Beth?" he asked softly, as he sat down on the edge of the bed. Bethany looked stricken, her lips trembling until she caught at them with her teeth, and Luke felt an awful premonition rise to chill his spine. Never had he seen her so terrified, not even when she had been chained in the dark cell of the calaboose. Even more strange, Peeto didn't seem nearly as frightened of the uncle who had abused him. Indeed, he was the one who was comforting Bethany.

"Pete? I want to talk to Beth alone for a moment."

Peeto seemed undecided about the idea until Luke's face took on an impatient look.

"Just for a moment, Pete, then you can come back."

Peeto glanced at Bethany again and reluctantly climbed down from the bed to take his leave. Luke immediately pulled Bethany into his arms, relieved when she came willingly, and stroked her soft curls.

"What is it, my love? What's frightening you? Tell me."

Bethany remained silent, her face buried in the fine linen of his shirtfront, and he held her close for a long moment. "I lied about Hugh," she whispered finally in a tortured voice. "He didn't mistreat Petie."

Luke felt as if she had struck him across the face. He could only stare at her as she burst into tears. He shook away his surprise, his arms tightening around her.

"I don't understand. What are you saying?"

Bethany couldn't bear to look at him, but she knew she had to tell him now. She had no choice. She sat up, wiping her tears with her fingers. "He didn't hurt

Petie like I said, but please, please, Luke, don't make me tell you anything else!''

Luke shook his head in confusion, trying hard to make sense of what she was telling him.

"I can't just let it go, Beth. Surely you see that. Not now when you're tearing yourself apart like this. You've got to tell me what's going on here.'' Luke waited but Bethany refused to look at him. "All right, then, I'll have to ask Pete. He knows, doesn't he, Beth?''

He started to rise, but Bethany clutched his arm to hold him beside her. "Please,'' she begged, tears flowing again. "Don't do that.''

Luke's heart twisted at the very real pain she was exhibiting, and he held her tight again, closing his eyes.

"Whatever it is can't be that bad, Beth. You have to tell me, or I can't help you. Don't you trust me? Is that it?''

At his words, Bethany lay quiet in his arms. Eventually, she spoke, her voice muffled against his shoulder.

"I didn't hit Hugh with the poker, Luke. Petie hit him.''

"Pete! Why?''

"Because, because . . .'' Bethany's explanation faltered pitiably as she swallowed hard, then she continued, her words very low. "He did it for me.''

Luke frowned, still not understanding. He waited.

"One night . . . Hugh was drinking a lot,'' Bethany began haltingly. "He always drank the most at night, all night sometimes, but this time he came into the nursery where we were. I thought at first that he was coming to see Petie, and I was glad because he never paid any attention to him."

She sobbed suddenly, and Luke stroked her curls as she continued. "But he hadn't come for that. He was so drunk, Luke, staggering all over and knocking things off the tables, and we both got real scared of him. Then all of a sudden he grabbed me, and he started . . . he started to tear at my dress." Her words came in a rush now, her voice trembling at the memory. "I couldn't get away. I couldn't fight him off because he was too strong—"

Fury such as Luke had never felt shot through him, flaming through his veins like liquid lava until his whole body was rigid with anger, every muscle rockhard, his face turning to icy, lethal granite. Everything began to make sense then—why Bethany had risked so much to steal away with Pete in the dead of night, why she had been afraid the first time he had made love to her, so many things he had questioned since he met her in Natchez.

"Hugh was the one who tried to rape you?" he managed to say in a stiff, unnatural voice.

Bethany's fingers tightened where they held his sleeve. "Yes, but Petie stopped him. He hit him with the poker to make him let go of me." She sat up, studying Luke's dark, angry face, her eyes shining with unshed tears. "I was so afraid. I was afraid he would die and they'd put Petie in some terrible place like the charity orphanage where I grew up. I had heard people whisper about Petie and call him a halfbreed and a savage, and I knew if they thought he had attacked Hugh, they would take him away from me. I had to run away with him. Don't you see, Luke I had to!"

Luke swallowed hard, aching inside when he thought how alone, frightened, and desperate Bethany must have felt that night in St. Louis. "Of course, I understand. You had to do it, and you did the right thing. But why didn't you just tell me the truth in Natchez when I first found you?"

Fresh agony rolled over Bethany's heart. "Because I wanted you to treat Petie like a son someday. I wanted you to love him, and I was afraid you wouldn't if you knew what he had done to Hugh. I knew you had left him once, and I didn't think you cared about him. I was afraid you wouldn't want a little boy who had almost killed someone!"

Old torments rose within Luke, ancient pain and rage and guilt, and he shut his eyes as he held Bethany's quivering body close.

"I killed a man when I was eight years old, Beth," he muttered against her hair.

Shocked, Bethany slowly lifted her face. Luke avoided her wide eyes, but he wanted to tell her. He wanted her to know.

"He was a Sioux warrior, and I stabbed him with his own knife," he went on, finding it hard to say things he had never voiced before. "His name was Panther Dog, and he killed my mother right in front of me." Luke swallowed convulsively as he saw it all again in his mind's eye. "He took his knife to her as if she was some kind of animal, butchering her, cutting away her blond hair—"

He stopped there, choking on the words, and Bethany could not stop her rising horror as some powerful emotion shuddered through Luke's frame.

"Luke, don't—" she began, but he went on in the same awful, strained voice.

"Let me tell you," he said gruffly. "Please, I want to tell you. After that, I was his slave for three years. He made me wear my mother's scalp around my neck on a rawhide strap. If I took it off, he beat me. Now I realize that he must have been crazy, but then I only knew he was mean and cruel." Luke was quiet a moment, and Bethany bit her lip, sick inside at the horrors he had experienced as a child and at the tragic irony that Luke had seen his mother die, just as Peeto had witnessed Snow Blossom's death.

"He kept me off by myself so I couldn't make any friends. No one in the tribe liked him anyway; they were afraid of him, too, I think. Except for Snow Blossom. She came to see me when Panther Dog was hunting. When he was gone, he tied me to a stake by a rope around my neck, like some kind of wild dog!"

A sob caught in Bethany's throat as Luke's fists clenched hard at the memory, but she stifled it, knowing he felt he had to tell her these things.

"One day after he left, the anger inside me built and built until I couldn't handle it anymore. I pulled and pulled until I broke my tether, then I ran into the woods and buried my mother's hair. I hid there all night, but he found me and whipped me until I couldn't walk. I waited until he fell asleep, then I crept over and took his hunting knife from its scabbard. I stabbed him with it, twice. I was so filled with hatred and anger that I didn't feel anything afterward—not guilt, not horror, not anything. I was just glad he was dead."

Bethany began to cry, heartbroken tears of loss for the childhood Luke had never had.

"Snow Blossom knew I did it, but she told the

elders she had seen a Blackfoot warrior kill him. They believed her, and I went to live in her family's tipi. That's when I began to learn their ways and see that there were good men among them. Panther Dog was a devil.''

Luke took Bethany's face between his hands, his eyes gentle. ''But I don't want you worrying about any of this anymore, Beth. Hugh will never bother either of you again, I swear. No one will ever know anything about what happened to you that night or what Pete did. Now, you stay here and rest for a while. I'll send Pete back in to sit with you.''

Luke kissed her gently. When he found Peeto waiting outside the door, he picked him up, hugging him tight for a long time, then set him on his feet and knelt beside him.

''Beth told me what you did that night in St. Louis, Pete,'' he said in a gruff voice. ''And it makes me proud. You're a brave boy, and I'm glad you were there to help her. Hugh's not going to hurt her again, I promise. Now, you go on in. Beth needs you.''

After his son had gone, Luke went downstairs in search of Hugh. He tried to control the rage he felt, rage seething and boiling with a need for release. He went methodically from room to room, then stopped in the doorway of the library, where he found Michelle sitting in a wing chair beside the fire while Hugh stood near the gallery door.

''Did you try to rape Beth when she was alone and defenseless in your house?'' Luke asked in a deceptively quiet tone.

The way Hugh guiltily averted his eyes was all the answer Luke needed.

Michelle gasped as Luke moved with the quickness

of a jungle cat, reaching Hugh in three long strides. The smaller man grunted as Luke's fingers closed over the lapels of his coat, nearly jerking him off the ground before he sent a steel-knuckled fist slamming toward his face. Hugh went flying backward against the wall, overturning a slender-legged table with a crash and a shattering of glass. But before he could crumple to the floor, Luke had him again by the front of his shirt. Luke bent over him, his face flushed with fury.

"If you ever touch my wife or son again, I'll kill you," he said, spitting the words out with harsh, barely controlled rage, then thrust Hugh away.

Michelle pressed herself deeper into the cushions, too frightened to move as Hugh slid into a crumpled heap on the floor and Luke stalked from the room without another word.

She waited a moment, not sure what to do, frightened by Luke's uncharacteristic savagery, but even more appalled by what he had accused Hugh of doing to Bethany. As Hugh groaned, then began to sob, she put her hands to her mouth, remembering how it felt to be hit with a hard, doubled fist. Her fingers went to the ridge in her nose that such a fist had made, and she shuddered, then moved toward Hugh Younger, taking her handkerchief from her skirt pocket as she knelt beside him.

"Monsieur? Hold this against your nose," she said softly.

"I'm no good," Hugh blubbered as he took it, blood running from his nose to soak the front of his white shirt and tan linen frock coat. His words surprised Michelle, but not as much as when he grabbed her hand and wept openly.

"Luke should have killed me! I wish he had! I want to die! I'm nothing without Anne! I never have been!"

"No one really wants to die," Michelle told him, then she pulled her hand away and rose to her feet. She left the room in search of Jemsy, who could help her get the distraught man up to his room.

I've made a horrible mistake and I wish it hadn't happened. I'm nothing without Aline. I don't know how—

"No one really wants to die," Michelle told him.
"We just think we do."

Chapter 19

Bethany did not see Hugh Younger again until the following morning. She was having breakfast with Luke, Peeto, and Michelle on the side gallery overlooking the goldfish pond when he came out of the house. Bethany stared at him, startled by his appearance. His left eye was swollen shut and there was an ugly black bruise spreading out over his nose and cheekbone. She looked quickly at Luke, but his face remained expressionless as he set down his coffee cup.

"Good morning, Hugh," Luke said noncommittally, watching Peeto get up and stand close to Bethany's chair. Luke felt a surge of parental pride at the courage his son continued to exhibit. He reached out to lay his palm on Peeto's dark curls.

"It's all right, Pete. Hugh won't hurt Beth or you again. What you did to protect Beth in St. Louis that night makes me proud. But now, you can run along if you want. Raffy's waiting by the kitchen."

Peeto stared at his father as if amazed by his words, then he gave Bethany a shy smile. Despite Hugh's presence, Bethany returned it, knowing how much Peeto had craved Luke's praise and attention. As Peeto ran off, she kept her eyes strictly away from

Hugh, then she was immediately alarmed as Luke put down his napkin.

"Hugh, I want to see you in the library as soon as you finish breakfast. Beth, I'd like you to accompany me into town tomorrow. Pete, as well, if you'd like."

"All right," Bethany murmured as Luke leaned down to brush her cheek with a kiss.

Bethany waited only a moment after he departed for the library before she made quick to flee the table herself, eager to be out of Hugh's company. She edged around Michelle's chair, hurrying across the gallery, but before she could reach the steps leading down to the fish pond, she was stopped by Hugh's hand on her shoulder.

"Wait, Bethany, please!"

Even his touch revolted her, and she whirled around, backing away from him until the stone banister ended her retreat. She stared up at Hugh's disfigured eye but all she could envision was that long-ago night in Peeto's nursery when he had lunged drunkenly at her, his hands squeezing and hurting, his breath sour in her face. She shivered with renewed loathing.

"Please, Beth, don't look at me like that. I didn't mean to hurt you. I was drunk and lonely, and I didn't know what I was doing. I only remember bits of it, anyway, and I wasn't even sure if they were real or some kind of ugly dream I'd had!"

Bethany stared at him without speaking, and Hugh continued on a desperate note. "I was so lonely after Anne died. I guess I just wanted somebody to hold on to for a while. If I could undo it, I would. Let me make it up to you, I'm begging you, Bethany. I've nearly stopped drinking now, and Luke and Andy are all the family I have left. Please!''

Bethany shrank away from his voice, his words, not believing anything he said. All she could think about was the pain and fear and hardship he had caused Peeto and her. She looked away from his pleading eyes, unable to bear the thought of living in the same house with him, even with Luke there to protect her.

Hugh leaned against the wall in deep dejection as Bethany turned to run down the steps and across the lawn. She would never forgive him for what he had done, he thought. Neither would Luke, and he really couldn't blame them. He turned slowly, to where Michelle still sat at the nearby breakfast table. She lowered her eyes as their gazes met, sipping from a small demitasse cup as Hugh returned to the table. She watched him surreptitiously as he slumped in a seat across from her. Her gaze lingered on the puffy, bruised eye, remembering when she had been beaten so badly that both her eyes were swollen shut. As always, images of the Hackett brothers made her hands tremble, and the fragile cup rattled noticeably as she tried to set it upon its saucer.

''Are you all right?'' Hugh asked, noting her pale face and attributing the fear in her eyes to his own presence.

''*Oui,*'' Michelle murmured, looking down at her lap, and Hugh let out a heavy sigh as he leaned back in his chair.

''You're a good friend of Bethany's, are you not?''

''*Oui.* I would do anything in this world for her. She saved my life.''

''Bethany Cole saved your life? How?''

"Please, monsieur, 'tis a painful memory."

"Forgive me," Hugh said at once, for the first time really looking at the woman across from him. She was pretty in a dainty sort of way, with her odd, yellowish eyes. She wore a plain black gown, as she had the day before, and he wondered if she had been recently widowed.

"May I ask for whom it is you mourn, and offer my sincere condolences."

"My father died nearly a month ago," she answered without looking at him.

"Your name is Michelle, is it not? May I be so familiar?" he asked, and at her nod, he continued. "Do you think Bethany will ever forgive me?"

Michelle's answer was truthful. "I cannot say, but she is very loving and unselfish. Please, *excusez-moi, monsieur.*"

Hugh watched her depart, then looked at the white wrought iron sideboard where a decanter of brandy stood on a gold tray. Every fiber in him leaned in that direction, urging him to drink it down, to let the fire warm his stomach and help him forget the cutting, neverending despair he still felt over Anne's death and, now, the hatred he received from everyone around him. His hands shook with the desire to take the bottle back to his room where he could erase from his mind the frightened look on Bethany's young face and the cold contempt in Luke's green eyes. He moved to the sideboard and lifted the bottle to his nose so he could smell the aroma that soothed him like nothing else could, then he gritted his teeth in self-disgust, forcing himself to set the brandy back on the tray. He hurried quickly away before he could weaken in his resolve.

* * *

Late that afternoon, as the sun sank low and the afternoon shadows lengthened across the lawns, Bethany pulled a warm red knit shawl around her shoulders as she sat beneath an arched wooden arbor covered with thick ivy. She had lingered there for most of the day, watching Peeto practice with his short bow and arrows. Tante Chloe had set Raffy to work in the kitchens, but Bethany hadn't wanted to remain so close to the house for fear of seeing Hugh again. Nor did she want Peeto to see him. He was just beginning to have a real home with a real father and a friend of his own age, and Hugh was only a reminder of the bad times in St. Louis. She wished he would just go away again and leave them all in peace.

A triumphant shout from Peeto interrupted her worried thoughts, and she clapped in approval at the sight of his arrow protruding from the trunk of a mimosa tree, very close to the center of the target he had made from her handkerchief.

Peeto jumped up and down, giving his Sioux yell, but his excited grin faltered as his gaze fastened on something past Bethany. When he quickly thrust his bow behind his back, Bethany turned and found Luke standing a few paces behind her. She colored guiltily, having been caught in the act of encouraging Peeto to practice his Indian ways.

"It's all my fault," she began nervously, coming to her feet to face Luke. "I know what you said, but I told him he could keep his things—"

To her dismay, Luke walked past her without answering and took the curved bow from the hands of his shamefaced son. But Luke's next words brought a sigh of relief.

"You were holding it wrong, Pete. If you put your thumb here, like this, you can improve your aim. Your grandfather taught me that trick. His name was Gray Sky."

Peeto's eyes grew wide as Luke took an arrow from his son's small fringed quiver, examining its feather for flaws before he laid it expertly against the string. His shot hit dead center and was still quivering from the impact as Luke put his arms around Peeto to help him shoot. Peeto's arrow nearly hit Luke's, and Luke patted his son's shoulder as he withdrew another arrow.

"Your mother, Snow Blossom, could shoot as well as any one of her six brothers," Luke said casually, smoothing back the feathers. "You look a lot like her, Pete, except for your eyes. She had big brown eyes."

Bethany's throat tightened with emotion. Finally, at long last, Luke was opening up to his son. She sat down to watch, not wanting to say or do anything to interfere with what was happening.

"Your mother and I were real good friends from the very first, like you and Raffy are," Luke said, letting fly another arrow. "She was my friend when no one else in the Mandan village would even talk to me. She even taught me her language."

Peeto was no longer watching Luke's expertise with the bow; he was listening raptly as Luke went on.

"I left the camp when I was fifteen because I could vaguely remember my father and Andy and Anne. But when I got back to St. Louis, I thought about Snow Blossom so much that I eventually went back with a military expedition. That's when I married your mother."

Another arrow thudded into the tree, as accurately

as the others, and Luke looked down at Peeto. ''I had to go on with Lewis and Clark, so I didn't know you had been born until I came back again. You were three then, remember?''

Peeto's eyes filled with tears. ''I remember you left, and we followed you. And I remember you saw us and came back, and then she fell and you were there close beside her.''

Peeto broke down, and Luke knelt, holding him tight.

''She fell that day, son. I didn't push her. We were arguing because she wanted me to take both of you back to St. Louis with me, and I couldn't do it. I'd seen the way the whites had treated me, and I knew it would be horrible for both of you. But she wouldn't listen. She tried to stop me and slipped on the rocks, but it was an accident, I swear it.''

Bethany started toward them as Luke stood with Peeto in his arms, closing his eyes as Peeto wrapped his little arms tightly around his neck. The child lay his head on Luke's broad shoulder, and Luke patted his back. Luke looked at Beth, stretching out his other arm, and she came quickly to the two people she loved more than life itself.

As they all three walked back to the house together, Bethany's heart took wing because all the barriers dividing them had been transformed into bridges that united them. There was nothing now that could keep them from being a real family.

Bethany was still wrapped in good feelings as she sat propped against her pillows. Luke had offered to check on Peeto tonight, and Bethany could not stop smiling. Everything was so wonderful that sometimes she was afraid it couldn't last, that something awful would bring it all to an end. But she shook those negative thoughts away as Luke crossed the room to her, snuffing the candles along the way. He left burning the one beside the bed, then swept back the filmy mosquito baire and slipped out of his dressing robe.

"He's sound asleep," he said, pulling the lacy drape back into place, then turning to plump his pillow. Bethany waited impatiently to be taken into his arms.

"What the devil is this?" he muttered, drawing out a charred green stone from beneath the pillows.

Bethany blushed as he held it in his palm, looking at her questioningly.

"A love charm," she admitted, embarrassed because she knew he was going to laugh at her.

"A what?"

"Oh, nothing. Tante Chloe gave it to me to make you love me."

Luke did laugh then, and Bethany was quick to defend herself.

"Well, it worked, didn't it? It brought you back to me after only two weeks!" she reminded him.

Luke leaned against the headboard, his green eyes glinting. His hand came up to slide beneath her hair to the nape of her neck. He drew her face to him, and their lips met and tasted, making Bethany sigh with pleasure.

"You're what brought me back, sweet. Not a charm, not a love spell, just you, my dreamsong," he muttered against her mouth. "So you can throw that dirty rock away."

Bethany allowed him to lower her to the pillows,

but she took the love gris-gris from his hand, smiling as she slipped it back beneath her pillow.

"Just to be on the safe side," she murmured, pulling him down to her lips again.

Luke gave a low laugh, moving until he lay over her, both hands entangled in her soft blond curls as he caressed her brow with his lips, then her cheeks and mouth and ears.

"Give me a baby tonight, Luke, please. I want to have your child so much."

Her whisper was breathless, and Luke felt the most indescribable tenderness for her roll over his heart. He smiled as he kissed her.

"You know I'll give you anything you want, anything at all."

"I want children, then, lots of children, one to fill every bedchamber of Cantigny."

That request brought a soft laugh from Luke. "That's about twenty children," he reminded her.

Bethany smiled. "Just one will do for now," she murmured. "One with your eyes and your hair and your smile—"

Luke's mouth stilled her whisper, and the room became quiet after that, except for their low murmurings of love and shared pleasure as the candle burned low, flickering one last time on the entwined couple in the bed before they were enveloped in darkness.

Chapter 20

In order to get Bethany and Peeto out of Hugh's company, Luke took them and Raffy into the Vieux Carré the following morning. He needed to visit the wharves, since the latest shipment of furs had arrived from his trappers in the Rockies. As he helped his wife and son from the carriage on the levee road, he gave a self-mocking grin, realizing he no longer liked to be out of their company. He would never have dreamed a slip of a girl like Bethany could tame his wanderlust the way she had.

"I need to speak to the captain of the *Duchess* about my pelts," he told Bethany. "Would you like to come along?"

Bethany smiled up at him, but Peeto was pulling her in the opposite direction, toward a vendor selling nougats.

"Petie wants some candy. We'll meet you there in a little while."

"Don't be long," Luke admonished, then strode off toward the keelboat alongside the landing.

Bethany watched him for a moment, thinking he was the most magnificent man alive, then she let Peeto and Raffy propel her toward the vendor's pushcart.

She retrieved several coins from her velvet drawstring purse and purchased each child a small sack of candy.

''Come on, boys, let's have a cup of chocolate, too,'' she suggested, then followed as they ran off to the closest dockside café.

The late-December morning was bright and sunny, with a cool wind blowing in off the wide, muddy river as they sat at one of the outdoor tables and enjoyed the sweet, warm beverage. Peeto and Raffy finished their drinks quickly, and Bethany remained behind as the children scampered off again to watch huge, heavy barrels of Kentucky whiskey being winched ashore from a flatboat moored next to the *Duchess*.

It was good to be on the waterfront again, she thought, remembering when she lived in the orphanage in St. Louis and had visited Captain Hosie on Laclede's Landing. The wharves around her now were even more busy than St. Louis's had been, with sailors and stevedors laboring over their duties all up and down the levee. A multitude of merchants and curious townspeople milled about as well, always on the lookout for a ship bearing goods in demand.

Bethany's gaze moved from one thing to another as she sipped her chocolate, while keeping close tabs on the boys, only vaguely aware of Luke's tall, broad-shouldered form on the deck of the keelboat. She was glad for an excuse to be away from Hugh, but at the same time she hated leaving Michelle alone with him. Although Bethany had tried to persuade Michelle to come to the wharves with them, she had refused, as she had refused to venture into any public place since she had seen Jack Hackett at the open market.

The thought of those terrible men initiated a wary look around from Bethany, but she reminded herself that Luke seemed to think his posted reward had driven them from the city. Such posters were likely to cause the capture of the criminal, Bethany knew from hard-earned experience. Memories of the calaboose still bothered her, until she remembered that Luke had decided to ask her to become his wife on that night. Such a development almost made her time in the dark, cold cell seem worthwhile, though she certainly had not thought so then.

Her eyes finally settled on a group of small, red-headed children walking along the docks with a sailor. Her hand moved to her flat stomach. She hoped so much that she was with child. Though it was too soon since her last monthly flow to know, she prayed that she was. She wanted a whole houseful of children, just as she had told Luke, enough to fill all the bedrooms of Cantigny and the schoolroom as well—especially the schoolroom. She herself would teach all her children to read.

Bethany continued to watch the group of children, gasping as one tiny little girl tripped on a plank and would have fallen hard if not for the quick hands of the sailor. Bethany smiled as he swung the child playfully into the air, the little girl's gleeful squeal audible above the other sounds on the wharf. Bethany's face suddenly went sober, and she sat very still for a moment. Then she was up and running toward the sailor without regard for propriety.

Luke glanced up from the bill of lading he was scrutinizing to check on Bethany's whereabouts and frowned when he found her gone from her place in front of the café. His concern grew more acute when he did not find her with Peeto and Raffy, who were sitting on a bale of cotton and watching the unloading

of the adjacent flatboat. He scanned the landing, relieved when he saw Bethany running through the
crowd. But he froze as she flung herself into the arms
of a tall, blond sailor. As the young sailor swung
Luke's wife off the ground and twirled her around,
Luke started down the gangplank, his eyes never leaving the happy pair across the way.

"Oh, Marcus, Marcus, I can't believe it's you!"
Bethany was saying to her childhood friend. "It's been
so long, nearly two years now! What are you doing
here?"

"My ship's in port, out yonder in the river. See?
The frigate *Wayward*. I've been all around the world,
Bethy—to China and New South Wales! You wouldn't
believe the fantastic things I've seen! But I've thought
about you often, and Captain Hosie. How are you?
And what are you doing down here in New Orleans?"

Bethany squeezed both his hands in hers. "I live
here now, with my husband. He's here, too. You must
come meet him!"

She turned to look for Luke on the deck of the
keelboat, and was surprised to find him only a few
paces behind her. The expression on his face was anything but pleased, and when his gaze dropped to
where she held Marcus's hands, she let go at once,
realizing what Luke must be thinking.

"Luke, Luke, come here! You must meet Marcus!
He's my best and oldest friend. He was at the orphanage with me. Remember, I've told you about
him."

Luke looked at the sea-bronzed face and sun-
bleached hair of Bethany's handsome young friend and
remembered, indeed, that Bethany had mentioned
Marcus. She had said he was coming back to get her.

He had been the one Bethany had said she would take as a lover when he returned.

"How do you do, sir," Marcus said, reaching out to shake Luke's hand. "Bethany's always been like my little sister, you know."

Luke relaxed a little, clasping the young man's hand, and Bethany laughed, glad to see Luke's smile, then looked down at the children with Marcus.

"Who are these children, Marcus?"

"They're the McCaffreys." He ruffled the red-gold locks of a little boy who looked to be around twelve. "This is young Daniel, and these are his little brother and sisters. That's Natasha, she's three, and Bobby's four, and little Becky, here, is barely two."

"Hello," Bethany said, smiling at each child in turn. "You all are very handsome with your pretty red hair," she turned to Marcus. "I was admiring them when I recognized you, Marcus. Aren't they sweet, Luke?" she asked, smiling up at him.

"Yes, they are," Luke agreed amiably, and Bethany turned back to Marcus as Peeto and Raffy arrived to look over the little redheads.

"Why don't you give them some of your candy?" Bethany said to Peeto as the three older boys eyed each other warily. Peeto opened his sack at once, generously allowing each McCaffrey to take a handful of sugary nougats.

"Do they live here in town?" Bethany asked.

Marcus shook his head, making sure the children were busy choosing candies before he answered. "They're orphans, Beth, like us. Their ship went down in a storm on its way from Ireland. We came upon them afloat in a longboat in the Straits of Florida. Their parents perished."

"Oh, no, how terrible," Bethany murmured, turning concerned eyes to the children. "What will happen to them?"

"My captain's taking Danny on as a cabin boy, but the little ones will have to go to the Ursulines, I guess. I'm supposed to take them there today. We ship out again in the morning, for Barbados this time."

Marcus's brown eyes met Bethany's gray ones, both of them remembering their years in the charity orphanage. Bethany's heart twisted.

"But, Marcus, they're all so little. They need a mother."

Luke watched Bethany's lovely face fill with sympathy, then she turned, her great, imploring eyes on him, and he felt himself weakening even before she voiced the suggestion he knew was coming.

"Luke, we can't let them go there. They need to stay together as a family until Danny can come back for them." She stooped, picking up little Becky and smoothing soft wisps of the child's coppery hair away from her freckled face. "She's so little, Luke. Look, she's just a baby."

Luke reached out, and the little girl put her small hand in his large one, and he felt a twinge of what Bethany was obviously feeling.

"Can't we take them to Cantigny, Luke? Just for a little while? I promise I'll work really hard to find a good home for them, one where they'll all be together. Tante Chloe will help me take care of them, and Michelle, too. Please, Luke."

"I think we can find room for them," he answered, chucking little Becky under the chin. "And, Marcus, you must come back to Cantigny with us tonight so that you and Bethany can have a visit before you set sail in the morning.''

''Thank you, sir, I would like that very much,'' said Marcus, and Luke was pleased by the radiant smile that Bethany bestowed upon him.

On the coast of Louisiana past the great Pontchartrain Lake, the ocean waves rolled in to break in foamy lines along the white sand. Hugh Younger watched Luke walk with Bethany along the beach, their laughter floating faintly to him on the sea wind. In the month he had been at Cantigny, he had been utterly amazed at the change in Luke Randall. Until now, he had never heard Luke laugh, even when they were children.

Although Bethany and Peeto still avoided Hugh like a deadly disease, he couldn't help but see how much the three of them loved each other. Much in the same way he had loved Anne before she had been taken from him. Andrew had been amiable enough to him, but Michelle was the only one who acted as if she liked him. His eyes found her where she walked along with Becky McCaffrey. Michelle reminded him so much of Anne, with her gentle ways and quiet smile.

Andrew had told him of the terrible things Michelle had endured, and Hugh knew she was still frightened of the Hackett brothers. He had barely been able to persuade her to come out to the beach today, and if it hadn't been for the children's pleas, she probably would have remained in seclusion on Cantigny. Michelle was too pretty and young to shut herself up, he decided. Though she was not very strong at the moment, emotionally or physically, it was her steadfast encouragement that had kept him from drinking since his arrival in Louisiana. Somewhat to his surprise he realized that the fact that she was a woman of color made no difference to him; more than anything, he did not want to see contempt for him in her amber eyes. Suddenly eager to hear her soft voice, he got up to help her with the children, just as Luke and Bethany collapsed together on a quilt a short distance up the beach.

"Oh, thank you for bringing me out here, Luke. The Gulf of Mexico is so vast and beautiful, just like Marcus described to us before he left," Bethany said, leaning back on her elbows. "It was worth the long carriage ride to see all the different shades of blue and green." She turned her face to him. "Have you ever been out on a ship at sea, Luke?"

He watched the never-ending sea breeze play with Bethany's loosened curls, noticing how her nose was growing pink from the day in the sun. He handed her the wide-brimmed straw hat she had brought with her.

"I sailed to Cuba once on business. For days, we didn't see land, or anything else except sea and sky."

Bethany looked back at the crashing waves. "I think that would frighten me. I like to have my feet on solid ground." She laughed. "But Petie's like a little fish now that you taught him to swim. Just look."

Luke gazed down the beach where Peeto and Raffy splashed and cavorted in the shallow waves. Along the shore behind them, three bright coppery heads dug in the sand close to where Michelle sat next to Hugh on a blanket. The McCaffrey children had ridden in the second coach with Hugh and Michelle. They are becoming very close, Luke thought, then his eyes sharpened as a towheaded child stood up among the other little ones. He frowned, sitting up to take a closer look.

"Who is that child with the blond hair?"

Bethany shaded her eyes, dutifully regarding her adopted brood, then she smiled as she adjusted her hat to shade her face.

"That's Betty Ann, of course."

"Of course," Luke said. "Who is Betty Ann?"

"Tante Chloe found her at the open market, the poor little thing."

"Bethany . . ." Luke began sternly, but she interrupted him.

"She was wandering around all alone. Her father just left her there to fend for herself. She's only seven, Luke." Bethany sat up on her heels, pulling her white skirts and petticoats out of the way as she sifted the white sand through her fingers.

Luke shook his head. "Beth, this has got to stop somewhere. You can't take in every stray in the city."

"Please don't call them that. They're not strays. They're just children without anyone to love them. I was like that once, before I met you and Petie."

Luke reached out to take her hand. "We were lucky to find you."

Bethany smiled and leaned down to kiss him, but her mind was still on the children.

"Luke, I've been thinking—"

"Uh oh," he said, pulling her down on her back, then turning to prop his head in one hand while he looked down into her face. "How many orphans have you found?"

Bethany laughed. "None. Yet. But I know there are more in the city who need a loving home." She hesitated as Luke's lips brushed her ear, making her momentarily lose her train of thought. She waited until he stopped.

"Eventually, even Cantigny will fill up." She looked at him, then continued in a rush. "So I was wondering if I could have the old mill to fix up as a home for the children. Michelle is so good with them, and she could live there with them, not in dormitories but in cozy little bedrooms with fireplaces and ruffled curtains. It would give Michelle a good way to earn her own keep. She has been uncomfortable living here on our charity, though I told her she's like part of the family."

Luke was silent, and Bethany anxiously tried to read a reaction in his eyes, with no success.

"I know you're too busy with your fur business and the cane and rice accounts and all, but I could take care of all of it, Luke, really I could. I'm a very good manager, if you'd just give me a chance, and it would provide the children with a real home instead of an orphanage. I would be willing to work hard if you'd just let me borrow enough money to rebuild the mill—"

At that, Luke sat up, impatient with her. "*Borrow* the money? For God's sake, Beth, you're my wife. You don't have to grovel to me like this. If you want a children's home on Cantigny, you can have it. With a hundred children, if you want."

"Just like that?" Bethany asked, amazed at his generosity. She had been prepared to use a little persuasion on him.

"It would be worth it to have a little peace and quiet in the house. I can hear those redheads yelling and laughing all the way down in my library," Luke said, though he smiled.

Bethany reached up to trace the dimpled groove in his cheek.

"Don't be so sure. Our own children will be just as distracting, and I'll expect you to pay more attention to them."

"I'd rather just concentrate on you."

"Good," Bethany murmured, meeting his kiss eagerly for several long moments. Then, as Luke's mouth left hers, she gave a secret smile. "You have about eight months or so before you'll have to divide your attention between us."

Bethany felt him tense, then he lifted his head slowly to look at her.

"Are you telling me what I think you're telling me?"

"Yes," Bethany said with a breathless smile. "Autumn will bring you a son, or a daughter, or both, if we're lucky."

She was in no way prepared for the enthusiastic hug Luke gave her or for the hoarse words he uttered against her hair.

"Why haven't you told me?"

"I wanted to be sure first."

"You're going to have to take better care of yourself. You can't carry Becky and Bobby around as you have been, you hear? Maybe we should get in out of the sun—"

Bethany stopped his words by placing her fingers on his lips, but she was more than happy with the pleasure she read in his expression.

"I won't do anything to hurt the baby. I've wanted your child too much for that."

"And I want you, well and safe and at my side," Luke murmured, his heart warm with the news, yet feeling a peculiar terror for Bethany. Childbirth could be a terrible ordeal for a woman. He had seen them die from it too many times in the Sioux camp. Even the thought of Bethany's going through such agony made his stomach turn over.

"Promise me you'll take care," he whispered.

She smiled. "I will give you a dozen healthy babies, you'll see. Come, let's wade with the children. They hardly know you because you're always working. You'll have to stop that when our baby comes," she teased, then was up, darting down the beach.

Luke took off after her, wanting to catch her and make her slow down before she fell and hurt herself.

Chapter 21

Bethany leaned against the ornate wrought iron railing of Andrew's house on Toulouse Street, her eyes sweeping over the people gathering below her balcony for the great Fat Tuesday parade of Mardi Gras season.

She was already dressed in her costume, which Luke had commissioned Madame Josephine to make for her, and her long, crimson velvet skirt swept the iron rail as she held her black lace mantilla out of the way. She peered down the street toward Rue des Ramparts, looking for Peeto and Raffy. Both children had been in sight just moments ago where they watched a juggler tossing yellow wooden pins in the air, but now they were nowhere to be seen.

She frowned, perturbed with them. She had given them explicit instructions not to stay long since Luke was expected home soon. She moved off the balcony into the white-and-pale-green bedchamber she and Luke used when they were in town, then out a different door to the iron gallery that faced the inside piazza. The cobbled stable was deserted, indicating that Luke and Andrew had not arrived yet from Cantigny, where they had been supervising the rebuilding of the old mill. The children would move in soon, and Bethany was more than pleased with the cheerful yellow walls and ruffled chintz curtains. No one would be lonely or frightened in those bright rooms.

Actually, Bethany would have preferred to remain at Cantigny with Tante Chloe and the children, but Luke had insisted that the family come to town for the fireworks and parades, and Bethany was pleased he wanted them with him. Except that Hugh had come as well, and she could do without his offensive presence.

She looked down over the railing to where Hugh sat on a garden bench with Michelle. They were hard to see in the gathering dusk, but much to Bethany's chagrin, she saw that Hugh was holding Michelle's hand. She frowned, wishing Michelle would stay away from Hugh like the rest of them did. The two had been spending a lot of time together, and although Hugh had stopped drinking and his behavior had been without reproach since his arrival, Bethany couldn't bring herself to trust him. She probably never would be completely at ease around him, though she understood Luke couldn't just cast him out of his house, especially when he was behaving so well. Michelle was just too kind and gentle to think ill of him. But she hadn't known Hugh before, and Bethany and Peeto had.

"Michelle!" she called down. "Have the boys come back through the gate?"

"Non," came Michelle's soft reply, and Bethany's frown deepened as she returned to the street balcony.

Ten minutes later, as darkness began to fall, she grew even more worried. After twenty minutes, she was fully alarmed. Not willing to wait another moment, she hurried down the narrow inside staircase with its carved mahogany banister and rushed down the long, narrow front hall. As she threw her black velvet cape over her shoulders, Michelle and Hugh entered through the French doors of the courtyard.

"I'm going to look for Petie," Bethany told them, turning for the door. "I won't be long."

"Not alone!" Michelle protested in dismay. "Luke told us never to go out alone at night. It is especially dangerous during carnival, Beth, with all the crowds about!"

"I have to. Petie and Raffy should be back by now. I'm afraid something's happened to them."

Hugh stepped out to block her passage. "Luke and Andy will be back any time now. Wait for them, and we'll all search together."

Bethany hesitated, twisting the laces of her cape with nervous fingers. "But it's getting so dark outside!" She looked toward the windows, suddenly determined to find the boys. Her chin tilted up in an obstinate fashion. "Move out of my way, Hugh. I'm worried about them, and I'm going now."

"Luke will kill me if I let you go out alone at night in your condition. At least let me go with you."

"Frankly, I'd feel a lot safer without you along," Bethany snapped, then half regretted her harsh words at the disapproving look on Michelle's face. Hugh was right, and Bethany knew it. Luke would be furious with her if she went out alone among the crowds.

"All right, come with me if you must," she said, "but let's hurry. Michelle, if Luke comes, tell him we've gone up the street to look for the boys."

Michelle nodded, standing on the front stoop as

Bethany stepped into the street with Hugh right behind her.

"Do you have any idea where they might have gone?" Hugh asked, peering at the revelers jostling and pushing through the narrow thoroughfare.

"They were up there near the intersection last time I saw them, but they might be at the sweetshop just around the corner. Raffy said once that the baker sells them a dozen sweetcakes for a penny."

Suddenly sure she would find the children at the Vermeil Bakery, Bethany hurried off in that direction, leaving Hugh to follow as best he could. He quickly caught up with her, and though Bethany didn't particularly like his touching her, she let him take her elbow as he shouldered a path through the crowded street.

A short conversation with Monsieur Pierre Vermeil informed them that the two boys had been there not long before, but had crossed the street to watch the blacksmith at his forge.

"Could they have gone home a different way?" Hugh suggested when they found the smithy closed for the celebration.

Bethany shook her head, undecided about what to do next. She wished Luke was with them. He would know what to do.

"Madame! Madame!"

Bethany spun around at the scream and found Raffy sprinting toward her, his eyes huge with fear.

"Dey's gots Marster Pete! Dey's gots me, too, but I's kicked dem and gots away!"

"Who? Raffy, tell me who!" Bethany cried, grabbing the child by the shoulders. "Who's got Petie?"

"Dere's two of dem. Big white mens. Dey done

taked 'em off to de graveyard yonder," Raffy cried, pointing wildly up the street. "Dey was real mean, and dey say dey's gwine to cut off'n Marster Pete's head and send it to de big marster!"

Bethany's blood ran cold. If it hadn't been for Hugh's grip on her arm, her legs would have crumpled beneath her.

"Run home, Raffy. As fast as you can," Hugh ordered, suddenly taking charge of the situation. "You, too, Beth. It's got to be the Hacketts! Maybe I can stop them before they get away with Pete!"

"No, no, I'm coming with you!" Bethany cried. "Run, Raffy, and bring back Luke and Andy. Hurry, hurry!"

Hugh was already sprinting up the banquette, ignoring the last stragglers on their way to the Place d'Armes, as he made his way to the tall, iron gates of the old Cemetery of St. Louis. Bethany rushed up just behind him, her heart in her throat.

"Pete!" Hugh shouted into a darkness lit faintly by a lamppost as he stepped inside the open gates. His voice echoed eerily along the high, whitewashed brick walls enclosing the rows of tombs, and Bethany stopped behind him, looking fearfully at the white crypts gleaming ghostly in the gloom. In her mind, she again saw Michelle's battered face after the Hacketts had held her captive, and her stomach twisted with icy horror to think of innocent Peeto in their hands.

"Petie, Petie! Where are you?" she cried in sudden panic, causing Hugh to whirl furiously on her.

"Dammit it, Beth, get back to the house where you'll be safe! I'll find him!"

"No need, boy. We's got the kid right here."

Both Bethany and Hugh jerked toward the gruff voice coming from the shadows, appalled to see Jack Hackett rise like a wraith not far away, his feet braced on a low tombstone. Braid Hackett stood a few feet behind him, one of his muscular forearms clenched tightly around Peeto's throat.

In the split second that followed, Hugh moved first, thrusting Bethany behind him as he charged at Jack Hackett. Bethany screamed as the outlaw lifted his right arm and pulled the trigger of the heavy, double-loaded flintlock pistol in his hand. Hugh lunged sideways as the bullet discharged, but he wasn't fast enough. The blast knocked him backward and he lay motionless at the base of a kneeling marble angel.

Bethany darted down an adjacent path past the crowded tombs, but Jack was quicker, despite his bulk. Her head jerked back as he caught a handful of her hair, and she screamed, falling to her knees, only to be jerked up again as Jack Hackett dragged her through the dark maze of graves.

"Stop, stop!" she cried, fighting him until his fist hit hard against the side of her head, rendering her dizzy. Rough hands clutched her, pulling her bodily atop a cold stone vault. Jack Hackett laid his gun on the slab, then held Bethany down with both hands around her throat.

"Did yer think we'd ferget ye, bitch?" he growled from between gritted teeth. "Yer the one who kilt our brother, Bucko, and yer man done broke Braid's jaw till he can't talk plain 'tall. We's been waitin' and watchin' fer a chance to git ye, and nows we's gonna see what ye think 'bout seein' yer family git kilt. How much ye think yore man'll up his reward after we's cuts up the two of youse? Randall ain't gonna like what we's gonna do to youse, that's for shore.''

Bethany nearly choked from his foul breath pouring down into her face. She struggled and screamed as his dirty fingers grasped the front of her bodice, tearing it to her waist with one sharp jerk. She kicked and clawed at him as his big, grimy hands mauled her bare breasts, and he yowled in pain as she managed to gouge her fingernails into one of his eyes.

''Hep me wit' her, Braid,'' Jack roared in rage. As Jack's brother moved to assist, Peeto broke free, aiming his small boot in a swift arc toward Jack Hackett's head. It connected with a horrible crack, sending the big man rolling. Bethany scrambled to one side, feeling for the pistol. When she found it, she fired it blindly at Braid. The powder flashed, and Braid yelped, ducking behind the nearest tomb. Bethany grabbed Peeto's hand, sobbing with fear as they ran down the intersecting paths, feeling their way in the darkness among the cold marble crypts and shrines. They had to hide! Hide until Raffy brought Luke!

Luke paced back and forth in the narrow hallway on Toulouse Street, stopping again in front of Michelle and Andrew.

''How long have they been gone?''

''Only about fifteen minutes,'' Michelle answered.

''And Hugh's with her? You're sure?''

''*Oui*, they left together—''

Michelle was interrupted as the door burst open and Raffy fell breathlessly to his knees in front of Luke.

"Dey's got Marster Pete, dey gots him! Doze Hackett mens!"

Luke's fingers closed around the boy's arms, nearly lifting him off his feet.

"Where? Where?"

"In de graveyard! De one of St. Louis. I's told de madame and Marster Hugh. Dey's gone dere to gets him."

"Oh, God," Luke said, whirling to face Andrew. "Go for the night watch, Andy, now! I'll see if I can find them in the cemetery."

Luke hurried to retrieve his pistols from the study, checking to make sure they were loaded before he rushed out into the night. He ran up the banquette toward Ramparts Street, cursing the crowd, but as he neared the intersection where the entrance of the cemetery was located, the streets grew quiet and deserted. The cemetery's front gates stood ajar, and he kept his finger on the trigger as he edged warily through the opening.

The moon had risen enough for Luke to make out the hulking shapes of the crypts. Deep shadows crossed the adjacent rows of tombs, and he pressed his back against the wall, not underestimating the Hacketts. They were bloodthirsty, sadistic murderers, and they had his wife and son.

He froze as a low, tortured groan sounded close at hand, then inched closer until he made out the shape of a body sprawled beneath a stone angel. The man's head and shoulders were hidden in the black shadow, and with his heart in his throat, Luke knelt to turn the face into the faint moonlight.

"Hugh! Hugh, can you hear me?" he whispered,

his eyes on the dark stain spreading over his brother-in-law's chest. "Where's Beth and Pete?"

Hugh groaned and his voice came hoarsely. "The Hacketts have them. Somewhere inside. You got to find them—"

"Hang on, Hugh. Andy's coming with help," Luke said softly. He listened a moment for any sound that might lead him to Bethany, but the night was quiet except for the faraway revelry of Mardi Gras merrymakers. Luke moved stealthily along the dark path. He drew up, every muscle rigid, as Bethany's terrified scream suddenly erupted somewhere deep inside the bowels of the cemetery.

Bethany jerked away from Braid's hand before her own cry had died away. She sent her fist against his face in a quick jab, and when he yelped in pain and grabbed his nose, she thrust Peeto into the narrow space between two stone angels, where they could fit easily, but a man Braid's size could not follow. She pushed Peeto down a path on the other side of the tall angels, and they ducked behind another tomb. Her heart drumming in her chest, she hugged the child close.

"I got 'em trapped like rats, Jack, behind them angels," Braid's voice shouted not far away.

"Come on, Petie," she mouthed into the boy's ear, then bent low, creeping quietly with him around an ancient burial site. She pressed her back against a rectangular crypt that stood six feet high. It had a flat top, overgrown with grass and weeds, and she held Peeto very close as she whispered into his ear.

"Lie down on top in the weeds where they can't

see you. And don't move. Promise me you won't move.''

"But what about you?" he whispered fearfully.

"If I get up there, too, they'll see us. Now go on! I'll find somewhere else to hide."

She boosted him up as best she could, waiting for him to settle among the high weeds on top of the vault. The sound of a boot scraping against marble sent her edging quickly around the opposite side of the crypt. She squatted down in the dark, holding her breath. Slow, stalking footsteps came closer, and Bethany inched farther away, fear making her heart pound in great, hard thuds. She drew up in horror as the stomach-turning smell of rancid bear grease filled her nostrils.

Braid!

Bethany looked around frantically, praying the men wouldn't see Peeto. She had to lead them away! If she could only make it to the outside walls where the stacked oven tombs were located, then she could feel her way along the bricks to the entrance gates.

Ducking down a path to a dark spot, she nearly fainted when she heard the Hacketts still very close to Peeto's hiding place. As she reached the high outside wall, she cried out, hoping to draw them away from Peeto, then felt her way along the front of the oven crypts. Her fingers moved along the bricks and hinged doors, groping for a foothold or crevice to use to scale the wall. She sank to her knees in terror as Jack Hackett suddenly appeared around the front of an ornate grave topped with double copper urns. To her horror, a lantern now swung from his hand, and she pressed herself back into the shadows, away from the flickering light. He stopped, looking around, and

Bethany held her breath. Then he suddenly thrust the lamp in her direction, illuminating her where she crouched close to the ground.

"Now whatcha gonna do, gal?" he cried with an evil sneer, guffawing harshly as Bethany fled in panic in the opposite direction.

A turn in the wall took her into the safety of darkness again, and when her searching palms found a door with a broken hinge, she fumbled desperately with the bolt, trying to open it. When it finally gave way, she crawled inside, desperate for any sanctuary from her pursuer. As Jack Hackett's taunting yell sounded just behind her, Bethany scrambled deeper into the oven. As the lantern glow appeared outside the door, she sat very still on her hands and knees, her chest heaving, and it took a moment to recognize the sickening-sweet odor of rotting flesh. She gagged, realizing that it was on a crumbling casket that she knelt. Horrified at the idea of being enclosed with a decaying corpse, she began to claw her way out of the oven crypt, despite the threat that awaited her in the fresh air.

"Not so fast, missy," came Jack's voice. Bethany began to scream as he blocked her exit from the oven tomb with his burly forearm.

"So ye picked yer own grave to save me the trouble," he cackled cruelly, lifting the hinged iron door that covered the opening. "I don't even need to waste me bullets, now does I?"

As the heavy iron door clanged shut, enveloping her in pitch blackness, Bethany screamed in absolute horror. She screamed and screamed, her body rigid with terror and the horrible smell of death, her own hysterical shrieks reverberating in her ears in the cramped echo chamber in which she was imprisoned.

It was Bethany's muffled screams that led Luke to her. As he rounded a corner deep in the cemetery, Jack Hackett loomed up in front of him, a lantern swinging in his hand. Luke didn't hesitate. He fired, and a black-edged hole appeared between the outlaw's eyes, freezing his cruel, leering smile into a mask of death.

Luke forgot about Hackett even before he fell, and began frantically searching the high vaults around him for Bethany and Peeto. He came to an abrupt stop as a gun barrel jabbed viciously into his back.

"You done kilt my brother and now I'm gonna kill you," came Braid's grunted threat through his misshapen jaw. Luke whipped to one side, going for Braid's pistol as a shrill Sioux yell ripped through the air and Peeto hurtled himself off the crypt where he had crept unnoticed, drawn by Bethany's cries. Braid turned and fired, and Peeto fell hard as metal ripped through his arm, spreading white-hot agony with it.

Luke was on Braid in an instant, his knees pinning the outlaw's chest to the ground as he drove his fist into Braid's face with all his strength. He brought his fist down again and again as all the anger, frustration, and hatred he felt came gushing out in blind rage.

Braid lay still in death before Peeto's cry of pain cut through Luke's bloodlust. He sat back on his heels, his chest heaving as he crawled to Peeto and lifted the boy against him.

Peeto struggled to free himself, clutching his bleeding arm with one hand as he pointed to the

nearby ovens. "They put Beth in one of the ovens! I
heard them! You've got to get her out!"

Shouting voices sounded at the front gates, and
Luke yelled for Andrew as he ran along the wall, his
heart growing cold when he heard Bethany's faint
screams somewhere in the endless tiers of oven crypts
that stretched along the outer walls.

"Beth! Beth! Where are you?" he called in hopeless horror, trying to pinpoint her muffled cries. In
the darkness, it was impossible to find the right crypt,
and as her cries suddenly died away, he went into an
absolute panic, forcing the locks on one door after
another, down the long line, iron hinges squeaking
and clanging in the night as he broke open graves that
had been bolted for decades and others that still
reeked of death.

Then Bethany cried out again, very close, and he
pulled open the door to release her horrible screams
of terror. He felt inside for her, his fingers touching
the velvet of her dress. He pulled her into his arms,
crying her name over and over as he clamped her
against him.

"I've got you, I've got you! Listen to me, Beth!"

Her shrill cries finally quieted, her stiff limbs suddenly going limp against him as she sobbed into his
chest. Luke picked her up and carried her through the
darkness to where several men with torches were
bending over Peeto.

"Is Beth all right?" Andrew asked in concern as
Luke stepped into the glow of the fires.

"The bastard locked her in one of the ovens," he
said, his own words hoarse with rage. "Is Pete all
right?"

"It's just a flesh wound, but Hugh's in real bad

shape. They've already taken him to Charity Hospital.''

Luke knelt beside Peeto, still holding Bethany in his arms. ''She's going to be all right, Pete, and so are you. The Hacketts are dead now. They'll never hurt us again.''

He pulled Peeto up, holding both his wife and son tight as they clung to him, weeping out their terror and fear.

Epilogue

Cantigny Plantation
February 1812

Bethany's eyes fluttered open as an infant's thin wail awakened her. She sat up at once in bed. Luke was no longer beside her, but she immediately found him across the room beside the cradles. She smiled as he reached down to pick up one of their four-month-old twin daughters, then drew on her quilted robe and left the warm covers.

"Sssh, little one," Luke was crooning softly as Bethany joined him. She shook her head in wonder, still amazed by what a wonderful father Luke had become, not only to the twins but to Peeto as well. Even the children out at the Mill Home received a good-sized dose of his warmth and generosity. As it turned out, Luke loved children as much as she did.

"Is it Tara or Shanna?" she whispered mischievously, knowing he found it hard to tell the identical twins apart.

"Shanna, I think," he answered, sitting down in the rocker near the fire. He lay the baby on his lap, smiling down into her cherubic face as she held tightly to two of his fingers and made happy, gurgling sounds.

A moment later, Tara decided she needed some attention, too, and Bethany tenderly lifted her other daughter in her arms, kissing her downy blond hair.

"Yes, my little love, Mama's here," she whispered, sitting down in a second rocker across from Luke.

The chairs in front of the hearth creaked in tandem in the quiet hours of early morning, and Luke and Bethany smiled across at each other.

"They're beautiful, aren't they?" he said with pride. "They look more like you every day with their blond hair and gray eyes." He chuckled. "I've never seen Pete so crazy about anybody in his life. He's like a little mother hen to them, and Raffy's just as bad."

Bethany laughed softly. "I know. Sometimes they get a little carried away with rocking the cradles, though. I'm sure Tara and Shanna must feel at times as if they're in a runaway carriage."

Luke laughed and soon both babies slept peacefully. Their proud parents laid them gently back into their beds and returned hand in hand to their own big four-poster. Snuggling beneath the downy comforter, Bethany sighed in contentment.

"I really miss Michelle and Hugh," she murmured. "Do you think they've reached St. Louis yet?"

"Probably. I suspect we'll receive a nice long letter from them soon," Luke replied, kissing her temple.

"I hope so, Luke. I'm so glad they're married and happy now. It would have been so awful if Hugh had died when—"

Bethany could not finish, and a shudder racked her body.

Luke knew well that she was remembering that long

ago night in the cemetery. "Don't think about it, love. It's long over now. Hugh and Michelle are happy and safe, and they've certainly got their hands full now that they've adopted the McCaffreys."

"I miss those feisty little redheads, even with all the other children we've taken in," Bethany said. "But Hugh and Michelle intend to have their own baby soon. Michelle told me she wants as many children as I do."

"I didn't think anyone wanted as many children as you do," Luke murmured with a smile. "And if you continue to give me babies with the ease that you had the twins, we'll have our twenty before we know it."

"You have a little to do with that, you know," Bethany reminded him.

"More than a little," he agreed, his mouth tasting hers. "Perhaps we should think about doing something to fill up a few more bedrooms here at Cantigny."

"Oh, yes, let's," Bethany agreed, before his lips stopped her words and thoughts. She closed her eyes, weaving her fingers through his black hair, and knew that Luke's Indians had been right to tell their lovely legend of the dreamsong. Luke was hers, as she was his, and the gift the gods had given them was more precious than life itself.

LINDA LADD

LINDA LADD lives in Popular Bluff, a small town in southern Missouri. On June 5, 1988, she will celebrate seventeen happy years of marriage to Bill Ladd, whose very special blend of strength and gentleness inspires many of her heroes. They are very proud of their two children, Laurie, who is fourteen, and Billy, who is twelve, and both spend a good deal of time chauffering them to various teenage activities or coaching their basketball or baseball teams.

In addition, Linda enjoys many hobbies, including traveling, tennis, and reading the magical words of Kathleen Woodiwiss and James Clavell. A history buff, she has a true love for all things old and lasting. She collects antique candlesticks and Victorian picture frames, and one of her fondest dreams is to someday restore an antebellum mansion in the south.

Her readers have always been very important to Linda, and she says: "I hope you have enjoyed reading DREAMSONG as much as I enjoyed creating Luke and Beth's very special love story. So many of you have written with warm words of encouragement, and I want to express my heartfelt thank you for your kindness and support. I write for people such as you, and if my books entertain you or bring a smile to your face, it makes all the hours spent at my word processor well worthwhile. I am now hard at work on the first book of a new series, and I'm very excited about it. I hope you'll find time to read it. Please write to me in care of Avon Books—your letters make my day!"

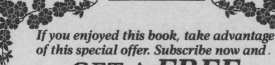